I0779251

MEANT FOR LOVE

Zoey

When I first met him, I got butterflies in my stomach.
I thought it was silly and pushed it aside. Avoided him.
Besides, I was taken—unavailable. Or so I thought.
That was before he hired me to take over his company's PR.
Now that we were working with each other, that meant he was completely off-limits.
Until one night in Vegas.

Nash

They say what happens in Vegas stays in Vegas.
Unless you ask the woman of your dreams to marry you while you are both drinking tequila.
And she says yes.
She thinks it's a mistake.
She's wrong.
Now I just need to get her on the same page.

BOOKS BY NATASHA MADISON

Meant For Series

Meant For Stone

Meant For Her

Meant For Love

Meant For Gabriel

Made For Series

Made For Me

Made For You

Made For Us

Made for Romeo

Southern Wedding Series

Mine To Kiss

Mine To Have

Mine To Hold

Mine To Cherish

Mine To Love

Mine To Take

Mine To Promise

Mine to Honor

Mine to Keep

The Only One Series

Only One Kiss

Only One Chance

Only One Night

Only One Touch

Only One Regret

Only One Mistake

Only One Love

Only One Forever

Southern Series

Southern Chance

Southern Comfort

Southern Storm

Southern Sunrise

Southern Heart

Southern Heat

Southern Secrets

Southern Sunshine

This Is

This Is Crazy

This Is Wild

This Is Love

This Is Forever

Hollywood Royalty

Hollywood Playboy

Hollywood Princess

Hollywood Prince

Something Series

Something So Right

Something So Perfect

Something So Irresistible

Something So Unscripted

Something So BOX SET

Tempt Series

Tempt The Boss

Tempt The Playboy

Tempt The Hookup

Tempt The Ex

Heaven & Hell Series

Hell and Back

Pieces of Heaven

Heaven & Hell Box Set

Love Series

Perfect Love Story

Unexpected Love Story

Broken Love Story

Mixed Up Love

Faux Pas

STONE FAMILY TREE
SOMETHING SO, THIS IS ONLY ONE & MADE FOR FAMILY TREE!

SOMETHING SO SERIES
Something So Right
Parker & Cooper Stone
Matthew Grant (Something So Perfect)
Allison Grant (Something So Irresistible)
Zara Stone (This Is Crazy)
Zoe Stone (This Is Wild)
Justin Stone (This Is Forever)
Something So Perfect
Matthew Grant & Karrie Cooley
Cooper Grant (Only One Regret)
Frances Grant (Only One Love)
Vivienne Grant (Made For You)
Chase Grant (Made For Me)
Something So Irresistible
Allison Grant & Max Horton
Michael Horton (Only One Mistake)
Alexandria Horton (Only One Forever)
Something So Unscripted
Denise Horton & Zack Morrow
Jack Morrow
Joshua Morrow
Elizabeth Morrow
THIS IS SERIES
This Is Crazy
Zara Stone & Evan Richards
Zoey Richards
Stone Richards (Meant For Stone)
This Is Wild
Zoe Stone & Viktor Petrov
Matthew Petrov (Mine To Take)
Zara Petrov

This Is Love
Vivienne Paradis & Mark Dimitris
Karrie Dimitris
Stefano Dimitris (Mine to Promise)
Angelica Dimitris
Zoe Stone & Viktor Petrov
Matthew Petrov
Zara Petrov
This Is Forever
Caroline Woods & Justin Stone
Dylan Stone (Formally Woods)
Christopher Stone
Gabriella Stone
Abigail Stone
ONLY ONE SERIES
Only One Kiss
Candace Richards & Ralph Weber
Ariella Weber
Brookes Weber
Only One Chance
Layla Paterson & Miller Adams
Clarke Adams
Only One Night
Evelyn & Manning Stevenson
Jaxon Stevenson
Victoria Stevenson
Only One Touch
Becca & Nico Harrison
Phoenix Harrison
Dallas Harrison

Southern Wedding Family Tree

Mine To Have

Travis & Harlow

Charlotte

Theo

Mine To Hold

Shelby & Ace

Arya

Mine To Cherish

Clarabella & Luke

Zander

Mine To Love

Presley & Bennett

Cadence

Charleigh

Mine To Take

Sofia and Matty Petrov

Mine To Promise

Stefano Dimitris & Addison

Avery

Mine To Honor

Levi & Eva

Cici

Mine To Keep

Grace & Caine

Meadow

SOUTHERN TREE

Southern Family tree

Billy and Charlotte

(Mother and father to Kallie and Casey)

Southern Chance

Kallie & Jacob McIntyre

Ethan McIntyre (Savannah Son)

Amelia (Southern Secrets)

Travis

Southern Comfort

Olivia & Casey Barnes

Quinn (Southern Heat)

Reed (Southern Sunshine)

Harlow (Mine to Have)

Southern Storm

Savannah & Beau Huntington

Ethan McIntyre (Jacob's son)

Chelsea (Southern Heart)

Toby

Keith

Southern Sunrise

Emily & Ethan McIntyre

Gabriel

Aubrey

Southern Heart

Chelsea Huntington & Mayson Carey

Tucker

Southern Heat

Willow & Quinn Barnes

Grace (Mine To Keep)

Charlie

Southern Secrets
Amelia McIntyre & Asher
JB Normand
Southern Sunshine
Hazel & Reed Barnes
Sofia (Mine To Take)
Kaine
Denver

meant for *LOVE*

NATASHA
MADISON

ONE

I PUSH OPEN the glass door and step out to the parking lot. The sun is slowly coming up. The waves crashing on the rocks not far away fill the quiet morning, along with the birds soaring in the cloudless sky. "It's going to be a beautiful day," I mumble as I walk toward my car, gym bag and protein shake in one hand. With my ringing phone in the other hand, I see it's my brother Caine's name flashing on the screen. The picture is of him glaring at the camera, wearing a tux, sitting on a stool—a beer in his hand taken at his wedding—when I answer. "Nash Griffin," I mock him since that is the only way he answers his phone, which irritates the fuck out of me.

"He's a comedian," he says right away, picking up on the joke. "I thought I'd find you sleeping."

"You thought wrong. I'm just leaving the gym," I tell him, opening the trunk of the car before tossing my bag in and walking over to the driver's door and opening it. Putting the phone on speaker, I start the car, and the Bluetooth picks up, but as soon as that happens, the FaceTime ring hits my phone.

He waits until he can see me before he talks. "You were just leaving the gym," he says, his voice in disbelief, "it's what… six o'clock there?" I see he's sitting behind his desk at the office, suit jacket hanging already on the back of his chair, tie a little loose with one button open.

"Yup," I confirm, putting on my sunglasses and exiting the parking lot. "Just a little after."

"And you're already done with your workout?" he asks, flabbergasted.

"We can't all be going for the dad bod," I joke with him, earning me one of his famous glares. "I was going to tell you when I saw you last that you've been letting yourself go." I roll my lips because I know he's going to come back and tell me to go fuck myself.

"Fuck you," he hisses, his face coming so close to the phone it's all I see, making me smile, knowing how well I know him. "I'd rather be home in bed with my wife than in a sweaty gym."

"But the question is"—I look around as more cars enter the almost vacant parking lot, which won't be like this for long—"would your wife want you to be in bed with her, or at the gym keeping that figure like it was when she fell in hate with you?" I laugh. When Grace and Caine first met, they loathed each other. More like my brother was a donkey who would say the wrong thing over and over again. I figured it out quickly. He did that because one, he was stupid, and two, he really, really liked her. She got under his skin like no one else. "So what's the answer?"

"I'd rather him be in bed with me," Grace's voice chimes in, then she comes into the camera view, rounding the desk to stand next to him. He looks up at her with a smile, his hand going to wrap around her hips while she wraps her arm around his shoulders. "All day, every day." She looks down at him with pure love written on her face.

"Well, if it isn't my favorite sister-in-law," I say softly, her eyes flying back to the screen and she tilts her head to the side. "How're you doing, sweetheart?"

"She's doing fine," Caine hisses, pulling her closer to his side, "and don't talk like that to her, all smooth and shit. No one wants to hear that early in the morning. And especially don't call her fucking sweetheart."

"I don't know. I can name a couple of women who would like me to call them sweetheart." I chuckle while Caine groans, and Grace just shakes her head. "What are you guys doing calling me at six o'clock anyway?"

"You are almost always at your desk by six thirty," Grace reminds me, "so thirty minutes isn't much of a stretch."

"A lot can happen in thirty minutes," I point out, and it's Grace's turn to be the comedian.

"Not too much can happen in thirty minutes that most women remember." Caine laughs out loud now, but not for long, when Grace turns her attention to him. "You remember that in the morning when you want to quickly get in there."

"Burn," I snap. "What I'm getting from this conversation is she's not satisfied in the bedroom." I make my way over to my office. "Caine, how does it make you feel that not only have you let yourself go but now you aren't even satisfying your wife?"

The growl makes me laugh each time. "Can you be professional for once in your life?"

"Hey," I say, "I answered the phone using my whole name."

"I know, so much different from 'Yo,'" Caine retorts while I pull up to the office. I park in my designated spot, seeing my name right above the company name, Cottrell Group. A company my parents started when I was born. They were both working for investment firms and decided to take their portfolio and see what they could do independently. They worked out of an office at home for many years until they outgrew it. Then they decided to open a branch in New York because of Wall Street. Their portfolio only grew. Caine and I got the bug to follow in their footsteps, so I graduated from the University of Philadelphia with a bachelor's degree in finance and economics. During this time, my parents expanded to California, Chicago, Texas, and Washington, DC, where Caine runs the show. I took over the California office, dipping my toe into the Texas office every now and again. Even though we have our own branches, we still like to occasionally drop in to each other's offices.

"Is this why you're calling?" I ask, getting out of the car and walking toward the building. A building we bought not too long ago and moved everything over to.

"No, I'm calling because we seriously need to discuss hiring someone to take over the PR of the firms. Someone who will handle all aspects of media," he huffs out on a deep breath. "Mom and Dad just let their assistants do it for the time being, but even now, they are done with it and don't see the need for it."

"Mom and Dad don't know anything about social media, so they don't see the need for it. I can see where they were twenty years ago, fuck, even ten years ago, but it's a different time. The new generation is coming up, and everything, and I mean everything, is done online."

"I agree," Caine says. "Which is why I'm handing it to you. The cool kid." He grins. "Besides, I don't want to handle it."

"You don't want to handle it?" I tilt my head to the side. "Or you can't handle it because of your age, Grandpa."

"At this moment, if you calling me Grandpa means you're going to take care of it, so be it." He chuckles.

"So this is how it goes?" I pull out the key to the door and unlock it before stepping in and disarming the alarm. "You don't want to do something, so you give it to me." I shake my head. "That's so generous of you."

"You're the hip one." He leans back in his chair as Grace bites her lip to avoid laughing. "I'm the dinosaur who still answers my phone with my name instead of Yo. I also don't know all those letter thingies."

"Letter thingies?" Grace asks before I get a chance.

"Yeah, like ttyl or byob or iykyk." He throws up his hands. "All these fucking alphabets."

I can't help but laugh at the last one. "That last one took you a whole five minutes of thinking before you pulled out your phone."

"More like thirty. He fought the hard fight." She grabs his face and kisses his lips. "You're perf." She abbreviates the word perfect, knowing it irks him.

"You know it's one more syllable," he mumbles as she shakes her head and stands. "It's not so hard."

"Before your brother irritates me even more this morning," Grace says, "I have a list of names of people I think you guys should reach out to."

I walk past the waiting area; the receptionist's desk is empty, and the chair is pushed in under her desk. Making my way down the corridor on the left-hand side, where the offices are, I go into the first one. "Send me the list of names, and I'll go over them," I tell her, walking to my desk and putting down my protein shake. "I'll set something up with a couple of them this week, and we can meet and see who we mesh well with."

"Mesh well with?" Caine says. "Does that mean who has experience enough to do the job?"

"It's something like that." I pull out my chair and sit down, turning on my computer. "You also have to ensure we're all on the same page. It's about experience and also about who vibes well with your company."

"That's what mesh well with means." Grace looks over at him, smiling. "In case you didn't get it."

"I got it," he snaps, and her eyebrows go up in a warning of sorts.

"Okay, Batman," she huffs. "Now if you will excuse

me, I have an email to send out."

She storms away from him as I smirk at the phone. "I don't know a lot of things about relationships, but something tells me she didn't like your tone."

"This is all your fault." He points at me.

"My fault?" I put my hand to my chest. "How did this become my fault? I was minding my own business when you called me to give me more work," I continue when the sound of pinging comes from my computer with the emails coming in. I notice the top email is from Grace. I click on the email and see the names she told me about. I scan the list of names. "Why isn't Zoey Richards on this list?"

Caine laughs. "You think Zoey Richards is going to work for us? That's like an HR nightmare. No way would you be able to keep your dick in your pants."

"Um, excuse me?" I look at him. "I'm not the one who banged my assistant."

"She's my wife."

"She was not your wife when you banged her the first time." I laugh. "Besides, I think I can control myself."

"You think?"

I shrug. "I mean, if she throws herself at me, I'm not going to say no." I wink at him. The minute I met Zoey Richards two years ago was the first time you could say I believed in love at first sight. She took my breath away. If someone asked me to paint a picture of my dream girl, it would be Zoey. From her strawberry-blond hair to her almond-shaped green-gray eyes to the soft freckles that span over her nose. To her amazing smile that just lights up her face, fuck, she's fucking gorgeous. To top it all off, she's smart, she's sassy, and apparently, according to everyone around me when we met, she's totally off-fucking-limits.

"That right there." Caine's voice disrupts my daydream about Zoey on the beach wearing her bikini while she smiles at me. "That look right there is why we can't hire her."

"What look?" I try to act like my cock didn't just get hard remembering her face.

"The look where your eyeballs turn into hearts and bounce in and out of your sockets."

I pfft. "Would it be better if I was a condescending prick to her on her first day?" I throw the first day he met Grace in his face. "Would that be better?" I don't even wait for him to answer. "Let me call her and see if she's even taking new clients." He just glares at me. "For all I know, you're getting your panties in a twist for nothing."

"Nash, I'm not kidding on this." His tone is very much like a father would use to tell his kids that he was done playing around.

"Aye aye, cappy," I say, saluting him. "Now if you will excuse me, some of us have to get the day rolling." I don't bother waiting for him to disconnect before I pull up her number on my phone, opting to text her in case she's in the Pacific Time Zone.

Me: Hey, Zoey, I have a question for you. Call me when you get a chance.

TWO

ZOEY

"WAIT A MINUTE," my cousin Zara says, slapping her hand on the table in front of her, "you told him what?" She's flabbergasted. Her eyeballs look like they are going to jump out of their sockets.

I put down the cup of coffee I've been holding in my hand since I got on the FaceTime call with her two minutes ago. I sent her an SOS text in the middle of the night when I couldn't sleep because I was replaying the worst night I'd ever had in my whole life. The minute she read it at nine o'clock in the morning, my phone was ringing. "We were having dinner." My hands start to shake when I relive it out loud and put it out in the universe. I mean, it's already out in the universe, but it was just between Josh and me, and now that I'm telling Zara, it'll be sort of reality. "I looked over at him and asked him where this was going."

"Just like that?" she balks. "Hey, can you pass the salt, and by the way, Josh, where are we taking this?"

"I mean, not in those words, obviously," I state. "More like, we've been with each other for over two years now, and it's like we've just started dating. You live at your place; I live at mine. We see each other a couple of times a week, but there is nothing more. I want to know where I'm going in the future."

I didn't think Zara's eyes could get bigger, but I was wrong. "And what did he say?"

"He was like, I love you, Zoey, you know this. I just, I like having my space, doing my own thing," I repeat the words that made my heart sink. "What we have is perfect. So I told him it wasn't perfect. Nothing that we had was perfect. Did we love each other? Yes, I know we do, but I want to know he can't live without me. I want him to want to rush home to be with me. I want him to be like, I don't know, my parents." I throw up my hands.

My parents met when my mother found a picture of her boyfriend's engagement photo online and then tweeted my father to crash the wedding with her. Well, that worked out so well they ended up not even going to the wedding but planning their own. "I want to know this relationship is going somewhere and I'm not wasting my time with him. Like, are we in this forever or is it just for the moment? Am I being selfish by giving him an ultimatum? I guess you can say that, but let's not waste anyone's time." I'm trying to give myself a pep talk without giving myself a pep talk.

"You're not being selfish." Zara tries to make me feel better. Our mothers are twin sisters and we are both named after the other sister; it is what makes our bond so unique. I mean, all of my cousins and I grew up more like siblings than cousins, but Zara and I, we were always just the two of us. "And you're right. If you don't know what you want after two years, then he's the problem and not you," she says softly, watching my face. "So how did you end it?"

"I ended it with, perhaps we need time and space away from each other. You do your thing, I do my thing, and we'll see if we are really meant for each other." I say the words as my stomach tightens.

"For how long?" She asks the loaded question I've been asking myself all night long.

"I never said." I pick up my cup of coffee again, my mouth going dry. "I waited a whole five minutes for him to talk me out of what I was saying." I swallow down the coffee that was hot but is now warm. "But he said nothing and just stared at me. It was more of a me saying this and more of him nodding and not saying anything. I mean, I gave him time, and when he didn't say anything, I just got up and left."

"You what?" she shrieks, and I have to admit that me leaving shocked even me. "Did he chase you?"

"He did not," I admit sadly.

"Fuck him," she snaps. "Fuck him and his bullshit horse he rode in on."

I laugh because it doesn't even make sense, but it makes enough sense to me that I get it. "Since he's in finance, I think he rides the bull down on Wall Street."

"Well, whatever he is riding, it's not going to be you."

I point at the screen. "He is definitely not riding me

anymore."

"Okay." She takes a deep inhale. "How are you feeling, for real?"

"Sad," I admit, blinking away the tears that threaten to come on full force. "I mean, I came home and took a bath with a bottle of wine."

"Oh my God." She puts her hand to her mouth.

"And then I cried for about two hours straight. I almost busted out Celine Dion's 'All by Myself,' but I refrained," I say proudly.

"You should have busted out Beyoncé and the 'Hold Up' song where she smashes everything with a bat."

"I should have," I agree, "but now it's said and done."

"I'm shocked he didn't even come to your place after you left him in the restaurant. I mean, maybe he was in shock, but when the shock wore off, he should have chased you home," she replies to me hopefully, and I just shake my head. "I mean, what a dick. Even if he did, you wouldn't answer."

"I would have." I don't bother lying to her. "I would have. I one hundred percent would have opened that door and taken it all back. If he gave me even one inch of indication he wanted me, I would have."

"We should go away this weekend," she says. "Go away to a spa."

"We are already leaving in a couple of weeks for our annual family vacation," I remind her, and she groans. "Exactly. We need to conserve all our energy for that one."

I'm about to say something else when I see a text

come through on my phone. It goes away after a second, but I think my eyes are deceiving me.

I click on my messages and see his name right away. Nash.

Nash: Hey, Zoey, I have a question for you. Call me when you get a chance.

My head literally spins at his message. Nash and I met a couple of years ago when he crashed one of our family vacations. He tagged along with his brother, Caine, who had just married into Matty's, my cousin, in-laws' family. To say I spotted him right away would be the understatement of the year. He had one of the best bodies I've ever seen, and most of the men in my family play professional hockey, so I've seen my share of good bodies. But it was his crystal-blue eyes that were mesmerizing. I could picture myself just being sucked into them. I won't even tell you about the number of tats all over his arms. The minute he shook my hand, I got butterflies in my stomach, which I thought was the stupidest thing ever. Then I did what any normal woman would do when they meet the hottest man they've ever set eyes on—I avoided him the rest of the vacation. Over the years, we've passed each other once or twice, and each time, I've tried not to spend any time with him. But every time I'm around him, I'm drawn to him, which I try to one thousand percent ignore.

"What are you doing?" Zara's voice makes me blink my eyes a couple of times. "You look like you've spaced out."

"Yeah, I just got a message is all. I have to get to

work."

"Okay, well, if you need me to come over and bring Chinese food, just say the word." She smiles at me. "We can make a voodoo doll and stick needles in his junk."

I throw my head back and laugh. "That actually sounds like fun. I'll call you later."

"Love you," she says, disconnecting.

I look down at the text again, reading it for the second time. He has a question for me. "What does that even mean?" I tap the table around the phone, wondering if I should even answer him. I don't think he's ever texted me since he took my number down the first night I met him.

I'm about to say something else when my phone pings loudly with another text, and I see it's from him. I about jump out of my chair and duck for cover, like he's right in front of me instead of in my phone.

Nash: Just in case you are wondering who it is. It's Nash.

I shake my head at his second text.

Me: Who?

I press send and wait for the bubble to come up, letting me know he's texting me, but instead, my phone rings with his name flashing across the top. Nash Griffin. Why does seeing his name excite me?

I think about sending it to voicemail, but I just literally responded to him.

I slide my finger across the bottom of the screen. "Hello," I answer and close my eyes for sounding too cheerful, like I'm happy he called.

"Well, well, well…" I hear his smooth voice across the phone, and I can picture his smirk as he talks to me. "If it isn't *the* Zoey Richards." I literally bite my lip not to smile but then fail.

"Well, well, well." I smile. "If it isn't *the* Nash Griffin." I play his game. "To what do I owe the pleasure, Mr. Griffin?"

"Oh, I like that," he says. "You need to call me Mr. Griffin more often." I roll my eyes. "Heck, I'd take you saying more than fifty words to me before you avoid the shit out of me."

I open my mouth in shock, looking down at the phone in the middle of my desk. "I do not avoid you." I can't believe he caught the game I was playing. I mean, I wasn't really playing the game, but still he actually realized what I was doing.

"Really?" He stops talking for a second. "Interesting."

I want to be not interested, nothing about this is interesting, but instead, I go on the defense. "Is this the question you had to ask me?"

"It is not." He chuckles. "I was calling because I need to discuss something with you."

"With me?" I ask, shocked. "What would you need to discuss with me?" My heart speeds up from a soft beat to a full-blown thumping.

"Caine and I were thinking of updating our social media and making it less…" He trails off as he thinks of a word, so I help him out.

"Dry?" I fill in the blank.

"It's finance. It doesn't get drier than that," he jokes

with me. "But we need someone who can revamp the website and do some social media for us."

"Okay." I lean back in my chair in my home office. "And you want me to do it for you?"

"Well, you always go with the best in the business, so yes, we want you to do it."

"You don't even know what I do." I stare down at the phone, watching the time go by, telling me how long we've been on the call.

"I know that you do public relations for all, if not most, of your family's social media accounts," he replies. "I know you have single-handedly turned three companies' PR nightmares into yesterday's news, and not one person even brings up the shit they got in trouble for." This man just shocks the shit out of me. "Now, do you want me to give you names, or are we good?"

I tap the table in front of me. "We're good."

"Good. I know you do most of the work remotely once you have everything settled. I also know you like to work one-on-one with the person at the top of the company, so that would be me." My stomach gets the same butterflies it did the first time I met him. "I know staying in LA for a couple of weeks or months while you work on our file would be a little bit of an inconvenience. But we would make it worth your while."

"I don't know if I can do it," I answer him honestly.

"Why don't you do something?" He cuts me off before I can say no. "Come down and take a tour of the office." I close my eyes because this is exactly what I need to do. Get out of New York City and away from Josh, not be here for him. As if I'm waiting for him to get his head out of his ass. I need to be unavailable for him is what I need to do. I need to focus on me and take what I need and not what he wants. I can hear myself cheering me on about being all brave and shit.

I don't know what the fuck I'm doing. Maybe I should hang up the phone and think about it before I just give him an answer. Except today, after the emotional events of last night, my mouth, my brain, and my heart are not on the same page. I shock even myself when the words come out. "Fine, I'll come out."

THREE

I'M SLIDING ON my jacket when the doorbell rings and my phone alerts me that someone is at the door. Something my uncle Matthew had installed when I moved into the brownstone he owned in New York. I look down at the camera and see the man standing there look up, no doubt listening to the recording telling him he's on camera.

I grab my Gucci backpack before I head out of my bedroom and run down the stairs toward the front door. Unlocking it and pulling it open, I see the man standing there wearing a black suit. "Ms. Richards," he says, "I'm Mr. Kent. I'll be taking you to the airport."

"Hi," I say, smiling at him. "I'm ready."

"If you have any luggage, I can take it now." I open the door, showing him the one bag that I'm taking for the four days I'll be in LA while meeting with Nash.

"I can take it down with me," I tell him, and he shakes his head.

"My mother would whoop my behind if I let a lady carry her bag," he states, stepping into the entrance and grabbing the rose-gold, stainless-steel carry-on suitcase I always travel with.

"Then by all means," I say, pointing at the bag, "have at it."

I wait for him to take the bag and carry it down the stairs before I lock the door behind me. I make my way down the stairs to the double-parked black Cadillac Escalade. The driver stands there with my luggage beside him as he holds the back door open for me. "Thank you, Mr. Kent," I say, stepping into the back seat. The door shuts behind me, then he walks to the back and puts my suitcase in the trunk.

I pull my phone out of my pocket right after I buckle myself in. At the same time, Mr. Kent gets into the front seat. "Let me know if you would like to stop for coffee anywhere," he offers over his shoulder.

I smile at him as he pulls away from my house. "I'm good, but thank you, Mr. Kent."

I look out the window. The music plays softly from the speakers as we make our way over to the private airport. The minute I told Nash I would meet with him, it took him an hour to message me over my flight information, along with the information of the car service he had picking me up. He did not miss a beat. By the end of the workday, it finally sank in that I was going to LA until Friday. Then I would come home and prepare for our family vacation next week.

Even this morning when I got up, I did not expect

Nash to text me.

Nash: *Fly safe. I'll see you when you get here.*

It was eight o'clock Eastern Time, which means it was five where he was. Was he getting up at that time, or was he getting home at that time? It could be either, and I couldn't put my finger on why the latter bothered me so much.

Me: *Sounds good.*

I press send, looking down at the phone, only putting it away once the SUV stops. I look out, seeing we are here, and the plane awaits us. I slide my phone into the backpack's side pocket containing my purse and my laptop and grab the door handle, but it's pulled open before I can open it myself. "Let me help you," Mr. Kent says, outstretching his hand for me to grab it.

"Thank you." I put my hand in his as I step out, hooking the strap to my backpack around my shoulder before I walk toward the plane. Mr. Kent unloads my bag as I walk up the four steps toward the inside of the plane.

"Good morning, Ms. Richards," the flight attendant says, smiling at me. "I'm Ricky, welcome aboard." "Good morning, Ricky," I reply, walking down the aisle that has one seat on either side, each facing another set of seats, and a beige couch right behind one set of chairs with a pillow and folded blanket on it.

"We are ready to go whenever you are," she says as I turn and put my backpack in the chair facing the seat I'm going to sit in. "As soon as we are up in the air, I'll have your breakfast ready for you."

"Oh," I say, surprised as I sit in the chair, "I don't

think I ordered anything." I know usually they send you a menu so you can order food before you get on the plane. But I didn't even think about it until this very minute.

She smiles at me. "Mr. Griffin took care of it."

"Oh," I reply softly, "all right." She turns around and walks back over to the plane door. I look out the window and see Mr. Kent has left already. I hear the door slamming shut before she walks into the open door to the pilots, saying something to them.

Reaching over and grabbing my phone, I see I've missed a text from Nash.

Nash: *See you in six hours.*

I shake my head and reply to his text.

Me: *I'm locked and loaded on the plane. Next stop LA.*

I don't wait for him to answer me. Instead, I go to my text thread with Zara.

Me: *I'm on my way to LA.*

Zara*: Um. Why?*

Me: *I'm going to check out a job.*

Zara: *Are you moving to LA?*

Me: *No. I'm literally going to check out if I want to take a job.*

Zara*: Ohhh, I like this play. Did you tell dickhead where you were going?*

Me: *Negative.*

Zara: *I love this journey for you.*

Me: *You and me both.*

Zara: *So who are you meeting?*

Me: *Nash.*

I wait for her to text me back, but I know she isn't when the phone rings in my hand. I can't help but answer the phone laughing. "Hello." I put the phone to my ear.

"Um, excuse me, you are going to have a meeting with Nash?" Her voice goes high. "Nash, Nash?"

"I only know one Nash." I ignore her as the plane starts up. "But yes, he called me to ask me to take over his PR and update a couple of things. I tried to say no."

She pffts out. "Yeah, I can imagine, 'oh no, I don't think I can do it, Nash,'" she singsongs. "Did you twirl your hair and bat your eyes for him?"

"Um, I will remind you I'm in a relationship." I look out the window, hoping the plane moves so I can stop this conversation.

"I will remind you that you just ended that so-called relationship, so it's like free rein," she counters back, "and this is Nash." Of course, she would bring up what I told her in confidence two years ago, after I met him, never thinking she would use it against me, but knowing that I would also use the play she is using right now.

"I know who this is, and I know I can't ever go there, especially if we are going to work together."

"So sleep with him before you get him to sign the contract."

"Zara," I snap, and she laughs.

"You can't tell me you aren't even a little bit curious as to what he can offer between the sheets."

"I'm not even a bit curious," I lie, literally through my teeth. It's a good thing we are on the phone and not face-to-face because she would call me out on it.

"Okay, well, I'm curious for both of us, and since I'm the one who is engaged, it's time you took one for the team."

"I have to go," I say once the plane starts moving forward. "We are about to take off."

"I want updates," she says. "Pictures, or it didn't happen."

"Eww," I respond and hang up on her, the sound of her laughter the last thing I hear before I shut my phone off to Airplane Mode.

The plane picks up speed before my back is pressed against the seat, and I look out the window at the sun in the sky shining down on the city of New York, where I was born and grew up. Well, I grew up on Long Island, but I've lived in New York City since I turned nineteen and attended NYU in public relations and corporate communications. It started when I turned fourteen, and my brother, Stone, and my cousin Christopher made me take over their social media accounts. I would post a couple of times a week and answer all questions and dm's, except for the disgusting ones asking me for my dick size. Even though once I wanted to grab a picture of a knife and send it back to them, saying it's about this long but not as razor sharp. Unlike me, they did not find any of this as funny. After I did the two of them, I sort of started doing a couple of my other cousins before I thought about doing it for real.

As soon as I graduated, I started working with my aunt Candace at her PR firm. She handed me my first client, my cousin Franny. She lived out in Dallas and had a sports television and radio division taking over all the PR they had to do. Then I was hired by my uncle Matthew for the television and radio division he had in New York and Chicago. I was then hired for a couple of foundations, and my client list grew so big I could pick my clients. The good thing about doing what I do is I'm not constantly working with the same people all the time. I set them up, ensure everything runs smoothly, then check in on them a couple of times a week as management. I literally love my job, and I'm good at it. When Nash called me, I had no idea he even knew what I did, let alone how good I am at my job.

The plane coasts into the clouds, and I look up as Ricky walks toward me, smiling. "I have coffee or tea or mimosa."

"I'll have a mimosa," I say, knowing I will be okay since I'm landing in six hours, "but just one." I hold up a finger.

"Perfect," she replies. "I have your fruit platter as well as a platter of cupcakes." I just stare at her. "Along with sandwiches from the bagel shop you love."

"What?" I ask, surprised and a little shocked. Well, not a little, like a whole lot shocked. "How?"

"It was on your list," she says. "I'll be back." She turns to go back to the galley, leaving me with my mouth hanging open.

"How in the hell did he know about my favorite bagel shop in New York?" I ask myself because there is no one else I can ask. "That is so fucked up."

"Also, if you want, I laid out a pillow and a blanket

for you in case you wanted to nap," Ricky offers once she comes back with my mimosa. I pull out the tray table from the side of the chair. She walks over to the seat in front of me, opening up that tray table, where she also puts a bottle of water for me. I take a sip before she comes back with a platter of fruit that looks so fresh, I just want to eat it all, but what I'm really looking at is the plate with my pumpernickel everything bagel in the middle of it filled with scrambled eggs and sausage.

"Thank you, Ricky," I say, grabbing a piece of bagel and taking a bite. I finish eating the bagel and grab my laptop, opening it up and pulling up the Cottrell Group file I started reading through yesterday, when I agreed to go see what they were all about.

I move from my chair to the couch to work, only looking up when Ricky comes over to tell me we are landing in ten minutes. I close my laptop and store it back in my backpack before sitting in my seat. I see the sun shining down in LA just as bright as in New York. My hands start getting clammy as I watch the plane descend, touching the runway. I close my eyes, trying to beat the nerves away as the plane slows down. Ricky gets up as soon as the plane comes to a stop, and I unbuckle my seat belt.

I stand, smoothing out my pink pants before walking over to put on my matching jacket. I grab the handle of my backpack and sling it over my shoulder. The door opens, and Ricky turns to give me the okay to step off. "Thank you so much, Ricky," I say before I walk out of the plane. Stopping on the first step, I see Nash standing there, or better yet, leaning on the hood of his black car. He's wearing dress pants and a white button-down shirt that is opened at the collar. His sleeves are rolled up to the elbows, and his arms are folded across his chest. One foot is on his bumper, and I swear he oozes sex appeal without even trying, which makes me even more annoyed. He stands when he spots me, smiling as he takes off his aviator glasses. "There she is," he says, his voice sending shivers up my spine as I walk down the stairs to the last step.

"Here I am," I confirm when I take my first step on the tarmac.

Nash closes the distance between us, and I can see his crystal-blue eyes. He wraps one hand around my waist before he bends his head to kiss my cheek, making my knees weak. "Welcome to LA, Zoey."

FOUR

I WRAP MY arm around her waist, pulling her against my chest, and look down into her green-gray eyes and the soft freckles on her nose before I bend my head. I want to kiss her plump lips, but I know if I do that, she might kick me in the balls. Instead, I bend and kiss her cheek, smelling the hint of her perfume. "Welcome to LA, Zoey." I let her go even though my hands itch to pull her back to me.

"Thank you," she says. "Glad to be here." She tilts her head to the side. "I think."

I put my head back and laugh before some guy wheels over her pink luggage. She goes to grab it but I beat her to it, her hand landing on top of mine. "I've got it."

"Oh, okay." She quickly yanks her hand back from mine. I can already see she is trying to move away from me, but I don't let her. I put my hand on her lower back, ushering her to my car.

"How are you feeling from the flight?" I keep the

conversation very neutral, knowing there will be time to talk about work stuff later.

"A little tired but I'm okay," she admits.

"Are you hungry?" I ask as I stop by the passenger side door. "We can get a late lunch/early dinner and discuss a couple of things."

I can see the wheels spinning in her head. "That sounds great." She shocks me. I was betting on her saying she would get room service. Score one for me, I guess.

"Great," I say, stepping forward and opening her door for her.

She mumbles, "Thank you," right before I shut the door on her and before she can tell me she's changed her mind. I store her luggage in the trunk before getting in the car.

"What do you feel like eating?" I ask, starting the car and turning the AC on.

"Surprise me." She smiles, and I just smirk, raising my eyebrows, knowing full well she isn't going to want me to surprise her with what I want to eat. Because what I actually want to eat is her. "You seem to know what I like since all my favorite food was on the plane."

"Ahh," I say, putting my glasses over my eyes so she can't see me gawk at her. "Just wanted you to be comfortable."

"Should we discuss how you knew?" She turns in her seat to look at me.

"It's not a state secret, Zoey." I pull out of the parking lot and into traffic.

"It's not, but you got me my favorite bagel. How did

you know?"

I think about lying to her and saying it was a good guess, but she might find out the truth, and then it'll make me look like a creepy stalker, so I tell her, "You post about that sandwich every Saturday on your Instagram. You always get it after Pilates." I don't have to look at her to see her mouth is hanging open. "I figured it would be a nice treat."

"That was," she confirms, turning back in her seat to look in front of her. "That was very thoughtful."

"My pleasure." I zigzag through the traffic, heading toward my favorite sushi restaurant, knowing she loves sushi also. She looks out the window as we make our way there, making me more nervous than I have ever been. I've done million-dollar deals without breaking a sweat, but being with Zoey in my car, my hands are all clammy, and my mouth is dry.

I pull into the parking lot and turn off the car. She opens her backpack on the floor between her feet and grabs a black purse. "Is it okay to leave this in the car, or should I take it inside?"

"We are going to sit right there." I point at the window of the small little sushi place. "The car will be in full view at all times."

"So if someone comes around and smashes your window, you'll throw your body at them to protect my laptop?"

I stare at her, trying not to burst out laughing. "Most definitely," I assure her, turning my head to the side and secretly laughing while I reach for the door handle and open the door. I'm rounding the car when she gets out of her side. I take her in again, just like I did when she was walking down the plane's steps. Her pink pants are loose fitting and have elastic at the ankle, so they look comfortable and classy, with a tight white shirt that shows off her perfect fucking tits. Tits that if you didn't know, you would think were fake, but I've memorized them since the first time I saw her in a bikini. It's also because I've seen her in said bikini that I know that what is under her clothes is one million times better than her with clothes on. The jacket hides all the goodness that is under it.

We walk side by side toward the door, and I pull it open for her before she walks in and stands in the small entrance. This place has five tables, which are always taken at lunch and dinnertime. Since it's almost dinner, only two tables are open.

"Take a seat." A woman sticks her head out from the back between the bead curtain.

I wait for Zoey to walk toward the table in the middle of the window looking outside. She sits in one chair, and I sit in the chair facing her instead of beside her. She puts her purse on the chair there. The woman from the back comes out with a pitcher of water in one hand and two menus in the other. "Have you been here before?"

"It's my go-to," I tell her. "Usually, I pick it up and take it home or to the office. I don't think I've ever actually eaten here."

Zoey looks up at the woman with a smile when she puts the menus on the table between us as she fills two glasses of water before asking, "Sake?"

"Sure," I say.

At the same time, Zoey says, "No."

"No or yes?" The woman who couldn't care less about our argument looks back and forth between us, and I'm sure she's counting to ten before she gives up and walks away.

I look over at Zoey, who just stares at me. "Sure, one." She holds her finger up, her nails square and perfectly manicured to a soft pink. The woman walks away from us, stopping at another table before I hear the sound of the beads as she steps into the back.

"What do you recommend?" she asks, looking down at the menu.

"I usually go with the chef's creation," I say, "the Dragon Komodo and the Moonlight."

Her eyes roam the menu. "I'll have the same, then."

I don't have a chance to say anything because the lady comes back with a little white-and-blue bottle with matching little glasses. She pours half in each glass before she grabs her pad. "What can I get you?" We order the same thing, and the woman nods before turning and walking to the back.

"So tell me about your company," Zoey says, and I shake my head.

"Nope, we will get into all that tomorrow at the office." I grab my glass of sake, holding it up. "For right now, I'll toast to you coming to LA to meet with me."

"Um." She grabs her glass of sake and holds it up. "To coming to meet with you, and you eerily stalking my Instagram."

I laugh, clinking my glass to hers before she takes a sip of the sake, and I follow suit. "I don't eerily stalk your Instagram." I put down my glass while she takes another sip and then licks her lips. I want to change seats and sit next to her, so I can pull her seat closer to mine and lean over and see if her lips taste like sake or heaven. Either way, I would win. "I was just observant."

"I think that's what stalkers usually say." She shakes her head as she laughs. "It was a very nice thing for you to do."

"It was my absolute pleasure." I take a sip of water. "I'm not going to lie. I thought you would say no."

She puts her hands on the table in front of her, folding them and almost leaning on the table. "Since we are being honest"—she sort of smiles—"I was going to say no, but—"

"I don't care." I hold up my hand. "Whatever the but was, I don't care. The only thing that matters is you are here, and we'll be working together."

"Maybe." She points at me. "I said I would check it out."

"And I'm going to persuade you to take the job, and if that doesn't work—" I start to say when I see the server coming out from the back. I stare right into her eyes. "I'm not afraid to get on my knees and beg." I wink at her as I see her cheeks get a bit pink.

The server puts down the plates in front of us. "This looks amazing," she says, picking up her chopsticks. "Which one should I try first?"

"Either one is good." I grab my chopsticks, pick up a piece, and put it in my mouth.

I am mid-chew when she moans, and I just glare at her. "This"—she puts her hand in front of her mouth—"is amazing."

My cock—no, my whole body—suddenly wakes up with that moan. "You're welcome." I wink at her. "But if you really want to thank me…"

"This next part is going to be fun." She points her chopstick at me. "Well, fun for me to say, not fun for you to hear," she gloats. "If and I said if I decide to work for you, there are stipulations."

"Oh? I like this already." I put my chopsticks down and clap my hands.

"One, no flirting."

"Okay, well, a rebuttal is coming in." I pick up my chopsticks and point them at her before grabbing another piece of sushi. "I don't flirt. It's just my charm."

"You want to know the funny thing?" She picks up another piece of sushi. "I think you believe that." I shrug. "Let me ask you this. If someone else was on your list and you wanted to hire them, would you fly her here in a private plane and pick her up?"

I avoid looking at her because there is no way in fuck I would do any of that. I would hand it off to my assistant, and she would do it all. I would not go out of my way to order her favorite fucking bagel. I would definitely not go and pick her up myself. "Don't compare yourself to anyone else, Zoey. You're in a category of your own."

"See." She picks up another piece of sushi, avoiding

looking at me. "You can't say stuff like that."

"So you want me to lie to you?" I ask, and she gasps.

"No, of course not."

"Okay, since we know I'm not doing number one, at least not on purpose." I give her a sly smile. "I'm assuming you won't want to stay at my house while you're here." Her eyes widen. "I'm kidding." I bite my lip as she stares at me. "Unless you really want to stay at my place."

She shakes her head and laughs as she picks up another piece of sushi. "I will not be staying at your place. My cousin Gabriella has a place near here. I think I can stay with her."

I grab my own piece of sushi. "I got you a condo not too far from where I live. That way I can give you a ride to and from the office."

"There is no need to pick me up. I can make my way there," she pushes back. "I just need to know what time you're in the office."

"I usually get in around six thirty, sometimes six… depending." Shock is all over her face. "Most of my clients are on the East Coast, so I try to be available for them."

"That makes sense." She chews. "Are you done at three, then?"

"Usually around three. Sometimes I stay until five." I shrug. "It all depends on what I have going on in the day really."

"Those are long days," she says softly.

"Long days for sure." I pick up my sake glass. "But

I'm very thorough when I put my mind to something." I wink at her.

She puts down her chopsticks in front of her, placing her elbows on the top of the table and folding her hands. Her eyes light up even more and her lips almost form a smile, but then as she blinks her eyes, a shield goes up. This Zoey is all business, and if I have to say, she might be even sexier than the friendly Zoey. "Just so we're clear, I don't get involved with the people I work for or with. We will be nothing else except co-workers. I work for you and with you. Period. There is no gray area. It's black and white in my books."

I put down my chopsticks and lean forward just a bit. "But I'm irresistible."

She shakes her head, looking down, and when she looks up there is a twinkle in her eye that wasn't there before. "You might just very well be, but you are also very, very off-limits." She picks up her glass of sake and does exactly what I did to her by winking at me. "And so am I."

FIVE

ZOEY

MY PHONE BEEPS as soon as I slip on my shoes.

Nash: *I'll be there in a minute. Do you want me to come up and get you?*

I shake my head; you have to give it to him for persistence. He isn't going to let up, which gives me stomach flutters and then scares the shit out of me.

Me: *I'll be waiting for you.*

I smirk right before I send the next one.

Me: *Downstairs in the lobby.*

I press send and take one last look at myself before heading to the lobby. I'm wearing cream-colored shorts, but they are so flowy they look like a skirt, sitting mid-thigh, with a long-sleeved silk top that has a flower print all over it. The gold strappy chunky-heeled sandals complete the look. I thought about leaving my hair down, but it's a mess this morning after coming home last night and crashing after I took a shower. So I pinned it up in a ponytail and then curled the ends for a beachy look.

I grab my light green purse and the black bag that holds my computer before grabbing the key to the door and making my way down. I press the elevator button and wait for the doors to open. The minute I step in, I swear a cold shiver runs through me. I press L and wait for the doors to close. I look down at my feet as I wait for the doors to open, and the minute they do, I see him.

The glass door shows me that he's parked right at the door. He's standing out by the passenger door with his phone in his hand. I watch him as I walk to him, his black suit tailored to his body. A body that I know you can bounce a quarter off because he's so fit, it's mouthwatering. His white shirt shows you a bit of his throat, and his black hair looks like he just ran his hands through it. I swear if I wasn't so stubborn about my rule of not getting involved with a client, I would walk up to him and grab him by his lapels and pull him to me while I shoved my tongue down his throat. I shake my head to get rid of the picture of making out with him at eight in the morning.

He must sense someone watches him because his head shoots up, and his smile comes out right away. He steps forward to open the door for me. "Good morning," he greets cheerfully.

"Good morning," I say, stepping out into the warm air.

"Did you find everything you needed?" he asks, and I stop beside the car to look at him.

"The condo was fully stocked." I tilt my head to the side. "Right down to my favorite cookies and chips."

"I just wanted you to feel like you're home," he says, and all I can do is shake my head in disbelief as he pulls open the passenger side door for me to get in. I slide into the seat and look over at him putting his hand on the roof of the car and leaning in. "I picked you up a matcha," he tells me right before he closes the door.

I look over at the cupholder and see there are two cups there, one with a straw in it and the other with a cover. I turn in my seat, waiting for him to get in. "You got me matcha?"

"I did," he confirms, reaching for his seat belt. "I got it iced and hot, not sure which you wanted."

"Um," I say baffled, "I can do either. Which one do you prefer?"

He starts the car. "Of matcha?" I nod. "I prefer it away from me and never in my mouth."

I can't help but put my head back and laugh. "It's not that bad," I say, picking up the hot one first. "It's an acquired taste."

"Yes, if your taste is eating grass," he deadpans, his face making a grimace that my nieces and nephews do when they taste something that isn't to their liking. "It's so gross."

"It's delicious," I assure him, taking a sip. "Mmm, so good."

"Okay, if we are going to do the rules and shit," Nash starts, pulling away from the building, "rule number one to you, no moaning in my vicinity." My eyes open as I roll my lips. "That might be my only rule," he continues. "No 'oh, that's so good. Oh, I like that. Oh, do that again,

Nash.'"" At the last one, I can't help but laugh until my stomach hurts.

"Noted," I return when he pulls into the parking lot. "I promise to never moan around you."

"Unless," he says, turning off the car, "you are okay with moaning my name, and then all your rules will be broken."

"I am not," I tell him, as if sitting across from him last night was easy. With him staring at me with his blue eyes and cocky grin, for once in my life, I wanted to say fuck all the rules and be like, let's do this. I mean, I would never even think of doing this if Josh and I were solid. Maybe this is a sign that Josh isn't the one for me. Maybe, just maybe, this is the sign I was looking for. I mean, not a sign I should get involved with Nash, but a sign Josh isn't the one for me.

"Well, you'll tell me if you change your mind?" Nash asks as he opens up his door.

"You'll be the first one to know," I assure him, putting my purse and black bag over my shoulder and getting out with both matchas in my hand.

"Here, give me one of those." He holds out his hand, taking the hot cup from my hand. "Trust me, I'll give it right back once we get into the office."

I follow him to the glass door as he holds it open for me, and I step in. I see the receptionist smile when she sees it's Nash. "Good morning again," she tells Nash and then looks over at me. "You must be Zoey." I smile at her. "I'm Lucille, but you can call me Lulu."

"Nice to meet you, Lulu," I say.

"This way." Nash directs me as he walks to the right-hand side of the receptionist. "We can put your things down in the conference room, and then I can take you around and introduce you."

"Um," I say when he walks into the conference room that has a projector at the far end of the wall, facing the long table that has about sixteen chairs. "What did she mean good morning again?" I ask when I put the matcha down first and then my bags in an empty chair in front of it.

"I came to work and then left to come and get you." This. Fucking. Man. He must see I'm about to say something. "Hey, I know your dad and your uncles. They would kick my ass if I let you take an Uber by yourself in a strange city."

"You came to work," I ask him, folding my hands over my chest, "and then left to get me so the men in my family wouldn't kick your ass?"

"Correct," he confirms right before he puts down the hot matcha.

"And you bought me matcha." I point at them on the table.

"Unfortunately, that's what you like." He shrugs.

"You're something else, Mr. Griffin."

"Rule number two, you can't call me that, ever." He takes off his jacket and tosses it on one of the chairs before he puts his hands on his hips. My eyes drop to his black Tom Ford belt before flying back to his face. "Unless…"

I hold up my hand. "I don't want to hear what your

unless is," I practically snap, "and you are literally ruining all the rules."

"How am I doing that?"

"You are flirting with me right now."

He shakes his head. "I'm not flirting with you. At least, I don't think I am."

"Well, you are."

"Really?" He tries to hide his smile, but what starts as a smirk quickly turns into a full-blown smile. "Interesting."

"What is?" I ask, my interest piqued.

"If you think that's flirting, then the guy you're with is doing it wrong."

A knock on the door has me about to jump out of my shoes. A woman pokes her head in. "Found you." She walks in, swaying her hips left to right in a maroon skirt with a champagne silk shirt. Her black hair is perfectly styled and curled at the ends. "You must be the great Zoey." She comes to me first, extending her hand. "I'm Kailyn." I reach out to shake her hand. "Nash's assistant."

"Nice to meet you." I smile.

"I hope you got in all right and settled in."

"I did, thank you," I say as she looks over at Nash with literal hearts in her eyes. Except he has no idea. He's totally oblivious to it all.

"I have cleared your schedule for the next couple of days," she tells him. "I also just confirmed your attendance at the Bankers Summit in Vegas from Thursday until Sunday."

"Sounds good," he says to her. "I think I have all my

travel schedule done for after." He looks at her, then looks back at me. "Let me show you the rest of the office."

Kailyn walks out of the conference room before us, but Nash waits for me to be at his side before he extends his hand to the other side of the hallway. "This is my office." He walks toward the left side of the office, right across from the conference room. It's the first office when you walk in from the waiting area.

"Is this where the magic happens?" I ask, stepping into the room. It's right then I notice I fucked up in my words.

"Not all the magic," he quickly answers me. "That magic isn't ever performed here."

"I walked right into that one," I mumble, then turn to him. "I meant all the brainstorming."

"Now, who's flirting with who?" He winks at me before he walks out of the office and down the hallway, and I love this concept right away. "On one side of the office are the individual offices." He points to the right. "In the middle area are all the assistants." I see four desks lined up, one right after the other, but with enough space between for privacy. "Then this," he continues and walks over to the left side, "is my favorite part that I just brought into the office." He proudly states, "It's a work-share space." Four desks are connected in the middle and then two desks at the end. "It can be lonely working all alone in the office, so I wanted them to be able to shoot off ideas and stuff here without it being stuffy."

"This is amazing." I look around and see pictures of the office workers all lined up. Some pictures are from the office, while a couple of the pictures look like they were taken outside at a picnic or something. "Every second month, we have team building. We either go bowling, take a cooking course, or just plain have a picnic."

"It must be great for the morale around here," I say, impressed when one of the assistants walks in and spots Nash. He holds up his hand to say good morning as he rushes to his desk to answer a call.

"I realized a long time ago that people are more encouraged to work with you when you listen to them." He puts his hands in his pockets. "Who wants to come to work and be miserable?"

"Not many big enterprises think like that," I say.

"Well, what can I say? I'm one in a million." He turns while he hides his smile. "In the back is the bathroom and kitchen area." He points all the way to the end. "Shall we get to work?"

I clap my hands. "Let's." I follow him back toward the conference room as people start trickling in. I notice they all stop and talk to him. He introduces me to everyone, and by the time we get back to the conference room, I'm fully invested in him and his company.

I pull out the chair, then grab my laptop and put my cell phone right next to me. I open the laptop, waiting for it to start, and look up, seeing he's walking back into the office with a folder in his hand. "I have this," he says, pulling out the chair beside me and sitting down next to me, "it's just little press notes that have been made over the years." He hands it to me, and I open it up, seeing the news clipping. "My mother sent that to me. She said it was before the web days."

I laugh at that. "So what's the summit?" I ask.

"It's lending and risk management professionals from California. It features the following tracks: regulatory compliance, risk management, lenders and chief credit officers, and finance. Everything that sounds like a good time." He laughs as he leans back in his chair. "Actually, you should think of coming with me. It would be a great place to see how I work and what we stand for."

I'm about to answer him when my phone buzzes from beside me. I look down and the only thing I can see is it's from Josh.

I ignore it and turn back to Nash. "I'm one of the speakers, so you can see how popular I am." He puts his crossed hands on his stomach. "You'll get an inside look at the West Coast section of the Cottrell Group."

My phone buzzes again, and this time, I see the message.

Josh: *Did you really take off to LA without telling me?*

The fucking nerve of this guy. It's been four fucking days since I gave him the ultimatum, and the first text he sends me is about me not being in New York. No doubt he saw my Instagram post this morning of the sunset with the caption, "Waking up in LA."

I see Nash's eyes on the phone at the same time as I turn the phone over. "You can get that." My eyes fly to his. "I don't mind."

"No, it's fine," I say, ignoring the buzz again. "He can wait for once."

"He?" Nash says. "Who is he?"

"Josh is my boyfriend," I reply, but then I quickly rephrase. "Was my boyfriend." Nash's eyebrows go up. "It's a bit complicated."

"Sounds like it," he mumbles, then taps his finger on the conference table. "So what do you think? Would you like to come with me?"

I think of all the reasons I shouldn't go to Vegas with Nash. I think about how I'm going on vacation with my family next week, and I need to get home. I think of the fact I should be as far from Josh as I can possibly be, and the word comes out almost in a shout. "Sure."

SIX

ZOEY

"YOU'RE OFF TO Vegas?" Zara literally spits out her coffee when I call her bright and early on Thursday morning. I nod as I walk from the kitchen in the condo toward the balcony. Sliding the door open and stepping out in the white robe that came in the closet, I sit in the chair looking over at the houses, and I can hear the soft waves in the distance.

"I'm off to Vegas," I confirm, sipping the coffee I just made before calling Zara. It's six o'clock here, and I still haven't gotten used to the time change. "It's going to be good for me to find out more about the company. I can network and see what everyone says about the company as well."

She throws her head back and laughs. "Is that what you're telling yourself?"

"That's the truth."

"How is Josh?" Zara asks, and I shrug.

"No clue," I answer her honestly. "He texted me

the day after I landed here to ask if I was really in LA without telling him." I laugh bitterly. "Not like, 'oh, Zoey, I miss you. I need to see you. Maybe we should talk.' Nope, it was all 'you left without telling me,' and then he followed up with 'how long will you be there?'"

"So he's texted you, but he hasn't called you on the telephone?"

"How else would he call me, on the can and string? Why do you say it like that, on the telephone?" I make fun of her. "But to answer your question, negative."

"He's not worth it," Zara says. "If that was Daniel, I would be like fuck this shit."

"If this was Daniel," I say of her fiancé, "you would have already burned his clothes while you were live on some social media platform."

"Word." She points at the screen. "Don't fucking piss on my leg and then be like, I think it's raining on a sunny cloudless day."

"What is up with you and these sayings today?" I laugh.

"Ugh, I spent two days with Uncle Matthew and Uncle Max. It's like all their old-time jokes have stuck on me."

I silently laugh at her. "I have to go and pack my bag to leave. I think I'm going to fly home before we take off on the family vacation."

"Did you pack any slutty clothes?" Zara winks at me.

"I'm here for business. I'm not going to wear slutty clothes." I get up, opening the door, and step into the cool living room before walking to the back where the only bathroom is. "It's strictly professional with Nash."

"Well, then you're doing something wrong," Zara declares.

"Now I have to go and get ready," I tell her, hanging up the phone before starting the shower. I'm packed and already waiting for him in the lobby when he swings in. I grab my backpack and wheel my luggage to the door. He steps out of his car looking like he just walked off a fashion runway.

He's wearing dark blue jeans with a white polo shirt, the tattoos on his arms on full display. If he's wearing a suit, you can't see them, but the minute he rolls up his sleeves, they come out. I push open the door before he has a chance to pull it open. "Hey," he says, looking me up and down. "Didn't I say dress casual?" he asks, and I look down at my outfit.

"This is casual," I tell him of the light peach wraparound dress with a gray sleeveless tank top. "I'm not even wearing heels." I point at white wedges. "Besides, this is as casual as it gets."

"You look fantastic," he compliments, and I tsk him. "Is that flirting?"

"Do you tell anyone else you work with that they look fantastic?" I watch him as he puts my bag in the trunk next to his.

"Technically, I don't," he answers, slamming the trunk, "but that's only because no one actually looks fantastic." I gasp at his bluntness. "So I can't say it."

I pull open the door, getting in and trying not to think of how much that comment means. I also try to block out how sexy he smells. "Are we flying there commercial or private?"

"Private," he says, putting his sunglasses on. "They will have your matcha on board."

"Good." I pretend it matters. "Or else I wasn't going."

"Is that all it takes for you to stay where you are?" He looks over at me for a second with a sly smile. "I'll learn how to make that green stuff if that's the case." This. Fucking. Guy. Again. I ignore the way my heart leaps to my throat and instead push forward.

"Do you even know how matcha is made?" I ask and watch his index finger tap the steering wheel when he stops at a red light.

"I know it's green, and you add milk to it, and it tastes like shit. But for you, I'll learn."

"You have to sift the matcha and then you need to get a bamboo whisk." I can't see his eyes because they are covered with his sunglasses, but I can bet they are crystal blue and are lit up with laughter. "Which has to be soaked into hot water before you use it."

"Then use a wire whisk." He speaks back at me, and I shake my head.

"It has to be bamboo." He nods and starts moving the car when the light turns green.

"Noted. Siri," he speaks to the car, "make a note to order a bamboo whisk."

Siri answers not too long after. "I made a note to order a bamboo whisk. Would you like to set a reminder?"

"No," he replies. "Go on, what's next?"

"You have to sift the matcha in one of those little

sifters," I instruct him. "That way, you don't have any clumps."

"Heaven forbid the matcha has clumps. It must ruin the whole taste of it." He laughs at his own joke. "Then what, you just pour in water?"

"No." I shake my head. "Then you have to add a bit of water and whisk it until it gets foamy."

"So it can shake out the taste of grass?" I laugh. "Got it."

"Then you add some milk." I skip a couple of steps, but he's not ever going to make me this, so it's moot.

"I think I can do that," he says, pulling into the parking lot I arrived at a couple of days ago. "When we come back, you can come over to the house, and we can do it together."

"I'm off on vacation after Vegas," I remind him, "a big family vacation."

"Oh, that's right." He gets out of the car, turning one last time before he shuts the door. "Caine is going also."

Stepping out of the car, I look over the roof at him. "And you aren't joining us?"

"I am not," he states, popping the trunk open, "it's a family trip."

"But you came that one year," I mention to him, and I'm about to grab the luggage when he hands me his own black leather backpack.

"Hold this." He holds it out for me, and I grab it while he unloads my pink carry-on and his black steel one. "I did, but that was only because he just started dating Grace and he was afraid one of her relatives would try to shoot him."

"If my cousin Matty didn't get shot after dating Sofia and then dumping her, and then finding her again when she was going to plan his wedding to another woman." I shrug. "I think he was safe."

"Grace broke up with him and went back to the family farm and he had to chase her."

I hiss, "With Casey there?" I mention her grandfather, who is very, very similar to my uncle Matthew. Actually, if you put them together, I'm pretty sure they can take over the world. Casey would do it underground. Matthew would do it in your face while you're watching your life implode, and he'll do it with a smile as if you guys are having a beer together.

"On his horse and everything." He shocks me. "Even I thought he would shoot me in the ass, and I wasn't even the one who Grace was dating." He slams the trunk closed before he extends his hand for his backpack. Handing it to him, I expect him to give me my luggage, but instead, he slides his backpack over his shoulder and then wheels both the suitcases side by side. "The plane is waiting." It's the only thing he says when I try to grab it from him.

I follow him through the gate toward the plane. The male flight attendant stands at the bottom of the stairs with another man, who is wearing shorts and a T-shirt. They smile at us when we arrive. "Good morning," the flight attendant greets us with a huge smile. "I'm Gerald, and I'll be your flight attendant this morning," he says. "Robert will take your bags for you, and we will be off as soon as you are ready."

I walk up the three steps to the plane, this one smaller than the one I flew here on. This one has just one seat side by side and a couch behind the one seat. "Left or right?" I ask over my shoulder.

"Whichever one you aren't sitting in," he replies. "Unless I sit down in the one you want and you sit on top of me."

I roll my eyes but my head screams *that sounds like a great plan*. "Rule number, I don't even remember which number it is, but I do know you are breaking it."

"Things get boring when everyone plays by the rules," he scoffs, taking off his sunglasses and folding them. He tucks them into the front of his polo shirt where the buttons are. "Don't you think?"

"I've always played by the rules," I retort, sitting in the chair on the left, "and I've been entertained most of the time." I am lying through my teeth. I have never, ever gone out of my comfort zone. I have never bent the rules. If there were rules, they were there to make sure and protect everyone from travesty. The only time I've bent the rules and gone out of my comfort zone was when I accepted to come here and work with him, and now I'm sitting on a plane with him going to Vegas. I've done all of this because my so-called ex-boyfriend had trouble with committing to me, and I wanted him to take a stand. Which, after a week, he still has yet to take. Sure, he said he wanted to be committed, but did he show it? No. Did he do anything to prove it to me? Not one fucking thing. Not even a fucking fruit basket. He has only shown me that I did the right thing.

Nash sits in his chair, taking his phone out of his back pocket before handing his backpack to Gerald, who lets us know he will stow it until after takeoff. I hand him mine also as I buckle my belt.

It takes us no more than seven minutes for us to be airborne. Gerald has enough time to hand me my matcha latte and Nash a bottle of orange juice. "Do you drink coffee?"

"I do," he says, taking a gulp of his orange juice, "in the morning, right before the gym."

"You went to the gym?" I ask, almost shocked when he nods.

"I'm usually there at around four thirty. If I don't, I'm usually on my treadmill at least."

"Every day?" My mouth hangs open at this knowledge.

"Every day except on Sunday. I try to go easy on Sunday."

"I mean, it's the Lord's day." I can't help but laugh at myself, making him laugh at me. The plane ride is so short I don't even have a chance to get my bag back from Gerald and neither does Nash.

When we land, he hands us both our bags and our luggage is already waiting in the black sedan that has the words Bellagio across the back. "I thought the summit was at Caesars."

"It is, which is why I'm not staying there. I never stay at the event space. It's just too much."

"Is it because if you bring a woman to your room, it's harder to get rid of her?" I ask, and he chuckles but doesn't deny it. "Such a guy."

I get into the back seat, trying not to let the thought of him bringing a girl to his room bother me or the fact that maybe he might be doing this on this trip. "You okay?" he asks when he slides in beside me.

"Yes," I lie to him, "just hungry." Which is the furthest thing from the truth. I'm so sick to my stomach that eating will make me yack everywhere.

"We'll go get a quick lunch before we have to check in at the summit," he suggests, and I look out the window. Checking in to the hotel goes smoothly. We are both on the same floor, side by side. *Great,* I think, *not only will I have to know if he's with a girl in his room but I'll also be able to hear it through the walls.*

I stop at my door and see his door is literally right beside mine. "How long will you be?" he asks, and I look back at him. "Until you are ready for lunch."

"I just have to fish out my purse, and I'll be ready to go. Should I change? Are you changing?"

"I'm changing after lunch," he tells me. I nod, scan the card, and hear the click of the lock. "Be out in a minute." He walks into his room at the same time I walk into mine, and both doors close with a slam after us.

Luckily for me, lunch is interrupted by phone calls from Caine and a couple from his parents, all of whom are not coming to this summit but want to give their input. When we get back to our rooms, he looks over at me. "How long will it take you to change?"

"Ten minutes," I reply, "maybe twelve if I have to iron my skirt."

"Whoever is finished first knocks," he says, "and then waits for them in the other room."

I roll my eyes and push open the door, making sure I don't dillydally, just to make sure when he knocks, I'm ready to go. I rush over to my bag, picking it up and tossing it on the bed. My outfit for today is on top as I bend to untie the ankle strap to my wedges before kicking them off. I grab the white linen, wide-legged pants, shaking them out and seeing they didn't wrinkle, and then the silk top I folded in two also doesn't look like it needs to be ironed. "Score," I cheer to myself, going to the bathroom before undressing and then slipping into my outfit. The silk top has long sleeves and big cuffs at the wrists, with two sashes at the neck that tie into a bow before the cleavage starts. I tuck the shirt into the high-waisted linen pants, then turn to grab the shoes out of the other side of the carry-on. The strappy gold heels finish the look, and I'm grabbing my purse when there is a knock on the door. "I win," he declares with glee in his voice, and his smile turns into a frown when I open the door and he sees me ready. "Fuck, it's been seven minutes."

"I got lucky, I guess." I put my phone in my purse before walking out with him.

"It's a seven-minute walk." Nash looks at me and then my shoes. "Do we need to cab it?"

"For seven minutes?" I ask. "You know I live in New York, right? I could run in these shoes and only at the end of the night would I complain."

"Good to know." He winks at me, then looks back

down at the shoes. "Those should be illegal at work."

"Umm, your assistant was wearing almost the same thing yesterday," I point out, and his eyebrows pinch together.

"Okay, I amend my statement. *You* shouldn't be wearing those at the office."

I scoff, walking side by side with him, trying to think of something to say, but all the words are jumbled in my head, along with whether he ever hooked up with his assistant. Do they have the friends-with-benefits deal? The real question is, why do I even fucking care?

I see what he's talking about the minute we step into Caesars. He's stopped about five times, and every time, he takes the opportunity to introduce me to whoever stopped him. I smile politely, shaking their hand and listening to their conversations.

Everyone is very respectful as we make our way over to the check-in desk, where they hand him a badge with his name on it and then mine with my name on it, Zoey Richards Cottrell Group.

"There might be something wrong with mine," I tell him as we walk away, and he looks down to see. "What if they think I work for your firm and ask me banking advice?" He chuckles as he puts on his badge. "The only thing I know is you save your money."

"Well, at least you've got that," he teases as we make our way to one of the speaking events. "You're already one foot in the door."

"Nash, this could embarrass you and your group," I whisper-yell at him.

"You know I own the group, right? Not one person is going to fire you." He puts his hands in his pockets, and I notice you can see some of the outline from his chest tattoo through his shirt. "Zoey," he says my name, "relax."

"You telling me to relax doesn't mean I actually relax." I lean over and whisper in his ear without getting too close.

He puts his hand on the lower part of my back as he ushers me forward into a room where someone is speaking, so I shut up. The rest of the day is filled with speeches about what is new in banking. I literally have no idea at all what they're saying. I try to keep up and take a couple of pictures of Nash with his clients who have come to meet him. They listen to everything he says, and he points out little things they haven't even thought of.

The day flies by and into the night. Even the day after, it's so much on the go I don't see the hours go by, and finally, on the last night, I'm ready for the long vacation with my family. "Is the gala fancy?" I ask as we walk out of the hotel on the last day after the last speaker just finished presenting.

"Semi-fancy. I know lots of them are bringing their wives and stuff, so they might be dressed up," he says, stopping when I stop.

"I need you to think back to last year and what people were wearing," I ask him, and he shrugs. "Okay, what about the hottest girl there? What was she wearing?"

He laughs. "It was semi-formal," he says. "Why?"

"I don't have a semi-formal outfit," I gasp.

"Then go get one," he states, opening his front jacket pocket and pulling out his credit card. "Here, be ready at seven."

"It's four thirty," I yelp. "And I don't need your money." I look around. "I'll be ready at seven."

"Do you want me to come with you?"

"No, go and gamble," I say. "Put twenty on red."

"You lost four hundred dollars doing that," he reminds me.

"My luck is about to change," I tell him before I turn and rush into a couple of stores, settling on a strapless, tight-fitting white lace dress. The cutouts of the dress show the white slip under it, and I pick up a pair of crystal slingbacks to complete the look. I'm just putting the finishing touches on my lips when he knocks at the door. I pull it open before I tell him, "I'm almost done." I turn before I see what he's wearing, but when I look over my shoulder, I can see from his eyes that he likes my outfit.

"You can't go like that." He points at me, and I look down at my chosen dress.

"Why not?" I smooth down the front of the dress. "It's so pretty."

"It's just too much." I look down at myself as I pick up the little clutch purse that holds my phone and lip gloss. "Ugh, it's going to be a long night."

I watch him turn and walk to the door, noticing he's wearing a black suit with a matching black shirt. "I need a drink," I finally say, "since this is officially off the clock."

He laughs as we walk toward the gala. "People are turning their heads looking at you."

"They are not," I mumble as we get to the reception, where I snag a glass of champagne and take a sip, the bubbles exploding on my tongue. "Refreshing."

"Nash." Our heads both turn when we hear his name and see a man approaching. "I was hoping to catch you here." He extends his hand. "I loved your speech," he says to him, and I smile at him proudly. Even though I didn't know what he meant, his speech was fantastic.

"Thank you," Nash says. "This is Zoey Richards." He turns to me, introducing me.

"Your new lady," he says, and I shake my head.

"Not his new lady. We work together." I smile, wondering if he's ever brought a woman to this event.

"That's a shame," the man says. "If I was younger…" I can't help but laugh.

"You are too kind," I say. "I'm sure you bat away the women with your charm." I look at him and then at Nash, who looks at me with a smile.

"I wish," he replies, looking at Nash. "You should fire this woman and then date her."

"Now, that is a great idea!" he declares. The man smiles at me, giving me a wink, and walks away.

I wait for the man to leave and finish my glass before I get the nerve to ask him, "How many women have you brought to this event? Every single time we meet someone, they ask you if I'm the newer model."

"One, they have not asked you that every single time." He turns to look around. "And the answer to your question is not many." He avoids looking at me. "Some I was dating at the time. Some I was testing the waters with."

"So you're a serial dater?" I laugh as a server walks around with another tray of champagne. I put my empty glass on it before taking a full one.

"Not really a serial dater." He waits for the man to walk away before he speaks. "I just haven't found the one who I want to spend more time with." I stare into his eyes. "I need someone who will keep me on my toes. Someone beautiful and kind." I take a sip of champagne, well, more like half the glass. "Someone who, I don't know, drinks matcha."

I about choke on my champagne when he says that before he takes me to our table for the meal. He pulls out the chair for me, and I sit down as he sits beside me. "Would you like white or red?" the server beside me asks.

"White, please," I say to him and then look over at Nash, who shakes his head. "You aren't a wine drinker?"

"I don't mind wine. I'm just not feeling it," he explains as I lift my glass of wine and take a sip.

"What do you feel like having?" The minute I ask the question, I hold up my hand. "Don't answer that," I say, taking another sip of wine.

He leans into me, and I swear I hold my breath when I smell him beside me and then feel his breath on my ear. "You ruin all the fun." I turn my head, and we are so close to each other it's making it hard to think.

Two things happen at the same time. Someone calls

him away, and my purse buzzes in my lap. He pushes away from the table, walking over to the man. My phone buzzes a second time. I pull it out to see it's from Josh.

Josh: *I miss you.*

Josh: *When are you getting back? We need to talk.*

I'm about to answer him when I see he commented on my Instagram post two hours ago when I took a picture of the fountains. I click on his picture and see he uploaded a story ten minutes ago, where he was in a club between two girls. "Asshole," I mutter to myself and put my phone away. Yeah, he misses me, my ass. I finish the glass of champagne, turning and seeing Nash coming to me.

"What's wrong?" he asks, and I just shake my head. "You went from happy to sad in the amount of time I left to say hello to a couple of people and come back."

I think about lying to him and playing it off, but I'm annoyed and pissed. "Why can't men who say they want to be in a committed relationship show they want a committed relationship instead of acting like he's a single man?" I look at him.

"Did you not hear what I said before? I'm searching for that same thing." He chuckles. "I'm also the last person you should ask that question to." I take a deep inhale. "But I will say that if I perhaps had someone"—he smirks at me—"someone I've wanted for a really long time, there would be no question about how committed I would be."

I listen to him say the words and feel the back of my neck burn before I laugh nervously, not sure what to say.

"That would be one lucky girl." The words are out of my mouth before I can even stop them. "We should do shots."

He looks at me, his eyebrows going up. "This could be interesting."

"We should take a shot every time someone says something about the girls you've dated. I'd be drunk for sure." I laugh, my head feeling a little tipsy.

"What about you and the boyfriend?" he asks, and I reach for my wine. "Is the situation still the same?"

"Not my boyfriend," I correct him before I take a sip of my wine, "per se. We are on a break." I smile. "And not like a Rachel and Ross break, a real break." I put my glass down. "Like you do your thing, let me do mine."

He watches me, his eyes going dark. "We should take a shot every single time someone says equity."

"Oh, good one." I point at him. "Very, very good." I clap my hands. "This is shaping up to be a really fun night."

He tilts his head to the side, puts his hand on the back of my chair, and smirks. "The night's just starting, Zoey."

SEVEN

NASH

I WATCH HER eyes move back and forth, her cheeks turning a little pink. "We should eat before we start taking shots," she suggests. "Otherwise you might be carrying me home over your shoulder."

I turn to her. "If that's the case, I say finish that glass of wine so I can carry you home with me." I lean in, hearing her breath hitch. "Except I only have the key to my room, so you'll be sleeping in my bed."

"I have the key in my purse." She about stumbles the words out.

"It would be rude of me to go into your purse." I move back to my seat as the chairs around us start to fill up. I look over at her in that fucking dress that had me hard the minute I fucking saw her in it. It hugs every single curve on her body, and being strapless, I have to wonder if she's wearing a bra, which makes it really fucking uncomfortable in my pants.

"I think I would be able to crawl back to my room,"

she states, and I raise my eyebrows.

"You on your hands and knees," I tease, picking up my glass of water, "that's something I've envisioned before."

"Nash," she says my name and laughs. "Rules."

"Broke the minute you opened the door in that dress," I mumble to her. She doesn't have a chance to say anything to me as the woman beside her compliments her dress. They put the plate of steak down in front of me, and I've never wanted to finish a meal faster in my life. The meal goes quickly with the closing speeches, then everyone slowly gets up.

"Where to now?" she asks, looking at me as she grabs her purse.

"To the bar." I motion with my head to the left. I put my hand on her back, laying claim to her. If anyone is looking her way, they will know she's with me. When we get to one of the bars, a couple of men stand at the counter with a couple more coming up behind us. "What do you want to drink?"

"Tequila," she says. "If we are taking shots and you aren't backing down."

"Trust me, Zoey, once I start in on something, I never, ever back down." I wink at her as I give the bartender a chin up. "Two shots of tequila," I order, then look around at a couple of people. "Anyone else?"

"We should," one of the guys near me states. "After four days, we deserve it."

"I agree," Zoey adds, trying not to burst out laughing. "It was a good time."

"Lots of equity talk," one of the guys adds, and I look over at her as she holds up a finger.

We take a shot of tequila, and she chases it with a sip of water. "What do you want to drink?"

"I'll have a vodka with a splash of soda water."

I turn back to order the drinks before I put my hand on her hip to lean in and whisper in her ear, "Are you okay?"

"Yeah," she confirms, "I'm having more fun than I thought I would."

"It's the equity," I joke, and she throws her head back and laughs. My lips tingle to lean forward and kiss her neck. I've never seen this side of her. Well, to be honest, she's always run away from me the minute she's had a chance. But now, having spent the past week with her, I am able to admit that everything I thought about when I met her was the truth.

The bartender returns with her drink, my glass of scotch, and two shots of tequila. She pulls away from her conversation with one of the wives to smirk at me. "Are you going to say equity just to get me to drink?"

"No, I'm going to say equity so I get to carry you to my bed." I wink at her and hold up my glass for her to clink on it. I down the shot, and she winces when she downs hers before she takes a sip of her vodka.

We stand side by side at the bar with a couple of people around us. I'm having one conversation on my right while she is having a conversation on her side. Her laughter makes me look over at her as she turns her head and laughs on my shoulder. I see the man from before, and he is holding up his hand. "I said what I said, and I'm not taking it back." Zoey turns back to him, and with her being so close to my arm, I wrap it around her waist to get her closer to me. "So are you going to work with me?"

"My calendar is full," she says to him, "but I have your business card, and if something opens up, you are the first one on the list."

"That's what they all say." He shakes his head and takes a sip of his bourbon. "But you, girlie, I believe you."

"She doesn't lie," I cut in to the conversation. "Not even a white lie."

"You need to convince her to come work for me," he urges, and I shake my head.

"Not a chance in hell I'm letting this one out of my sight."

"I thought she wasn't your girl."

"She's not my girl." I turn to her and wink. "She's her own girl, but she's also my employee, so technically, she's mine."

"Smart man," he says and walks away.

"Nice save." She looks at me and takes a sip of her drink. "Also, I am my own girl."

"Do you want to sit?" I ask, pointing at an empty table in the back. Two cushioned chairs face a small round table.

"Sure." She walks away from me toward the table. She sits down on one of the cushions, and I sit next to her, but I move the table farther away from us so I can scoot my chair closer to her.

"I don't want this night to end," I admit as I take a sip of my scotch, putting my ankle on my knee.

"It has to end sometime," she says softly as she puts her purse on the table in front of her but leans back into the cushion, looking at me.

"Does it?" I ask. I would make a deal with the devil not to have this night end and we both stay exactly where we are.

"Yes, yes, it does." She turns a little toward me.

"What would your boyfriend say if he knew you were here with me?" Every single time I mention this guy, I hate him more and more, and I've never even fucking met him. But I know I'm jealous he's had her for the past two years.

"One." She takes a sip of her drink, and I see she's a bit nervous. "He's not technically my boyfriend. We are still trying to figure things out." Even though she's saying the words, she's not convinced of it. I give her a minute to take another sip of her drink. "I mean, I know what I want, but after two years, you would think he would have it figured out already."

I look into her eyes, the promises unspoken. "What do you want?" I ask her the loaded question. I wait, my heart hammering in my chest, my tongue heavy in my mouth to promise to give her everything she has ever wanted even though I don't know what that is.

"I don't really know." She finishes her drink and leans forward to put the empty glass on the table in front of her. "No, forget that," she quickly adds. "I know exactly what I want. I want the whole fucking thing." Her hands are animated when she's talking, and I want to take one of them and hold it in mine after I kiss it to get her to relax. "I want to marry a man who has my back and supports my career. A man who is proud of me and who I'm proud of. A house with a white picket fence"—she rolls her eyes—"which sounds dumb."

"It doesn't sound dumb," I say softly, taking a gulp of my scotch, but she doesn't even hear me. She just continues talking.

"I want two point five kids." I roll my lips to stop laughing at her, knowing she would probably glare at me, but with all my drinks, it escapes me, and she glares at me.

"Baby, you can't have two point five kids."

"I mean, I want to have two kids and be pregnant with another. And you know what?"

"I'm all ears." I reach out my hand and put it on her leg, expecting her to toss it off, but she's so worked up over this that she either doesn't notice or is okay with it.

"When I have kids, I want to be a stay-at-home wife. I want to put my career on the back burner while I become the PTA president or whatever it is they are called. I want to go on field trips and drive them to school and pick them up. I want to be there when they have horrible days because a kid was being mean to them, and I'm not too afraid to say I'll go toe-to-toe with their mother if they pick on my kids." She's so fucking gorgeous that I can't say a word. "I want to be there when they have the best day and have them tell me all about it. I want to do all of those things. That's what I want. I also want a man who will be okay with me staying home and doing that and not look down at it, thinking it's going to be a walk in the park. I want a healthy sex life." She shrugs. "You know, the basics."

"Then you should marry me." I say the words I've wanted to say to her since the first time I met her, and she smiled at me. "I don't know if I can give you all of that, but I know I can give you the whole picture in color, and what I can't give you I'm going to bust my ass to give you." Her mouth gapes open. "I will give you the white picket fence, the two point five babies. You can stay home, work part-time, whatever you want to do, you do, but I want to go on the record by saying that I want an above-average, healthy sex life."

I wait for her to say something, and her laughter fills the bar. "Yeah, right."

I sit up, putting my glass on the table beside hers, turning to her, my hand slipping off her lap. "I'm one thousand percent serious right now. Marry me, Zoey."

"No way." She sits up, not turning to me, her head moving side to side as if she can't believe what I'm saying. "Are you crazy?"

"Never been more sure of anything in my life." I tell her the truth, my heart hammering in my chest as I make the biggest deal of my life. "Marry me." I see her hand shaking a bit as she stares at me. "Come on, Zoey, it'll be fun."

She pffts at me, but I move closer to her, my hand coming up to touch her face. My thumb rubs over her cheek like I've done a million times in my head. "Come on, Zoey, live a little," I urge, getting closer to her, our knees touching each other. "Make all my dreams come true, and then watch me make yours come true." I put my forehead to hers. I've never even kissed this woman, and I want to spend the rest of my life with her. "Marry me." She puts her hand on my wrist, her touch soaring through my body. "What do you say, Zoey, will you marry me?"

I don't know how long I wait. I don't even know if I'm breathing. I don't know how many people are around us. I don't hear the slot machines or the laughter from nearby people. I don't see anything but her eyes turning a soft green gray, and I don't hear anyone's voice but hers when she whispers, "Okay."

EIGHT

NASH

IT'S AS IF the room around us comes to a standstill, or at least that's what it feels like. I hear myself breathing, or better yet panting. I swear I hear every single thump of my heart beating as I wait for her answer. Willing her to say yes, silently begging her to say yes. Praying to whoever is listening to me or looking down at all the sinners in Vegas. One beat, two beats, three beats, and I see her lick her lips, and then as if the gates of heaven open and angels start to sing, she whispers, "Okay."

The heart beating in my chest soars, and I move my head to the side, slamming my mouth down on hers. Her mouth parts in shock, making it easy for my tongue to slide into her mouth, and when it does, it's as if I'm soaring. Her tongue hungrily twirls with mine as we both take what the other is giving. My hands never leave her face, and I angle my head to the side to deepen the kiss. Her hands come out to grip the lapels of my jacket, pulling me toward her. If we weren't in the middle of a busy bar, I would have pulled her on top of me. I rub my nose with hers as I disengage from the kiss. Her eyes flutter open as I see her lips are wet, making me lean in and suck the lower one into my mouth while my tongue comes back out to invade her mouth for a second time before I let the kiss go again. Her eyes remain closed for a good two seconds before she opens them. "We have to go." She stares at me as I drop my hands from her face and pull the phone out of my pocket. "Let's go."

"Where are we going?" she asks as she stands beside me and bends down to collect her purse from the table in front of her.

"We're going to get married." I reach for her hand, and she doesn't pull back. Instead, she slides her hand in mine as we walk through the crowd to the exit. I'm practically running out of the hotel, and looking over my shoulder, I see her giggle. The lightness in her eyes is everything, and I have to stop moving. She crashes into me, but it's worth it. "Fuck, I've wanted to do this ever since I met you," I tell her as I put one hand on her hip and the other on her neck.

"What?" she asks, her eyes roaming my face.

"Kiss you whenever the fuck I want," I share before I tilt my head to the side and make out with her in the middle of the lobby. People zoom by all around us, but I'm lost in her taste. The kiss is long, it's wet, and it's fucking glorious. "Fuck," I curse when I let her go.

"Was that not good?" she asks, leaning into me, my hand on her hip going to the top of her ass.

"That was so good that if we don't leave, I'm going

to fuck you on that table." I motion with my head to the side where a round table sits.

She laughs with her hand on my chest. "Nash, that kiss was good"—she tilts her head to the side—"but it wasn't panty-melting." She nips the bottom of my jaw. "I think you can do better."

"Oh, baby," I say, and her eyes go darker, "I'm making it my goal for you to try to remember a time my mouth wasn't attached to you."

"Now is a good time to start." She tilts her head back, waiting for my kiss, and I don't let her wait long. Whereas the last kiss was hard and wet, this one is just as wet but softer until she presses her tits into my chest. Then my hand on the top of her ass goes south, grabbing her ass and squeezing it while I pull her to me. Both of us moan at the same time, drowning out the other one.

"How's that for a start?" I bend to kiss her neck.

"I mean, it's a start." She winks at me as I turn to walk out of the venue and toward our hotel. We zigzag through the crowd, her hand never leaving mine while we go through the revolving door together. Her laughter makes my hard cock turn to granite. I walk over to the concierge desk, and the man looks up at me with a smile.

"Good evening," he greets us. "How can I help you?" He looks at me, and then at Zoey standing right beside me.

"We want to get married," I reply to the man, and Zoey turns from beside me, moving her fingers in mine so she's got her front against my side. "Now."

I want to say the man is surprised by this request,

but it's Vegas, and I'm sure he gets asked this hourly. "I see," he says. "Well, let's start with the first thing. I'm assuming you are both over the age of eighteen." I don't have to answer because Zoey snorts from beside me. "You both need a valid driver's license, passport, or Social Security card."

We untangle from each other. My hand goes to the wallet in my inside pocket, tossing the

license on the top of his counter. Looking over, I see Zoey toss hers right next to mine. He nods at us. "The marriage license fee is seventy-seven dollars," he states, and I toss my black credit card right next to the other two. "Perfect, now you need to take the marriage license application to the Clark County Marriage Bureau," he instructs, looking at his watch. "You have about two hours until they close." He holds up his finger but only to pick up his phone. "Good evening, this is Curtis from the Bellagio. I have a couple who are on their way to pick up a marriage license." He stops talking. "I can email you all their documents to start the process, but they will be handing in the original one, as well as their two pieces of ID." He looks at us and smiles.

"Yes," Zoey says from beside me, "I think that's a good sign."

He hangs up the phone and looks at me. "Okay, I need you both to fill this out while I scan your IDs," he directs, handing us a form. "While you do this, I will also have a driver ready to take you there and wait for you."

"We need a chapel," I say, grabbing a pen to fill out the form. "Whichever one you know." I look at him.

"Whatever the cost. I want whatever package you have, just bigger and better."

"Of course, we can have it here. I know someone who can marry you right after you leave the courthouse."

"Oh, we need Elvis." Zoey leans in to say in my ear, "We can't get married in Vegas without it being Elvis."

"My wife would like Elvis." I wink at her as I turn back to Curtis. "Also, the honeymoon suite, is it available?"

"I would have to check the availability," he says, turning to his computer and clicking on a couple of things. "We have one available." He reads the screen.

"We'll take it," I tell him as I finish filling in my information and then hand the pen to Zoey, who starts on her side.

He nods. "Now, would you like a photographer?"

I look at Zoey. "Oh, yes!" Then she gasps, "I need a bouquet."

"She needs a bouquet," I tell the man, who tries not to smirk and just types something on his keyboard.

"I'm assuming it will just be the two of you?" he asks.

"Yup," I confirm, tapping the counter, "just me and the wife."

Zoey looks at me and giggles before she looks back down and continues filling out the form. I gasp, "We need rings."

"Oh, I want a ring," Zoey declares. "Do I get a ring?" She points at herself.

"You get two rings," I tell her, and she looks at Curtis, smiling ear to ear.

"I get two." She holds up two fingers. "Score."

"The first thing we need to do is get you over to the courthouse," Curtis informs us. "When you get back, I will have everything in your suite waiting for you." He looks over at the door and gives the man standing there a chin up, and he comes rushing over. "I will also transfer everything from your rooms to the suite."

"This is so easy," Zoey says, tossing down the paper. "No wonder so many people get married in Vegas."

"This man is going to take you to get your marriage license," he says. "Once you present yourself with the paperwork and your government IDs, it should take fifteen minutes." He hands me both licenses and the form, along with my credit card. "I will have someone here upon your return."

"Ohh," Zoey whispers, "we get to make out in the car." She slides her hand in mine as I rush her out to the same SUV that picked us up. I toss the paper to the side before grabbing her face and pulling her to me. I don't know how long it takes to get there, but we make out the whole time. We walk into the building, my eyes scanning for the sign. It takes us two minutes to hand in everything and then she tells us to take a seat.

"What type of ring do you want?" I ask, leaning and kissing her neck. I move up to her ear, sucking her lobe into my mouth. She gives me a soft moan. "I know what wedding band I'm getting you," I tell her.

"Ohh," she says, "I get to give you a ring also."

"Anything you want, baby." She leans in to kiss me, but the clerk calls our name. I walk up with her hand in mine and grab the paper before walking outside. The driver waits at the curb, and as soon as he sees us, he pops a bottle of champagne, making Zoey laugh. I stop moving to look at her. "I promise to make you laugh every single day of our lives." She comes to me and puts a hand on my cheek. "Among other things." She chuckles.

"Challenge accepted, Mr. Griffin." She nips my lip before she tilts her head to the side and kisses me. "Let's go get married," she urges, walking down the steps toward the driver who is holding a full glass in one hand and waiting to fill the other. I grab the full one and hand it to Zoey while he fills the second glass. "We need to toast."

I hold up my glass. "To the best night of my life."

"Our life," she corrects me, clinking my glass before downing her whole glass of champagne. I shake my head, finishing my own before we get back into the car. She turns to me when I get into the seat, her hands going to my face. "I have a secret," she whispers, looking into my eyes and smiling big as she says it. "I've wanted to make out with you all night long." I don't bother answering her. Instead, I lean in and wait for her to bend her head to mine, my tongue ready for hers when she slides it into my mouth. The sweetness from the champagne is all over it, and this kiss is more needy than the ones we had driving over here.

When we return to the hotel, Curtis waits for us in the lobby with a woman beside him dressed almost the same, but instead of pants, she's wearing a skirt. "Mr. and future Mrs. Griffin," he greets us, "we have everything waiting for you." I reach into my inside pocket and hand him the marriage certificate. "Claudette will take you to your room and get everything ready. Elvis will be here within an hour, whenever you are ready."

We follow Claudette up to the suite. "Welcome to the penthouse suite," she announces, opening the door for us. I see balloons that fill the whole ceiling as soon as we walk past the wet bar and powder room. "Mr. Smith will help with your rings." She points at the man sitting at the dining room table with a black tablecloth on the surface and rings all over it.

A butler is on the side of the wet bar, holding a silver tray with two glasses of champagne. "This is so pretty." Her eyes light up as she looks around the room. "And the flowers…" She points at all the vases of white flowers all around the room. "It's magical."

I walk up to her, pulling her into my arms. Her hand drops her purse to the floor as she places her palms on my chest. "Are you happy?" I ask her the loaded question. It's a question that is heavier than the will-you-marry-me question, and that one was huge.

She smirks, looking down at her hands, then she looks up at me, and her face fills with the biggest smile I've ever seen. Over the years, I've seen her smile many times, in person and on her Instagram. It's as if her smile is engrained in my brain, but this smile right here is a new one. One I've never seen before. One that makes the corner of her eyes crinkle. Her eyes are almost a crystal blue, with shades of yellow in them, and the smile has filled her whole face. It's a smile I'm going to do everything in my power to see every single day of my life. "I've never been happier."

NINE

ZOEY

MY HEAD TURNS to the side, and I can feel my head pounding as my eyes try to open, but they feel like they weigh over a hundred pounds. I open my mouth and then close it, trying to get some saliva so I can swallow, but it feels like I'm in the desert on the hottest day of the year, and someone threw sand in my mouth. The moan escapes me when I finally do crack them open a bit, the light from the sun almost blinds me, making me close my eyes again.

I try to get up, and the minute I lift my head, my body falls back down into the mattress like a dead weight. "I'm never drinking again," I mumble the words, taking a deep inhale before trying it again. But this time, as soon as I sit up in bed, I open my eyes and immediately go down. It isn't even a fight at this point. I also do it because my head spins, and then the light from the sun feels like it's burning my brain. "Ugh." I turn my head to the side and open them slowly, putting one hand over my face.

I look over at the side of the bed and see Nash's naked back, his head turned away from me. My eyes go wide when I see the sheet at the base of his back but only on one side. One leg is out of the cover and cocked up, along with one beautiful perfect ass cheek. His smooth, tanned back makes my mouth water. "Fuck, fuck, fuck," I groan before turning my head to the other side of the room.

My eyes scan the room and see the dress I wore last night tossed on the floor with one of my shoes near it. I'm not sure where the other one is. I think I remember Nash taking one off and tossing it over one shoulder before he took the other one off and tossed it over the other one before his mouth devoured my pussy, making me forget everything I was saying at the time. I swear I get wet just thinking about it. I attempt to sit up again. This time, the sheet falls off me, leaving me naked. I quickly reach for it again, bringing it up to my chest to cover myself even though I think I saw a hickey near my nipple. I look over at the side table to see if there is a water bottle. I see two glasses of champagne, both of them empty, and right near them are two bottles of water. I reach over, grabbing one and twisting open the blue top, tossing it to the side and downing the bottle of water. My eyes go to the side of my dress where I see a veil and a bouquet of white roses and baby's breath with a white-and-blue ribbon.

I hear my own voice in my head. "I want white roses and some greenery," I told the woman doing the bouquet live in our hotel suite. "And I'd like to have a blue-and-

white ribbon," I said excitedly before I looked over at Nash, who was sitting down at the table picking out my wedding band.

I shake my head and start to laugh. "That didn't happen." I lift my left hand up and almost drop the bottle of water as I stare at my left finger. The big square diamond in the middle with diamonds all around the band. The center diamond is massive, but the wedding band is even more massive. It's an eternity band, but each diamond is oval. The sun shines on it, and the reflection just sparkles on the ceiling. "This can't be real." I put my hand in a fist and bring it to my face. "This is fake." I bring it even closer. "This can't be," I say, looking over at Nash. "Who buys real diamonds in a hotel room?" I chuckle to myself.

I'm about to shake Nash awake when he groans from beside me. I watch him turn from facing the wall to facing me before he flips onto his back. The sheet that was half covering him is not covering anything at all but half of a leg. His body is on full display as the memories of after the wedding barrel into me.

I'm pretty sure I've worshipped and kissed every single inch of his body. Trailing it with my tongue after or maybe even right before we went into the shower, where he placed my ass on the cold tiled seat and then ate me until I came twice before he stood and fucked my face. My eyes roam his chest, going down and seeing his hand with the black wedding band on his finger. It's matte in the middle and shining on the top and bottom. The memory of the night before comes back to when we stood in the middle of the secluded little balcony overlooking the fountains.

I stand in front of him with my left hand in his left hand as his right hand slipped the ring onto my finger. "Zoey, I give you this ring as a sign of my undying love for you." I don't even think I took a single breath as he said the words. "With all that I have and all I can give you, I am honored to forever call you my wife from this moment until my last dying breath."

Elvis cooed and said, "All right now." I just remember looking down at the ring and blinking away the tears that threatened to come, but I refused to cry on what was one of the best nights of my life.

When it was my turn, I grabbed the black wedding band I chose for him, and holding his big hand in mine, I placed the ring on his finger. "I give you this ring as a sign of my love." I smile at him, and all I can remember is how happy and proud I felt. "With all that I have, I am honored to call you my husband from this moment until forever."

He didn't even wait for Elvis to pronounce us husband and wife. He grabbed my face and gave me the most amazing kiss I've ever had in my life. In. My. Life. It was sweet and soft, with lots of tongue. He claimed me like I've never been claimed. I felt the flashes from the camera coming one after another, but I was so lost in the kiss I didn't care. The minute he let go of my lips, he pulled me closer to his chest, lifting his hand in the air while I raised my bouquet over my head. Both of us laughed as we did it. The flashes came again, following our every move.

"Morning, baby," he mumbles from beside me. My eyes blink a couple of times, going from his hand to his face as his hand closest to me rubs my naked back, softly trailing his fingers up my spine, my body shivering under his light touch. When I look back at him, his eyes are closed.

"Um," I say, not sure what even to say. "Water?" I ask him, holding out my hand with the water bottle. He sits up next to me as my hand shakes with nerves, and my head feels like it's going to explode.

He takes the bottle from my hand and leans in to kiss my neck before finishing off the bottle. "Thank you, baby." His voice is soft, making my hands itch to reach out to touch him.

"So last night," I start to say nervously, "that was fun, right?"

"I'd say." He props the pillows behind his back and leans against the headboard, and the only thing that comes to mind is me grabbing on to it while he ate me out from the back before he fucked me hard. The soreness is apparent between my legs. "What word means more than fun?" He doesn't even cover himself. My eyes go to his chest and then down to his cock that is at half-mast right now, and my mouth waters to take it into my mouth. He's above average in length, but his thickness is where it's at. I had trouble getting my mouth around it, and every single time, I made it my mission to try to get more and more of him down my throat. "Best night of my life."

"Yeah," I say, blinking as my mouth gets dry, "what

happens in Vegas, right?"

My head screams, *oh my God, oh my God*. My heart pounds in my chest so hard I'm expecting it to come right through and flop on the bed in a bloody mess. "Should probably stay in Vegas." I look up to see his face go from soft to hard. "I mean, we could—you know—not tell anyone about it and it'll be like, remember that time we pretended to get married in Vegas?"

"Pretended?" His voice comes out hard, and then he laughs. "You think we pretended to get married?"

"Well, we did," I tell him, and he smirks and nods, like sure we did.

"I mean, it was lots of fun." I try to think of the words to say without telling him it was a mistake. Because, regardless, spending the night with him was not a mistake. I've done a lot of things in my life I regret, well, not that many, but last night was not one of them.

"I'd say it was a lot of fun. A lot more fun than I thought I was going to have on this trip."

I turn my body, holding the sheet to my chest. "So about the wedding. He wasn't really a reverend, so it was sort of a fake wedding, right?" I start to say, and he sits back up as I try not to freak out, knowing I just fucked up.

"It's not a fake wedding, Zoey," he bites out, making me angry.

"Of course it was a fake wedding." I gawk at him. "All weddings in Vegas are mostly fake." I throw up my hand that has my wedding ring on it. "I mean, not all weddings. Obviously, people come here to get married.

But they know they are getting married here, but ours was fake. Elvis wasn't even a pastor. I think he was even half drunk. He slurred most of his words and"—I open my eyes big—"he wanted me to promise to never step on your blue suede shoes." I gape at him and roll my eyes. "Or treat you like a fool." I wait for him to say something. "To love you tender and never return you to sender. Ugh, Nash." I put my hand on my head. "So obviously, it's not real."

"He was ordained." Nash laughs. "It's pretty real."

"Nash," I snap his name.

"Yeah, baby?" he replies softly, and I glare at him even though he's making my stomach get all mushy.

"Don't." I point at him. "The wedding was fake. It's Vegas."

"Zoey," he sings my name, the smile on his face big and annoying, and I wish I hated his face. I wish I didn't know what his hair felt like when I sink my fingers in it. I also hate that all last night's memories are now returning to me like a movie playing.

"Nash." I try to remain calm. "Everyone knows that weddings in Vegas don't really count if you are drunk. People go out and are like 'let's get married' and then the next day they are like 'that was fun but…'" My voice trails as I try not to freak out even more.

Nash sits up even more, but only to swing his legs out of his side of the bed, standing in front of me naked in all his glory, and I was wrong when I pictured him naked that first time I met him. I thought his body couldn't get any better than it was. I was wrong. He is leaner, more cut, his thighs meatier than I remembered. And his cock? They should make molds out of it. "Zoey," he calls my name, and I look up from his cock to his face. "Hate to break it to you, baby, but the marriage is real." I open my mouth to say something, and he holds up his hand. "Got the paper in my pocket that says we got married, and let me tell you, it's as real as it gets."

TEN

I PUT MY hands on my hips as I look at her with my wedding ring on her finger. "You're wearing my ring." I point at her. "I'm wearing yours." I hold up my hand. "And I'm going to keep wearing it."

"But you bought this in there." She points at the door that leads to the living room and the dining room. "It's not real."

"It cost me forty thousand dollars," I reply, and she gasps. "Trust me, those are real."

"Are you out of your mind?" she asks, and I just shake my head. "You have to be out of your mind, Nash." She looks at her hand. "You have to take them back."

"They engraved our initials in them," I point out, and she looks at me shocked. "You said we had to, so it'll always be there." I take a deep inhale. "I'm going to go and take a shower and then we are going to order some breakfast." I start to walk away from her. "Unless you want to come shower with me?" I wink at her. "We did a lot of married things in there." She closes her eyes and flops down on the bed. "Look at the room service menu and order something."

I walk toward the bathroom. "What do you want?"

"Whatever," I toss out, walking into the bathroom and turning on the water. My head throbs a bit. I figured she would freak out today, but I didn't expect her to think it was fake. I shake my head, looking around the bathroom. There are towels thrown everywhere because we took a bath, and she ended up riding me until we both came. The water was like a fucking tidal wave at the end. I had to put towels down to mop up all the water, even stepping on them now they are still soaking wet. The tub is still full of water, and a single loofah floats in it. I pull the plug up to drain the water and push all the towels to the side before turning the shower on.

I step in, chuckling at the conversation we just had. I let the water run over my neck that is getting tight thinking of my wife in the other room, freaking the fuck out. My wife. Holding out my hand, I see her wedding band there. What a fucking night. I turn off the water after I finish rinsing the body wash off me. Grabbing a towel and wrapping it around my waist, I take another one and run it over my head, drying my hair. Stepping back into the bedroom, I see her in the middle of the bed now with the room iPad in her lap. "This can't be real," she murmurs, looking up at me, and I see she has little red spots all around her lips from spending the night attached to my mouth. Every five minutes, my mouth was attached to hers, sometimes less. "It's not a fake wedding." She looks up at me. "I am never drinking again."

"You weren't that drunk when we got married," I point out. "I can't say for sure after we were married when we had our reception."

"A reception?" she shrieks.

"Yeah, Curtis set it up. We had cake," I tell her. "Then after he left, you took the icing and said you wanted to eat it off my…" She covers her face with both hands. "Then you pulled down your top and rubbed it all over your nipples." I smile. "Best cake I've had in my life. We did the garter toss right after."

"There was no garter toss." She peeks through her fingers.

"You're right." I smirk. "I placed your ass on the table after that and ate your pussy right before I took it off with my teeth. You wanted me to put it in your mouth while I fucked you."

She puts her head back and groans as I'm sure the memories are coming back to her when I hear my phone ringing. "Is that mine or yours?" I ask, and she just lifts both hands in the air, letting them fall back on the bed. "I think that's mine." I walk toward where the ringing is coming from.

Right out of the bedroom, I see the balloons all over the room, along with all the white flowers that seemed to multiply after we got married. The cake is in the middle of the table, right next to where her ass print is now showing. "Do you want any cake?" I shout back to the room, grabbing my jacket that is right next to one of my shoes.

"No, I don't want any cake!" she yells back. "I'm never eating cake again."

I laugh as the ringing stops, and I take it out and see it was Caine. "Did you order room service?" I ask her as I walk back into the bedroom, calling Caine back and putting it to my ear.

"Do you think I ordered room service?" She side-eyes me. "Does this look like I've ordered room service?"

"Baby, you look amazing, like you always do." I sit on the side of the bed, and I'm about to hang up on Caine to recreate a couple of moves from last night when he answers.

"Please tell me that picture you sent was a joke," he blurts, not even bothering with a hello.

"What picture?" I ask him, not sure what he's talking about. I look over at Zoey, who sits up in bed now.

"The picture of you and Zoey at the altar kissing with Elvis behind you," he says, making everything in me stop cold.

My eyes go big as I cover the phone with my hand. "We sent my brother a picture of us at our wedding," I whisper-hiss at her.

"Stop it right now." She throws the covers off her, and all I can do is stare at her body as she gets on the bed on her knees. Her hair is wild after taking a shower and me pulling it. She's got hickeys all over her body because I made sure I claimed every single fucking inch of her. From the top of her head to the tips of her toes, my mouth has been everywhere.

She reaches for me, and I think she's going to kiss me, but instead, she snatches the phone from me. "Tell me it's a joke, Nash," Caine says.

"One second, let me see what I sent you." I put the phone on speaker as I open my texts, seeing the top one to Caine. Opening it up, I see the picture in question. It's when I let her mouth go and looked at the camera with my hand up over my head. I felt like I won at life at that moment. "It's a nice picture." I look over at her as she looks down and just shakes her head.

"Wait a second." Caine's voice gets loud. "Is this real?"

"Oh, it's real," I confirm.

At the same time, Zoey says, "It's not real."

"Would you stop saying that?" I look at her as she sits beside me.

"Oh my God," Caine says, "have you two lost your minds?"

"I have to let you go," I tell Caine. "The wife and I are about to have our first fight, which will be followed by makeup sex." I wink at her, seeing her face go red, and I have to wonder if it's from embarrassment or the fact she wants me to fuck her as much as I want to fuck her.

"Oh my God," Zoey hisses at me, trying to grab the phone out of my hand at the same time my brother laughs. "Give me that phone."

"Call me later," Caine states right before he hangs up. I hold the phone higher in the air as she stretches her hand up to get it from me.

"Have I told you how fucking beautiful you are?" I

ask her the minute she stops struggling with me to get the phone. I toss it to the side of the bed, not giving a shit if it falls or breaks. I put my knee on the bed, getting onto the bed with her, and the towel falls from my hips as I make my way closer to her, my cock ready for her. Crawling until I'm in front of her, I grab her face in my hands and bend to kiss her. My tongue slides into her mouth, and she puts her hands on my chest. I love when she does this because I want her to feel how my heart beats for her. I want her to feel what I feel. I move my hands from her face to the sides of her neck, and her hands slide lower on my chest.

"We shouldn't be doing this," she mumbles when I let her lips go so I can bend and take one of her nipples in my mouth. Her back arches into my touch. "We really shouldn't be doing this."

"I don't know about that," I counter, moving from one nipple to the next. "I think we should do this again." I bite down on her nipple, my eyes moving to watch hers as her eyes flutter closed. "And again." I suck her nipple into my mouth, and at the same time, my hand comes up to pinch the other one. She moans out my name, and I swear it shoots right down to my cock like a lightning bolt. "And again." I move back up to her mouth, my tongue coming out and licking her lower lip at the same time as her tongue comes out to touch mine. "Spread your legs for me, baby."

She falls back on her back before she lays her feet down on the bed and opens her legs for me, exactly like I told her to. "That's my good girl," I praise, and her eyes get hooded when I say that. I crawl between her spread legs, putting my hands on the bed beside her arms. Her hands come to my face as I close the distance to her lips. I slide my tongue in her mouth at the same time as one of my hands holds my cock and runs it through her slit. Her wetness coats the head as I move down to her entrance and slide in.

She lets my mouth go to moan. "Yes," she says as I move my cock in and out of her, her pussy tight and wet. Her tongue slides into my mouth as I continue to fuck her slower than I did the last time. She lifts her legs, putting her feet right at the base of my back to make me sink deeper into her. "Hmm." She looks between us as my forehead touches hers.

"You watching me fucking you?" I ask, and she breathes out, not answering me. "Taking my cock like a good girl," I tell her, and her hands go from my face to my arms to my back. My hips move faster as she gets tighter and tighter, the wetness leaking out of her. I have to concentrate so I don't come before her, as that's never an option. I slam into her hard as my balls slap her ass. "Are you going to come for me?" I ask, her eyes watching my cock slide out of her and then disappear again. "Come on my cock like a good girl, baby." Her hips move to match my thrusts this time. "Show me how much you like when my cock fucks you," I urge, pressing my chest to her as I slide my tongue into her mouth, and she sucks my tongue like she sucks my cock.

"I'll come on your cock," she barters, "if you come in my mouth."

"Right down your throat," I tell her, and she nods. Her pussy makes it hard for me to move now. "You're really going to suck the cum out of me?"

"Yes, I want to suck the cum out of you," she moans right before she closes her eyes. I feel wetness all around me as her pussy spasms, dripping down my balls as I slam into her over and over again. This orgasm lasts longer than the last one did, and I swear I can feel another one coming. "I think I'm there again."

"Then ride it, baby," I urge her, and she thrashes her head side to side.

"I don't think I can," she says. Instead of answering her, I just fuck her harder, throwing her leg over my shoulder so I can sink into her deeper. "Oh, God." I close my eyes, trying not to come inside her, making her ride out her second orgasm. "Yes," she cheers, her pussy not stopping the spasming as it strangles my cock. "Nash," she says, and I groan. "Not in my pussy. I want it in my mouth." We've been together less than twenty-four hours, and she knows the sounds I make when I'm close. "In my mouth."

"Then you better get ready," I warn, pulling out. Her legs fall to the sides, and she sits up at the same time as she swallows my cock. "Fuck," I hiss. I don't know which one I like coming in more, her pussy or her mouth. Her hand grips the bottom of my shaft as she fists me and sucks me at the same time. My hips fuck her mouth at the same pace I was fucking her pussy. She moans when I hit the back of her throat, and it vibrates through me, pushing me off the edge. I come in her mouth, right down her throat, and like most of the times before when I was in her mouth, she swallows everything I have to give her. Her hand slows down when I finish shooting in her mouth. She looks up at me as she pulls my cock from her mouth before licking the head like it's a lollipop, the tip of her tongue sliding into my slit to take whatever cum is left in there. "Hmm," I say right before I move away from her touch and see her sitting there, her legs open, her pussy glistening. "Time for me to eat breakfast," I announce, and her eyes light up at the same time as they darken. "Lie back, baby, and let me eat," I say right before she lies down and I devour her pussy.

ELEVEN

Zoey

I SUCK HIS cock into my mouth, then let it go before I spit on the head of it and crawl up, straddling him. I lean down and put one hand on his cheek as I bend to kiss him. I could kiss him every single fucking hour of every single fucking day. I don't even need him to touch me, just kiss me, and I think I would be happy. He puts his hands on my hips before reaching between us to position his cock so I can sit on it. "Ride me, baby," he invites between kisses as I move my hips up and down, getting him all the way inside me. Filling me like I've never been filled before. He literally fucked me not less than thirty minutes ago before he came down my throat. He then proceeded to eat my pussy like it was his last meal, taking me to the edge over and over again. Making the orgasm build inside me so hard that when he finally sucked my clit and rubbed my G-spot as he finger-fucked me, I think I saw fucking stars. I've never been with a man who draws it out. Usually, they just want to get it over with, but not fucking Nash. He savors it, makes it last so fucking long every single touch feels like he's setting me on fire.

"That's it," he urges, his hands moving with my hips. I kiss him like it's the last time I'm going to kiss him. The kiss is as wet as he's making me. His hands move to my ass as I ride his cock, my forehead on his as I watch his eyes as I take him slowly. "That's it, baby, take me." I get up a bit on my hands as I move faster on him, my tits hanging near his mouth. "That's my girl." He sucks my nipple into his mouth as he moves to the other one. "Taking my cock the way she wants to take my cock." Just his words make me wet. I move faster and faster, feeling it coming, which is impossible because I think I've had four orgasms in less than ten minutes. But the bottom of my stomach gets tight, and I can't help but move faster, as if I'm chasing it as it tries to run away from me. When his hands stop moving my hips, I groan. "You were going too fast," he informs me as his hands move from my hips to my tits and he plays with my nipples. "Enjoy the ride."

"I was enjoying the ride," I groan, moving my hips slowly, the feeling lingering, "I was almost at the end of the ride."

"I know." He smirks. "But you just got on." I rotate my hips, his cock twitching inside me as I bend to kiss him again. The kiss is slow and less frantic than it was a couple of minutes ago, which makes me want to ride him harder than I did before. I suck his upper lip into my mouth. "Baby," he murmurs, "I want you to sit on my cock."

"I am." I slide my tongue into his mouth again as I move my hips, looking into his eyes as I move again.

"No, sit up," he orders me. "Sit straight up on my cock." I move my hands to his chest as I sit straight up on his cock, and I swear he fucking touches my fucking throat. "That's what I'm talking about." All I can do is feel the way his cock fills me more than it did before. "Tell me what you feel."

"I feel full," I admit to him. "I feel like I'm coming out of my skin." His hands move from my knees to my hips, just with his fingertips, the touch so light if I wasn't watching, I wouldn't know, yet the touch soaring through me.

"Listen to your body," he urges me, and I just stare at him. "What does your body want to do?"

"It wants to ride your cock," I tell him.

"Put your hands on my knees," he instructs me, and I reach behind my back, arching a bit as I do it, and the way his cock is curved inside me makes me shiver. "Your body wants to move, doesn't it?" he asks, and I can't answer. The only thing I can do is nod. I sit on his cock without moving, and I swear I'm about to come all over him. He sticks his thumb in his mouth before moving it to my clit. "Move up and down twice, slowly," he urges. I do as he says, his thumb moving as slow as I'm moving on his cock. My eyes close in ecstasy because his cock rubs my G-spot at the same time. "What do you feel?"

"Heaven." It's the only word that comes to my mind. "I need more."

"Then take more, baby," he says. "Two more." This time, his thumb moves side to side instead of in a circle. "You want more than two?" he asks, and I groan because all the words are fucking lost. "Now you can ride my cock." He gives me the go-ahead. "Feel my cock rub your G-spot?" he asks me as his thumb rubs faster and faster. "Every single time you get a touch tighter," he says. "If you think my cock feels like heaven"—I watch his face—"I wish you could feel what your pussy feels like."

"Tell me," I ask, hoping it's just as good for him as it is for me.

"It feels like my cock is rubbing on satin." His thumb never lets go. "Like it's wet and tight and velvet smooth." His hips move up to meet me when I thrust down. "Like your pussy was made for my cock, and my cock was made for your pussy." I have to close my eyes, the power of his words, the way his cock rubs inside me, the way his finger manipulates me. My whole body tingles. "I can feel you're close. Even your clit is getting hard, baby." I swear I ride him harder than I thought I could. "Fuck, baby, get what you want." I can't even say the words because I feel like I'm coming apart. My pussy contracts, and my clit pulses, my body fucking trembling as this orgasm shoots through me. My body moves on its own, taking everything he has. "That's my girl," he praises as he helps match my thrusts to ride it out. When I'm at the end, he holds my hips down on his cock and groans out his own release inside me.

"That was…" I say, leaning forward on him. "That

was…" His arms wrap around my waist. "That was"—I breathe in his scent, and my stomach contracts—"that was the last time." I close my eyes as he moves under me before I hear the laughter roar out of him. "I'm not kidding."

"Me either," he says, turning me on my back and sliding his cock out of me. "That was the last time this hour." He gets off the bed. "Don't move, I'll bring you a rag."

I watch him walk with his perfect ass, perfect body, perfect fucking cock into the bathroom before I look up at the ceiling. I listen to the water running, trying not to think about how nice it is that he's going to bring me a rag to clean myself with instead of lying in the bed and making me get up to clean myself. He walks back in with the white rag in his hand. I extend my hand to his, but he washes me off instead of giving me the rag.

"Um, I think I can do that."

"I'm sure you can," he replies as he washes me gently, "but I can also." He finishes washing me, bending and kissing me on the landing strip I have. "I'm assuming you didn't order room service."

"When would I have had the time to order room service?" I sit up, grabbing the sheet and covering myself with it. "Before or after I went on the internet to see if our wedding was real?"

He walks over to the closet and comes back out wearing a robe, and my brain screams out *nooo* while my eyes watch one of my favorite parts of him being covered. "I'll order the food, then," he says, reaching for the iPad and lying back down on the bed with me.

I can hear ringing coming from the living room, and I know it's not his since I think he tossed his phone somewhere on the bed, and then I might have heard a clunk when he was stretched out eating my pussy. "That's mine," I say, tossing the covers off and rushing to the living room in search of the ringing. Rushing to the door where my purse was tossed to the side, I open it to see it's not there. The ringing stops, and I stand, taking in the area, the strings of the balloons hanging all over the room. It smells like a flower shop with all the roses around the space. I'm about to go back when the ringing starts again, and this time, I follow it and find the phone right under Nash's pants that came off after I gave him head beside our wedding cake.

I turn the phone over and see it's my father, and I swear to everything I'm a sixteen-year-old girl again who just smashed their car into the garage by accident. "Oh my God. Oh my God. Oh my God." My eyes just watch the phone. "Maybe he'll hang up," I wish out loud, but I know I have to answer him. Maybe he's just calling to see how I am and if I'm ready for the vacation. "Hello," I answer, trying to pretend as if I'm not keeping a huge secret. "Hey, Dad." I put him on speakerphone and close my eyes.

"Please, for the love of God, Zoey." His voice goes from low to high-pitched by the end of it, and I look up to see Nash coming out of the bedroom with the second robe in his hand. He walks over and holds it out so I can slip my hands into it. "Tell me you're not married to

Nash."

"It was a mistake," I say softly.

"It was a mistake." His calm demeanor has left the building. I'm pretty sure it left the building the minute he found out what I did. "No, a mistake is I took the wrong flight. You getting married to someone is a lot more than a mistake."

"Evan," my mother says in the background, "would you—" He must look at her or glare at her because I don't hear her anymore.

"We're getting divorced." I look at my phone and not at Nash, who chuckles and doesn't miss a beat of this.

"We're not getting divorced." He doesn't even pretend to whisper, nope, not him. He's fully letting my father know that he's in this conversation.

I glare up at him. "Can you not talk to me when I'm on the phone?" I ignore the way he grins as I close my eyes and walk back to the bedroom, sitting on the bed. "Dad, I swear I thought it was a joke."

"Zoey." His voice goes low. "Are you serious?"

"Yes," I admit, "I swear I thought it was a joke." I inhale. "Who actually gets married in Vegas?"

"Um," he sings, "your aunt Allison and uncle Max. It's not like your uncle Matthew doesn't bring it up at least once a week."

"Yes," I say, "but that's different. They knew they were getting married."

"Did you not know you were getting married?" he asks, and I look at Nash, who is now standing in front of me with his arms crossed over his chest, his wedding band catching my eye.

"Well, I knew we were getting married," I admit, "but I just thought it was fake because it was Elvis." My voice goes loud. "And he wanted me to be in a hunka, hunka burning love." I should stop talking at this moment, but I can't. "I'm sorry, Dad."

"For what?" My father's voice is softer now.

"Not my proudest moment," I say. When I feel the tear about to leave my eye, I brush it away. I've never wanted him not to be proud of me.

"It'll be a funny story when we look back on it." He tries to make me feel better, and the knock on the door has Nash turning and walking back out of the room. "We'll talk more when I see you."

"Gives you time to calm down," I try to joke with him, laughing through the tears.

"Or gives you time to come up with a better excuse," he counters. "I love you, Zoey, and I'm always proud of you. Some moments more than others, but always."

"Thanks, Dad. I love you," I say before I disconnect the phone and look down at my notifications, seeing I have about twenty-five missed calls and over one hundred missed text messages. Fifteen different family chat threads are going crazy, and then I spot the one with Josh's name flashing on the top, so I open it up and see.

Josh: *You need to call me right fucking now, Zoey.*
Josh: *What's up with your Instagram?*
Josh: *WTF did you do?*

I switch open my Instagram, and right there at the top of my profile is a picture of Nash and me from last night.

It's the same picture he sent to Caine with the caption: Introducing Mr. & Mrs. Griffin.

"Oh my God." I don't even bother reading the comments because I see a couple from my cousins Michael and Dylan, and I just can't deal with this right now. I hear the door slam and look up when Nash comes back into the room.

"Do you want to eat in here or at the table?" He points toward the door and doesn't even wait for me to answer before he switches topics. "And just saying, we aren't getting divorced."

I put my head back. "You haven't even had one serious relationship in your life."

"Until now." He points at me. "I'm pretty serious about this relationship right here."

"Okay, well then, let's go with we don't even really know each other."

"Fine, I'll give you that. We don't know each other as well as other people who get married know each other." He stands in front of me. "Give me ninety days for you to fall in love with me. For us to fall in love with each other."

I gawk at him. "That's not how this works," I point out. "Usually, you get to know someone, and then you get married. You know, go out on dates."

"I'm not going to be dating my ex-wife," he scoffs. "I'm going to date my wife."

"That makes absolutely no sense, Nash."

He walks to me and puts his hands on my cheeks. "You were crying?" he asks softly, his thumbs wiping away where the tears must have left marks. "I don't like it." His words throw me off guard.

"Can we focus on one conversation at a time?" I tell him, trying not to get sucked into his charm.

"Yes," he says, "we aren't getting divorced because we are going to be dating."

"Again," I huff, "that makes no fucking sense."

"It makes all the sense in the world, baby." He bends to kiss my lips. "Besides, who dates their ex-wife?" He shakes his head. "Now that's just weird."

TWELVE

I SEE HER eyes moving from my eyes to my lips and back to my eyes. "Now, let's go eat," I urge, kissing her softly. "We need to keep up our strength."

"No." She shakes her head. "We don't need to keep anything up because that's not going to happen again."

"I mean, not right now." I grab her hand in mine, and I don't expect her to follow me, but her fingers wrap around mine exactly how she did last night. We walk out of the bedroom hand in hand, both of us wearing the hotel robes, as I lead her to the table the room service attendant put all the food on. "I didn't know what you ate, so I ordered one of everything," I say once we get to the side of the table. "I also got you a mimosa," I tell her, walking over to the bottle of champagne in the ice bucket. Picking up the bottle of champagne and popping it, the sounds make her jump a little as the top spills over, so I move closer to the bucket. "Baby, give me a glass." I point at the two crystal glasses set on a silver tray with orange juice and pineapple juice.

"I said I wasn't drinking again," she reminds me as she hands me both glasses.

"What's the worst that can happen?" I wink at her as I pour half of the glass full before the bubbles fill it up the rest of the way, then hand it back to her. "We're already married. Unless you want to have a baby?"

"Are you out of your mind?" she shrieks, grabbing the glass from me before sliding into the chair in front of her. "A baby?" She shakes her head. "This"—she points at the table before grabbing the pineapple juice instead of the orange juice—"is one reason we should get divorced." Filling the rest of her glass with the juice. "My husband would know what I eat for breakfast."

"What do you eat for breakfast?" I ask, pouring my own glass of champagne. "To my wife." I hold up my glass, and she reluctantly clinks her glass with mine. "The best wife ever," I declare, pulling out the chair right next to hers. "Top of the charts, baby." I wink at her as I take a sip of my champagne.

"Okay, what did you get?" She ignores me as she sips her mimosa before looking at the five plates covered by domes.

"Pancakes and French toast for sweet, a plate of scrambled eggs with sausage and bacon and of course white toast, wheat toast, and an everything bagel."

"So literally one of everything," she notes, picking up a dome.

"Basically," I confirm, watching her grab a piece of pancake and then opening another one to scoop some eggs on top of the pancake in a line. I watch, fascinated with what she is doing as she opens the lids until she finds the sausage and bacon, putting one piece each on the pancake. "What are you doing?" I ask her as she starts to roll it.

"It's a breakfast taco," she says, smiling. "A husband would know that."

"You learn something new about your spouse every single day," I inform her. "My parents still learn something new about each other every single day." I grab a pancake and copy what she just did. "Speaking of my parents, I should call them."

"That would be nice. Unless they are on Instagram, then they probably saw it," she says, taking another bite of her concoction. "Apparently, we posted it on our Instagrams last night or this morning."

"What picture did we use?" I ask, and she just stares at me.

"It doesn't bother you that we posted we were married on your Instagram?" she asks as if posting her on my Instagram is the end of the world.

"Nope. Saves me from doing it tomorrow," I state. "I do have to call Kailyn and ask her to postpone all my meetings for the next two weeks." I make mental notes to do all the things. "When is the family vacation?" I ask her as I take my own bite and agree it's pretty good. "You know what this is missing?" I take another bite. "Hash browns."

"Vacation is in two days," she answers, dipping her taco in the maple syrup container. "I have to go to New

York and get my things."

"We'll go back to LA together." I chew. "I'll grab my stuff, and then we'll go together to New York."

She stops mid-chew. "Wait, you're coming with me?" Her eyes move side to side.

"Baby, it's practically our honeymoon." She rolls her eyes. "Now hurry up and eat because I want to get to know my wife better." I take a bite of my taco. "I have some chocolate sauce and champagne, and I want to know if it tastes the same on a person."

"You aren't getting me all sticky with that." She laughs.

"Okay, fine, you can eat it off me. Either way, I win." I wink at her, and she shakes her head.

By the end of the meal, I even add in the maple syrup, and she is a sticky mess. Well, we both are.

The next day, we fly back to LA, and we are there for literally an hour before we have to fly to New York. "Mrs. Griffin," I say when she gets into my car after being away from her for a whole hour, "you didn't even give me a hello kiss."

"Isn't Mrs. Griffin your mother?" She turns so her back is against the door. "I'm sure she will give you a hello kiss."

"Very funny," I deadpan, leaning forward to kiss her, and she kisses me as if we haven't seen each other for a day instead of an hour. Her hand comes up to hold my cheek as our tongues slide into each other's mouths. "Hi, wife," I say softly against her lips, "you ready?"

"As ready as I'll ever be," she replies, and we make

our way over to the plane that will be flying us to New York. "There are a couple of things we need to discuss."

"We're on vacation," I say. "Can we discuss things when we get back? Right now, I want sun, sand, and sex with my wife."

She laughs. "You can have that without me."

"But I don't want anything without you." I take her hand and kiss it. Grabbing our bags, we make our way to the plane, and the flight attendant is there waiting for us.

"Mr. and Mrs. Griffin, welcome aboard. We have a delivery," she says, looking at Zoey, who looks at me and then at the attendant with a confused look.

The white box is in the middle of the tray table. "Um, are you sure it's for me?" she asks as she walks and sees her name on top of the card. "What did you do?"

"I didn't do anything." I pretend I have no idea what's in the box as she unties the white ribbon and opens the box. She moves the tissue paper to the side and sees the jean jacket folded in the middle. "What is this?" Her eyes are bright, and a smile fills her face as she takes it out of the box.

"Turn it over," I tell her, and when she does, she throws her head back and laughs.

"Very funny." She shows me the back that is all glittered with the name Mrs. Griffin. "Thank God you put your name on there. Now they know where to return me in case I get lost."

I snort. "As if I would let you out of my sight," I say as she puts the jacket back into the white box.

We sit in the seats side by side, and when we are able

to, we get up, and I drag her over to the couch. "Come make out with me."

"I'm not making out with you." She shakes her head.

"Why not? We can just make out. It doesn't have to lead to sex," I say, grinning, "unless you want it to."

"You are out of your mind," she says, sitting on the couch. I sit next to her, extending my arm over the back of the couch, and pull her to me. It takes a minute before she's making out with me. We're side by side at first, and then I slowly pull her onto my lap. By the time we land, she's lying on top of me. I think we spent a total of ten minutes not making out with each other.

My cock is hard like a rock. I can tell she's on edge because when we get into the foyer of her house, she drops to her knees and takes me into her mouth. I give her one minute before I pick her up by her armpits and slam her against the wall. Her legs wrap around my waist as I move my pants down my hips. She picks her skirt up, moving her panties to the side so I can slide into her.

"You better hurry," I urge her as I thrust into her. "It was a long six hours." I don't have to say another word because she bites down on my bottom lip and comes at the same time as I do. "Fuck," I groan when I slide out of her, and her legs fall to the floor. "That was the longest foreplay of my life."

"The plane ride tomorrow is only four hours," she mentions. "It'll be better."

"I almost asked for a blanket so I could finger-fuck you," I admit, and she gasps. "Exactly, I don't want to die before we go on our honeymoon. After that, I don't think I'll care." I slap her ass as we walk in the dark house. "I need a shower and bed."

We slide into bed, and even though she tries to pretend she hates to be held, she is in my arms and asleep in less than a second. The flight the next day is about the same, except she would set timers so we stopped making out for a full twenty minutes.

In the truck on the way to the resort, I don't care what she says, I pull her into my lap and make out with her the whole way. "We need to test out the bed first," I say to her as the truck comes to a stop. "I need to get into you."

"You've been in me twice today," she reminds me as she steps out of the truck.

"That doesn't count. We weren't in the same time zone as we are now." I grab her hand, bringing it to my lips as the driver takes the bags out of the back of the trunk.

I look around the lobby, spotting Caine walking our way, wearing shorts and a white polo T-shirt. "Well, well, well." His voice echoes in the empty lobby. "If it isn't my brother." He stops in front of us and then looks at Zoey. "You must be my new sister-in-law."

I watch Zoey, who laughs nervously before she side-eyes me. "I guess that would be accurate today." She smiles but sarcastically adds, "Not sure about tomorrow." I can see she's anxious now as she looks around to make sure that it's just the three of us. "I need a drink," she admits.

"Isn't drinking what got you married to my brother?" Caine says, laughing.

"You're right." She laughs with Caine, and I close the distance between us, wrapping my arm around her waist and pulling her to my side. "I'm never drinking again in my life."

"Doesn't matter to me. The damage is already done." I wink and smirk at her as I hold up my left hand.

"I'm going to go see my family," she says, putting her hand to her stomach, so I know she's nervous.

"Do you want me to come with you?" I ask, and she shakes her head.

"Me, I know they won't harm." She gets on her tippy-toes and puts her hands on my shoulders. "You, it's a toss-up." She walks away from me, and I snatch her wrist in my hand, pulling her to me. "What the—"

"Kiss," I demand, bending and kissing her lips softly. "Now you can go."

"One of these days…" She pretends to be irritated as she walks away from us, mumbling something I think has to do with me and my death.

I watch her as she walks through the lobby to the back of the hotel. "I thought I was crazy getting involved with Grace," Caine says, and I look back at him as he shakes his head, "but Zoey?" His face fills with a grimace. "The whole family is like big and beefy." He motions to his arm, exaggerating the muscles.

I chuckle, trying not to let it get to me. "Your in-laws have guns. And not just like one or two."

He nods. "Yeah, but, like, it's one shot, and I'm a goner." He laughs. "For you, it's drawn out. If one gets tired, they tap out, and another one comes to kick your ass."

I move into the lobby, going to the desk and giving the woman my name. Of course the whole hotel is booked out for the family. "Like, seriously, what the fuck are you thinking?" Caine asks when she hands me the keys to my room.

"I don't know what I was thinking," I answer him honestly. "All I knew is we were sitting down and she looked more beautiful than anyone I've ever seen in my life. All I could think was I want to make her mine."

"So you ask her to date you. Jesus, you don't marry her." He shakes his head. "That makes more sense than 'Hey, let's get married.'"

"I was in the moment." I shrug, and I'm about to say something else when I look over and see Stone and Christopher coming my way. "Oh, fuck," I mumble, "here we go."

"I'm going to be very fucking pissed at you if you make me fight on my family vacation," Caine hisses as they get closer. Stone's face is full of fury, while Christopher looks like he's trying not to burst out laughing.

"There you are," Stone says, then looks around. "Where the hell is my sister?"

"She went that way." Caine points to the right. "She just left. If you hurry, you might catch up to her."

"You're really married?" Stone asks, crossing his arms over his chest.

"Yup," I answer, trying not to be rude but also trying to tell him I'm no pushover.

"What the fuck?" he seethes.

"It was spur of the moment." I look at him and then Christopher.

"I wasn't invited either," Caine adds, pointing at himself. "I think they wanted it intimate."

"They wanted it intimate?" Christopher laughs at Caine's words. "They weren't even dating."

"Well, we're married." I hold up my hand. "I'm sorry we did it without telling anyone, but…" I smile when I think about that night. "I won't be sorry I married her." He just stares at me. "I will say, best fucking thing I did in my whole life, hands down." I slap Caine's shoulder. "Now, if you guys will excuse me, I'm going to go find my wife."

"You mean my sister," Stone grumbles, and it's then Christopher just bursts out laughing.

"I'm sorry, dude, I tried to keep from laughing." He slaps Stone's shoulder. "I was ready to pounce, but you sounded like Uncle Matthew right then."

"Shut the fuck up," Stone growls. "This isn't finished," he tells me, and I look over my shoulder.

"I hope when you have the chance, and you think about you and Ryleigh"—I turn to look at him—"and how if you had the chance to make her yours permanently, would you have taken the chance for her to change her mind or would you have married her on sight and not cared about anything else but her?" He doesn't say anything. "That's what I thought. And between us, you can be pissed at me about all of this but just don't take it out on Zoey. You want to be pissed and take out your frustration, I'm more than happy for you to take it out on me. Whatever you want to dish, I'll take it." I stare into his eyes. "But you treat her like you always have."

"She's my sister, you know that?" Stone reminds me.

I nod at his statement. "Yeah, she is." I smirk before the smile washes off my face, and he sees I'm not playing with this. "I will take her far away from here if anyone makes her fucking sad." My voice is tight. "Because now that's my job, to keep her happy and safe." I see him watch me. "Since, you know, she's *my* wife."

THIRTEEN

Zoey

I WALK OUT of the lobby toward the pool, where most of my family members have probably gathered. At least most of them. If not, they're at the beach, which means I can go to my room to regroup before meeting them.

I look up at the hotel and see the balconies that overlook the beach, knowing all of them have been rented for our family. The family vacation started before I can even remember. Since most of my family was in hockey, the only time everyone was officially off was in June, so all family vacations were done during that time. It was a time everyone always dreaded, but once we were there, it was always, and I mean always, the best time. The kids would run on the beach or go to the pool, and the teenagers would always be in some type of war with one another, competing and playing games to see who was far superior. Then leading to the adults getting involved to negotiate, but slowly, it would end up with the adults included in the game.

I see a server coming out from the side with a tray filled with mixed drinks. "I'll have one of those." I hold my hand up as he walks my way, wearing his uniform of blue pants and a Hawaiian shirt.

"This is the specialty drink—" he says, handing me a napkin.

"Is there booze in here?" I ask as I take one of the tall yellow drinks off his tray. The wetness from the glass feels good against the heat of my hand.

"There is tequila—"

"That's all I need to hear," I say, taking a sip of it. The cool slush concoction hits my tongue, and the sweetness follows. "This could be trouble." I hold it up to him. "I taste no tequila."

He smiles at me. "Trust me, there is lots of tequila. But if you want, I can bring you more so you can add it."

I look at the drink, then look up when I hear voices. "Last time I drank tequila, I ended up married." I laugh nervously before taking another sip. "So I might take you up on that offer."

He nods at me and hightails it away from me. "Wait, did he think I was going to marry him?" I ask myself as I see him stopping next to my mother and my aunts Allison and Zoe, who I'm named after. All three are wearing black bikinis, not identical, but all with white linen cover-ups. Each of them is wearing a straw hat to hide the sun from their face with sunglasses. I hope when I'm older I have the confidence they have and also their style. I mean, it's normal for my mother since she's the stylist to the stars. She started working as a personal shopper when she was younger, then started Zara's Closet. Now she's one of the most sought-after stylists in Hollywood. She even has a staff of fifty working for her.

Neither of them sees me yet, but it's as if my mother knows I'm nearby because she quickly looks my way, then puts both her hands to her mouth. I wait for it, knowing the soft and sweet Zara isn't going to stay for very long. "In three." I take a sip of my drink. "Two." The minute I say two, her hands fall from her face, and she whips off her sunglasses. "One."

It takes Zoe and Allison a minute to look my way, and their eyes go to me when they do. Zoe's face mimics my mother's, while Allison rolls her lips, trying not to smile in my direction. My mother makes her way to me like a bull chasing the red flag in Spain. "Jesus." I look over to see my cousin Zara walking my way, wearing a bikini top and cover-up around her hips. "Prepare to be hung out to dry," she mumbles quickly before the women get here. "The plane ride here was so much fun." She grabs the drink from my hand. "Thanks for that."

"Zoey Allison Richards," my mother says between clenched teeth.

"I don't even think that's your middle name," Zara shares, "but you were often compared to her, so she might be confused."

"I thought my middle name was Parker." I make the mistake of speaking, and my mother's eyebrows pinch together even more.

"Don't you start with me," she huffs. "Do you know what we've been through these past two days while you were radio silent?" She leans in.

"I wasn't radio silent." I hold up my hand. "I spoke to Dad."

"Oh, trust me, I know. Who do you think had to tame his ass?" She folds her arms over her chest. "Who do you think had to talk him and your uncles from signaling the phone chain, followed by getting on a plane and tracking you down in Vegas?"

"Um," I say softly, "you?"

"You got that right." She unfolds her arms. "It was me." She points at herself. "Me, your mother, who had to find out you got married when your brother called and almost had a coronary on the phone. You decided to send him a picture of your wedding at four o'clock in the morning." I really have to take the time and go through my fucking texts and see who else I sent it to.

"If I can just cut in here for a second. She also posted it on Instagram, so it's not like she was trying to hide it," Zara defends. "Should we not take this time to congratulate her on becoming a bride?"

"Stay out of this," both her mother and my mother snap her way.

"Hey, don't take it out on me. I have a man who asked for my hand in marriage, and we are getting married next year." She holds up her hand.

"He never asked for your hand in marriage." Her mother glares at her. "And why is that?"

"Okay, I think we're getting off topic here." She looks at me. "It's Zoey's day."

"Thanks." I look over at her.

"Just helping you out," Zara says, as if she actually helped the situation instead of infusing it even more.

"Why don't we just take a second," Allison suggests, "and one, ask her if she's okay." She looks at me. "Are you okay?"

I shrug. "I guess so," I answer, not sure what to say.

"She guesses so." My mother pffts. "Seriously, Zoey, what the hell were you thinking?"

"She was caught up in the moment," Allison declares. "You are there with the love of your life, and you just want to be together forever."

"Um…" Zara holds up her finger. "I don't think we are at the love stage in their relationship."

"Seriously." I practically stomp my foot. "Shut up," I hiss at her.

"What?" She holds up both hands. "I'm helping."

"Help by shutting up," her mother says, "and minding your business."

"Fine," she pouts, taking a sip of the drink she took out of my hand. "I'll just be here for moral support."

"Listen." I hold up my hand. "I'm so sorry you found out the way you found out. It was not cool."

"It was totally not cool," my mother agrees, her voice going soft. "You're my only child."

"Um…" Zara holds up a finger. "What about Stone?"

My mother rolls her eyes. "I mean only girl. You are my only girl, and I've waited for this day my whole life. To get to go with you and argue over dresses." Her voice cracks. "And then I'll just let you choose whatever you want because it'll be perfect no matter what." She blinks.

I'm about to hug her when my cousin Zara mumbles, "Incoming."

We all look over to see my uncle Max and uncle Matthew walking my way with my father beside them. All of them are wearing swim trunks and a button-down linen shirt. "They look like that Michael Douglas movie with all his old friends that go to Vegas for their last hoorah," Zara whispers to me, "but then they probably think they are on the runway for *GQ*."

"You"—my aunt looks at her—"don't you say a word."

"I'm drinking and enjoying myself. Jesus, Mom," she retorts, taking the straw in her hand.

"Just say sorry and maybe shed a tear. That might help," Allison suggests. "Definitely cry. It works every single time."

"Not every time," my mother states. "When we put Nair in Matthew's shampoo, he was not having us crying." She stands up straight and walks in front of me. "Let me handle this."

"There she is," my father says, making his way in front of the other two. "We've been waiting for you."

"That sounds creepy AF," Zara mumbles, and my aunt nudges her.

"Okay." My mother holds up her hand. "She just got here." She looks at Max and Matthew. "So you'll have to save the interrogation for another time. Like, maybe when they leave."

"I don't think I can say anything," Max admits, holding up his hand. "I eloped with Allison, so I was just coming to congratulate my niece."

"You mean, stole my sister." Matthew glares at him.

"It's been over thirty years," Max says. "It's safe to say it was a good idea."

"Thank you for your congratulations." I walk up to my uncle Max and give him a hug, and he kisses my head. "I'm sure we will have to have a meeting and a huddle." I walk over to Matthew. "I'll even promise not to interrupt you." I smile up at him, and he shakes his head.

"He got a hug, and I got nothing." He grabs me and brings me in. "I blame your father anyway," he says before kissing my forehead.

"Don't care," my father counters. "Leave my daughter alone." I walk to him and hug his waist. "Go unpack and meet us on the beach. Your grandfather is looking for you."

"Did you guys tell him?" I gasp and look at everyone. Matthew looks up at the sky as if he's looking for a clue.

"Traitor."

"He has Instagram," Matthew finally says. "Maybe if you wanted to keep it a secret, one should not post on social media."

"I'm going to change. Where is my room?" I ask them, knowing my uncle Matthew has everyone's room number ready to rattle off by heart.

"Seventeen thirty." My father grabs my key card from his pocket. "I wanted to make sure you saw me as soon as you got here." He points over to the side where the rooms are. "Just walk through there. Every person has a bungalow over the water."

"As if I could hide anywhere." I hold out my hands. "We're the only ones at this resort."

I grab the key card from him. "I'll meet everyone at the beach," I say, turning and making my way away from them before they realize they let me off the hook faster than they should have. I was expecting a little bit more pushback. "Wow." I look over my shoulder. "They are slipping in their old age." I make my way over to my room, wondering where in the hell Nash ended up. Walking on top of the wooden pathway that leads to all the bungalows, I spot ours at the very end. Scanning my card before stepping in, I gasp. If my luggage wasn't in the middle of the room, I would think this was a mistake.

The room is filled with white roses like in the hotel suite where we were married. Every single surface area in the little living room is covered in roses. I walk toward the back of the room, seeing the king-size bed facing a wall of windows that gives you a view of the turquoise water. A hot tub is on the side, with two white lounge chairs right in front of a ladder that leads down to the water. A white square box with my name on it sits in the middle of the bed.

I pull the card out and read the note.

Happy honeymoon, wife.

Love,

Your husband

I shake my head, sitting on the bed to open the box to find a white satin button-down top with matching shorts. It feels like heaven on my hand, and I see it's embroidered on the left-hand side with my name, Zoey Griffin. "This is ridiculous." I ignore the way my stomach feels when I read the name as I shake my head, putting the top down when I hear the door slam. "Hello!" I shout out.

I watch Nash walk into the room, and his hair looks like he's been running his hands through it a million times. "I was looking for you." He comes over to me, bending and kissing my lips. He walks over to stare out the window before he opens the sliding door all the way. "I just had a head-to-head with your brother," he says, shocking me.

"There isn't even any blood on you." I get up, putting my hands on my hips.

"Why would there be?" He turns to look at me, his eyes a softer blue in the sun reflecting off the water.

"You stole his sister and married her without telling anyone," I huff. "Wow, it's like he doesn't even love me. He didn't even hit you once."

He chuckles. "We did exchange some blows," he admits, and now my eyes go big. "Verbally."

"Maybe you coming here wasn't a good idea," I say softly.

"We're married," he informs me, "and I have ninety days for you to fall in love with me. You being here for two weeks cuts into that time."

"I never agreed to the ninety days," I remind him. "We still have a lot to talk about." He walks to me, and I can see the look in his eyes, so I hold out my hand. "My cousin is waiting for me on the beach, and if we do what I think you want to do, everyone is going to know we are in here having sex."

"We're married," he scoffs, "and this is our honeymoon. Of course we're having sex."

"Can you stop saying that?" I throw up my hands and walk back out to get my luggage. "And I think we should perhaps not share a room while we figure this out."

"Okay," he says, surprising me, "I'll just sneak into your room at night."

I open my luggage, grabbing the first bikini I find, and go into the bathroom to change, closing the door behind me. He laughs as I undress and slide on the white bikini bottom with two gold straps at the sides. The matching top is white, and the straps over my shoulders are gold. When I walk out, he's sitting on the bed with his phone in his hand, and he looks up. "Hmm," he hums, taking me in from head to toe. "I'm going to fuck you in that bikini before we leave."

"Great." I pretend to be annoyed. "Good to know."

He smirks, then looks back down at his phone. "I have to call my parents." I stand by my luggage. "The news has hit them."

"Oh," I squeak, wondering how this will make me look. What kind of woman marries a man without meeting their family? My heart sinks when I think of the fact his mother could hate me. "I'll just leave you to your phone call," I offer, needing to get the fuck out of here. "I'm going to be on the beach."

"I'll find you," he assures me, and I'm about to walk out of the room when he calls my name, "Zoey." I turn around. "I should give you the heads-up that I sort of maybe threatened your brother." I blink slowly. "I told him if he made you sad, I would take you away from here, and I'm not kidding."

"You said what?" I'm not sure if I actually heard what he said.

"If your family wants to be pissed at anyone, they can be pissed at me. But I will not let them shit on you."

"Um," I say, putting my hand to my stomach to stop it from freaking out, "okay."

"If I see you sad, we're leaving." He looks back at his phone. "And I'm not backing down on that. They'll get over it, but in the meantime, they will not make you feel sad."

"Okay, Nash." I walk over to him without even realizing my feet are moving. "Thank you for that." I stand between his legs, and his hands run up the back of my thighs to my ass, and then he holds my hips. "Also, same goes for you, I guess. If you don't feel comfortable with anything."

"I can handle that, baby, but you've already cried once, and I'm not interested in seeing that face again. Ever." The air vacates my body, leaving me almost panting. "I'll meet you on the beach, yeah?" I nod and bend to kiss him. My hand automatically comes up to hold his face, something I've always been doing with him, and I don't even know why. It's just an extra touch, but it's an extra touch I love doing. Which is silly and which I will not think about.

I let go of his lips and grab my phone before walking out of the room when he says, "Hey, Dad." I want to sit and listen to the conversation, but I don't think I have it in me if they start shitting all over me. I walk away with my head down, heading toward the sound of music and the daybeds by the beach water littered with my family members. Luckily, Zara spots me and waves me over. I have to stop what feels like a million times before getting to her. Everyone is laughing at the fact I eloped, and not one person has said anything negative. Some even give me a high five for doing it the way I wanted to do it.

"I got you a drink," Zara says, "but I drank it, so the guy is coming back."

"My sister-in-law." I see Ryleigh approaching, followed by Gabriella and Abigail. "I'm so excited." She gives me a hug and gets on the bed next to Zara. "I want to know all the details."

"Oh, yes, I want to know all the details." Gabriella slides onto the bed, followed by Abigail. "One, let me see the ring." She leans over, grabbing my hand and gasping. "Oh, he did good."

"Damn," Ryleigh says, "he is not playing."

"It was," I start to say and stop when the server comes back with a pitcher of strawberry mojitos, and we each get a glass. I take a sip. "It was a mistake," I finally say. "I thought the Elvis guy was a fake."

"Shut up." Ryleigh snorts, laughing. "But Nash is here."

"He is." I look around. "He wants me to give him ninety days to fall in love with him."

"Oh, like *90 Day Fiancé*," Abigail says. "Just you're married already."

"This is crazy." I take a bigger sip of my drink. "Two weeks ago, I was dating Josh, who I was with for two years. Who I'm in love with." I speak the words and immediately feel a guilt I've never felt in my life.

"Didn't you break up with him because he didn't want to commit?" Zara says, earning her a glare. "I'm just saying, he was with you for two years, and you didn't even have a toothbrush at his place. You asked him to give you a drawer, and he acted as if you wanted him to build an expansion on his shitty two-bedroom condo." She looks at me. "And then you have Nash, who married you in less than a week and refuses to let you go. He has my vote."

"Mine too," Gabriella agrees. "Josh is a thirty-five-year-old still living his dreams of being frat boy president. Every single time I saw him, he was like 'want to play beer pong? I bet I can win.'"

I can't help but laugh because he used to say that a lot. "When he saw I was pregnant, he was like 'bummer, I guess I'll drink for you,'" Abigail says.

"Has he even reached out to you since you got married?" Ryleigh asks me.

"He called me a couple of times and sent me a couple of messages," I admit. "I just have yet to call him or text him."

"I think once you tell him you're married," Zara says, "that will nip that in the bud. He'll go his way, and in twelve years, he'll settle down with a twenty-four-year-old because that's how old his brain will be by then."

"You should get that phone call out of the way now,"

Ryleigh urges, "before the husband comes and doesn't leave your side."

"I think you're right," I agree, grabbing my phone. "I have to call him sometime anyway."

"Or you don't. You block him and forget him." Zara shrugs, and everyone looks at her. "It's just a suggestion."

I get off the bed and walk over to the water's edge, off to the side where no one is, and pull up his number to call him. My heart pounds so hard in my chest, and I feel like I'm doing something I shouldn't be doing, which is silly.

"What the fuck, Zoey?" he questions as soon as he answers the phone. "It's been four fucking days."

"I'm sorry," I say, moving my foot over the sand. "I'm on vacation with my family."

"And your husband?" he snaps, and I stand straight as if he just threw ice water on me.

"Um…"

"It's a joke, right?" His tone is tight and angry. "Just to piss me off."

I snap, "The world doesn't revolve around you like you think it does." I finally let him have it.

"It's not funny, Zoey," he hisses.

"You're right, it's not funny," I agree with him.

"So now what?" he asks. I look out into the water, seeing Stone and Ryleigh as they are laughing together, and then look over to see Gabriella on top of her husband Romeo's back, saying something to make him laugh.

"Well, we agreed we needed space," I remind him. "You agreed to it by not even trying to call me the next day."

"So you married the first man you meet?" His laugh comes out bitterly.

"I've known him a while," I counter and close my eyes because it shouldn't matter. I did nothing wrong.

"You've known me for two years. It seems you forgot who I was." His voice sounds weird. "Time to show you." It's the last thing he says before he hangs up on me. I look down at the phone, wondering if the call dropped or something, but I see I have all my bars.

"What the hell?" I stare at my phone when a text comes through.

Josh: *Have a great vacation. I'll see you when you get back. Love you, Zoey.*

My eyes stare at the message on the top of my phone. "Hey." I look up to see Nash come to me wearing just his shorts and nothing else. "Are you okay?" he asks me, and I turn my phone over in my hand so he doesn't see it.

"Yeah, I'm fine." I put on a fake smile. "I was just checking my voicemail." I hold up the phone, lying to him and feeling that feeling again. "How was the call with your parents?"

"Okay," he says, and I can see there must be more to it. "We have to have dinner with them when we get back home." He looks out into the water. "Want to come in the water with me?"

"Sure, let me go put my phone down, and I'll be right in." I turn to walk away, but I don't make it far when his hand grabs my wrist, stopping me.

"We just lied to each other," he says, and my heart sinks, "and I don't like it. In fact, I fucking hate it." He closes the distance between us. "I know you weren't checking your voicemail because I saw you talking, and you know that everything isn't okay with my parents." He puts his hand around my waist, pulling me to him, not caring who is watching. He's openly affectionate with me. "If we are going to do this, then you have to call me out on my bullshit, and I have to call you out on yours. And…" He pushes the hair off my shoulder before he bends to kiss my neck. "We have to be all in, or we aren't giving ourselves a fair chance." My heart speeds up. "Give me a fair chance, Zoey." He looks down at me, into my eyes. "Give us a fair chance."

I don't know if it's the way he's looking at me, or if it's just because I'm pissed at the conversation I just had with Josh, or if it's the fact that as soon as I'm in his arms, I feel like I've never felt before. Whatever it is, it makes me whisper, "Fine, I'll give us a fair chance."

FOURTEEN

NASH

I WATCH HER eyes while she agrees to give me a chance, while she agrees to give us a chance. The minute she says the words, I swear I about jump off my feet and pump my fist in the air, but instead, I kiss her softly, not the way I want to kiss her. "Go put your phone away, and then we'll talk in the water."

"Okay." She turns and not even going far just dumps it on the first table she sees. The section of the beach is closed off for the family, so it's safe. "I'm ready." Then she walks to me, pinning her hair up on top of her head before sliding her hand in mine as we walk into the warm water.

I stop when I'm at my waist and duck down the rest of the way before I pull her to me. "Let's talk." I grab her hips, pulling her to me, and she wraps her legs around mine. "I'll go first." Her hands are outstretched by her sides as she moves them around in the water. "My father is not happy with me, and my mother is even more annoyed with me." I see the worry in her eyes, and it washes over her face. "They think it was irresponsible and stupid, to say the very least, and disrespectful to you."

"To me?" she says, shocked.

"Yes." I nod. "I married you like you were some dirty little secret instead of showing the world how proud I was that you were my wife." I see her swallow down the lump she had forming in her throat as her lower lip trembles. "And if I have to admit it, they are a little bit— but not a lot—right."

"Nash." Her voice breaks as she puts her hands on my arms, the warm water moving us up and down.

"No, Zoey, they are right because you aren't some dirty little secret." The words make my blood boil. "So I have to agree with them on that. They were right. And I voiced that, maybe not politically correct, but I said what I said, and we'll deal with that when we deal with it."

"When we get back, we'll invite your parents over and have dinner with them, and I'll let them know you didn't get married by yourself. I sort of helped." I can't help but laugh. "Even though I thought it was fake."

I kiss her neck, tasting the salt. "Thank you, baby," I say softly. "Now who were you on the phone with?" I already know in my gut that I'm not going to like the answer. She avoids even looking at me when she starts talking, and all I can do is bask in the fact she's here in my arms, at least for now anyway.

"I called Josh," she admits, and even though it feels like she just kicked me in the balls, I have to not make her regret she told me.

"I see." I try not to make my voice go so tight.

"He saw my Instagram post, and he's been calling and texting me." I nod instead of saying anything. "I owed him a phone call."

My eyebrows rise. "You owed him a phone call?"

"We were together for two years," she says and finally looks at me. "Two weeks ago, we were still dating."

"And where does that leave you now?" My anger creeps up as I extend my hands to the sides as I move us in the water, closer to the shore.

"It leaves me in the water with my husband, telling him I'm going to give us a chance."

"And you told him this?" I ask, and she nods.

"I mean, he did hang up on me."

"What a dick. I mean, if I ever meet him, I'm going to shake his hand for sure." My admission shocks even myself.

"What?" she asks, shocked. "Why would you do that?"

"If he hadn't fucked up and pushed you away, I would have never gotten my chance to be with you." I smile at her. Finally, the heaviness of the last five minutes leaves me. "So I owe him at least a beer."

"Good to know I'm worth a beer at least," she deadpans, and I wrap my arms around her waist even tighter, pulling her closer to me and kissing her neck again.

"You're worth a bit more than a beer," I joke with her, "but if he doesn't know that by now, I'm not going to tell him."

"So you are going to safeguard me?" She now leans in, wrapping her arms around my neck, laughing.

"I'm going to do whatever I have to do to make sure you stay mine." She stares at me. "And word to the wise, baby, I won't play fair. I'm going to play dirty, but you'll like it." I kiss her with a huge smack. "Most of the time anyway."

"Are you guys having your honeymoon in the water?" I look over and see Caine walking toward us. "'Cause if you are, that's fucking nasty. You guys have your own private beach in front of your cabana. Why are you out here with kids and shit?"

"We are not doing anything but having a conversation," Zoey quickly points out and unwraps her legs from me. "Now I'm going to go out and have a drink with my brother and kick him in the balls for not defending my honor."

She turns, giving me a kiss before walking out of the water, and I watch her strut her stuff. "I'm right here," my brother says, making me laugh, "and you get to go home with her."

"Yeah, I do," I declare proudly, then I stand. "You speak to Dad?"

"Oh, yeah," he says, "called you a fucking idiot."

"Meh," I reply, "he's called me worse."

"Oh, I know." He laughs. "Trust me, I know."

"Mom got in on the action this time also," I say, and he gasps. "Yeah, she's not happy either. Called me a dickhead since that's what I lead with all the time."

"Dude." He laughs. "Seriously, though, what the hell is going on?"

"Nothing, we are two people who—"

"You haven't even dated her. Did you even sleep with her before you married her?"

"We saved it all for the wedding night," I admit proudly. "We shared our first kiss after we got engaged, so all this me leading with my dick is not even accurate."

"You kissed her after you got engaged?" He's shocked at this piece of information. "You have done lost your damn mind."

"No, I haven't." I shake my head. "I've never been clearer. We are two people who like each other enough to get married."

"Like each other enough to get married," he repeats my words, hoping it makes sense, and I know it doesn't. "Should you, I don't know, date and get engaged and then married?"

"Now you sound like Mom and Dad."

"I mean, I hate to agree with them in general, but they might be right about this."

"Listen, I know it's unconventional," I admit, "but she just agreed to give us a chance."

"What the fuck does that even mean?"

"I asked her to give me ninety days to fall in love with me, and she agreed," I say proudly.

"That's the stupidest thing I've ever heard in my life." He shakes his head.

"It's not." I stand by my words. "All I need is time to show her how good it can be."

"So you're going to woo your wife?" He can't help but laugh.

"Obviously, I'm not going to woo my ex-wife." I shake my head with a grimace on my face. "That's just fucking weird."

"You can't fuck this up." His voice goes low, and I know he's not joking now.

"I'm not going to fuck this up," I assure him.

He groans, rubbing his hands over his face. "Have you met you? Your longest relationship was four months and that was because she was gone for three."

I hold up a finger. "First of all, she was gone for two months, and she wasn't Zoey," I explain as we make our way out of the water. "She's like no one I've ever met before."

"You've known her a week."

"How long before you knew you were all-in with Grace?" I ask him and see his jaw get tight. "Was it before or after you hired her to be your assistant, and she started driving you crazy?" I hold up my hand. "The minute I met her on the beach that first time, I knew I was going to marry her." He gawks at me. "I know it's crazy to say, but I just knew if I would ever marry someone, it would be her. Then spending this week with her, I knew I was right. She's everything I've looked for in a woman and more. She's smart, she's kind, she's fucking hot, and the sex is out of this world." I turn to him. "I'm already half in love with her."

"Thank heavens for that. I would hate for you to be married and not already be half in love with the woman."

"Exactly," I say, slapping his shoulder. "Can you imagine that? It would not even be worth it."

"Mom dropped you." He points at me. "Must have dropped you on your head when you were a kid. Had to."

I laugh and look over to find Zoey with Stone. "Got to go make sure my wife is okay."

I don't even wait for him to answer as I walk toward them, getting there just as he grabs her around her neck and gives her a hug. "Hey," I call, looking around to see if I am going to be somehow attacked.

"Hey," Zoey says, and I look over, seeing Ryleigh coming our way, "I was having a chat with my brother." She lets him go and comes over to me, standing beside me. "Giving him shit for not even fighting for me."

"I wasn't going to hit him," Stone counters. "I was just going to rough him up, but then who was going to contain my wife?"

"Contain your wife?" Ryleigh surprises him from behind. "Contain me?" She folds her arms over her chest. "If you had hit him, I would have gladly helped him press charges on you. And actually, represented him."

"Gorgeous," Stone sighs. "I think that's like illegal or something." He wraps his arms around her waist and brings her to him.

"Now, have you stopped being mad at her?" she asks him, putting a hand on his chest while he side-glares her. "Don't give me that look, Stone Richards. She's a grown woman."

"She is," Zoey cuts in, "and as much as I'm lucky to have a younger brother and then sad because you didn't even take a swing at him, thank you for being in my corner."

"See," Ryleigh says, "now I'm going to go and take a nice bath and get ready for dinner. Are you joining me?"

"Eww," Zoey says, "did you just ask him to go and do nasty things with you?"

Ryleigh looks at her. "You're staying in the honeymoon suite. You don't think that you'll be having sex every single day, three times a day?"

Zoey gasps at the same time Stone groans, "I'm not." He shakes his head.

I look down at Zoey. "We should also go and get ready for dinner." I slide my hand in hers. "We're full of salt and stuff."

"Are my ears bleeding?" Stone asks Ryleigh as he turns and just leaves us on the beach, dragging Ryleigh with him.

"Are you okay?" I ask her, and she looks up at me, and I can see she is. There's not an inch of sadness on her face.

"I am." She smiles, her beautiful face just lighting up.

"Then my job is done." I crinkle my nose. "At least for the next hour."

FIFTEEN

Zoey

"BABY, ARE YOU almost ready?" Nash shouts from the bedroom while I slip on my skirt. "I hear your cousins outside the door whispering, not really whispering, about if we are doing it."

I laugh as I adjust the top of my skirt and then slip on my slides. "I would be ready if you hadn't come in and taken a shower with me." I rush out of the bathroom, seeing him lying on the bed, one leg on the floor, one leg off the bed, his white sneakers not touching the bed. His blue eyes seem even more blue with the little tan that he's gotten in the past two days since we've been on vacation.

"Um." He sits up, and my mouth waters when I look at him. His beard is longer than I'm used to seeing him with, but sexier. "You wearing any panties under that?" he asks of my skirt that goes to my mid-calf but is pulled up on my left hip with a huge slit showing most of my leg. The matching beige-colored, one-shoulder halter top completes the whole look.

"Of course I am." I put my hand on my stomach to ignore the way it goes up and down like the soft waves in the ocean.

"Perfect." He grins as he gets up, and I take him in. He's wearing black shorts that look like they've been cut mid-thigh, but I know they probably cost over four hundred dollars to be cut like that. His shirt is bluish green, the top three buttons left open, showing you the tan chest that not too long ago was pressed up against me in the shower. The cuffs of his sleeves are rolled up until his elbows, his silver Rolex watch on his left wrist, and of course the wedding ring that he's never, ever taken off. Not even to put sunscreen on. He walks the distance to me, putting his hands not on my hips but on the side of my ribs, where he can touch my skin. "I'm going to slide them to the side when I fuck you later." I roll my eyes, pretending I didn't just get wet with his words. "I like your hair like this." He raises a hand into the back of my head, fisting it. "It's wild and looks like you just woke up."

"I had no time to do anything," I inform him. "We literally got dressed in ten minutes. I didn't even put on mascara."

"I was done in five." He kisses my lips. "And you don't need makeup." He slides his hand in mine and turns toward the front door. I can hear people outside our door as we get closer and closer, and when he opens it with his free hand, I see them all standing there. "Told you."

"Finally," Stone says. "We were standing here forever."

"We got here two minutes ago." Ryleigh smacks his abs. "And you were like 'ewww, they're probably doing it.'" She looks at him. "It." She tries not to laugh at the word he was using but can't help it, and all he can do is glare at her.

"She's my sister," Stone defends, and then Romeo comes over and slaps his shoulder.

"Not so fun anymore, big guy?" He shakes his head, going to grab Gabriella's hand.

"If it makes everyone feel better," I say, stepping out, "we weren't doing it."

"Yeah," Nash adds, "we did it in the shower before you guys got here." I gasp, ripping my hand out of his while the girls all laugh and the guys literally look in front of them. "Baby." He wraps his arm around my shoulders as we follow the rest of them toward the lobby, where there will be golf carts ready to take us to one of the local bars. "We're on our honeymoon. Everyone knows we're doing it." The way he says it makes me laugh and shake my head.

"They can think. They don't have to know," I say softly, and he just shrugs.

"Where is Abigail?" I turn, asking where my cousin is. She was the one who was dying to go out.

"Passed out in her bed from drinking all day. Tristan tried to wake her up, but she told him to do it again," Gabriella says, laughing.

When we get to the lobby, I'm shocked that most of

my cousins and their significant others are waiting there for us. "I thought you guys were opting out," I tell my cousins Michael and Dylan, who are standing side by side wearing the same outfit, matched with the same scowl.

"Your fault," they both say at the same time.

"It's like their wedding reception," Michael mimics his wife, who glares over at him.

"This isn't our wedding reception." I turn to Jillian and Alex, who are standing together with Jillian's twin, Julia.

"Yeah," Nash agrees, "our wedding reception will be bigger. Probably next year."

I swear my head whips around so fast I would think it's going to roll off. "What?"

"Oh, trouble in paradise already?" Christopher teases, joining us, holding Koda's hand in his, her new engagement ring on her finger. "You can't do it next year. We're getting married."

"Wow," Koda says. "Good to know."

"Then this winter break, I guess," Nash voices.

"There is no reception." I walk over to a golf cart and get in. "And tonight can be Koda and Christopher's engagement party."

"No way," Christopher says, "that's next week."

"What?" Koda snaps.

"It's nothing big." He tries to blow it off. "Besides, we're all here, and my parents want to do it. If you don't want it, go tell them." He motions toward the hotel.

"Oh, trouble in paradise already, buddy?" Nash slaps

his shoulder while he walks over to the golf cart and sits next to me. His hand goes on my knee.

"Can we go?" someone asks as we all get into the golf carts.

We get to the bar in less than five minutes, and I need a drink by the time I get there. During the whole ride over, he's had his hand on my knee, but he's been moving his fingers lightly back and forth, sometimes going higher than he should but then moving back down again.

A long table is set up for us. We all grab our seats, and the margaritas are already coming out and being served. "Okay, okay," Grace, Caine's wife, says from in front of me, grabbing her own drink. "I have so many questions, and Caine said I can't ask them." She smirks at him. "But he's not the boss of me, so I have to know."

"Oh, we should all ask them one question." Zara looks at Grace as if they've discovered America. "Good idea."

"I'll go first," Sofia, my cousin Matthew's wife, says from beside Zara. "How long were you two dating?"

I swear, my family has never been quiet in their lives. Not once have you been able to sit down at a dinner and hear your own thoughts. Now, suddenly, in the middle of this bar-slash-restaurant, every single fucking mouth is shut, and all eyes are on Nash and me. He puts his arm around my chair. "Um…" I say, looking at him and seeing his smirk. "Um…" I have to laugh because the answer is ridiculous, even for me. "Ten minutes, maybe? I don't even think."

"Hold on." Stone slaps the table and holds up his hand. "You guys weren't dating?"

"When did you think they were dating?" Christopher looks over at him. "She was dating Jarod like a month ago."

"I think his name is Jordan," Dylan chimes in, then looks at his wife, Alex, who shakes her head. "Jacob?"

"Nope," she replies, taking a sip of her margarita and smiling, "not even close."

"His name was Joshua!" Zara shouts.

"His name was Josh," I correct, "and we broke up."

"How long before you got married did you break up?" Caine's voice breaks the laughter as he leans back in his chair, his eyes staring straight at me.

"Hey," Nash warns him, and he turns to look at him with the same look, "watch your tone with my wife." The way he says it, his voice is tight, and the laughter at the table seems to have died down. It feels like everyone is on alert. Even Zara beside me feels like she'll be ready to fight, and she's been half drunk since she got here.

"No tone." He leans back. "Just a question I'm sure everyone is dying to ask."

"Caine," Grace says his name, "chill."

"It's okay," I assure her, avoiding looking at Caine or Nash, because I'm sure he'll see the tears that are forming in my eyes, and then he's going to be like King Kong and take me away from everyone. "We broke up a week before."

"Oh my God." Grace slaps her hands together. "That is even better than I thought it would be."

"I have a question," Dylan breaks in. "How the fuck did you break up with Jordan?"

"Josh," most of the people at the table correct him.

"Whatever his name is, we've met the guy twice." He shakes his head, then continues his question, "Then you end up dating for ten minutes and get married."

"That's not fair," Gabriella blurts, "that's like two questions. You get one."

"We broke up two days before I went to LA to work with Nash for their company." I hold up my hand to Caine. "And then we ended up in Vegas."

"I've ended up in Vegas before," Stone says, looking at Christopher, "but I've never gotten married."

"That's not a question," Zara scoffs, "so simmer down."

"How did he propose?" Koda asks. "Like you went from working to let's get married. That's a merger and a half." She laughs at her own joke.

"We were at the bar," Nash starts, and I look over at him, his eyes looking into mine. "She was finally giving me the time of day and not ignoring or brushing me off—"

"I did not ignore or brush you off." I interrupt him, and the girls snort because I totally was, but I didn't know it was that evident.

He chuckles, ignoring what I just said. "I knew before she was beautiful, but her sitting in front of me at that moment, I knew I'd never seen anyone as beautiful as Zoey. I also knew I wanted her to sit by my side for the rest of my life." His thumb moves up and down on my arm. "I knew I wanted to marry her. So I asked her."

"Oh my God," Grace coos, "that's so romantic."

"That is so much better than the sex tour you took me to," Ryleigh says to Stone. "Take notes."

"Oh my God," Michael says, putting his hands on his head, "did you guys even have sex before you got married?"

"Michael," Jillian, his wife, hisses at him.

"Yeah, not everyone knocks up their one-night stand before they marry her." Alex looks at her brother, who glares over at her.

"I'm not the only one that happened to," Michael defends, "look at Stefano and Addison." He points at Stefano, who shrugs and kisses Addison's temple as she holds her pregnant belly.

"I didn't even kiss her until after she agreed to marry me," Nash shares, and now my brother is the one slapping the table.

"He's insane." Stone looks at Nash, then looks at Christopher. "You what, held her hand?"

"Did we hold hands?" Nash looks at me, and the whole table bursts out laughing, even Caine. "I don't even think we held hands."

I stare at him, and the lightness in his eyes lets me know it's going to be okay. It's going to be awkward, but it's fine. "I think we side-hugged once."

"I mean, a side hug"—Stone throws up his hands—"how could you not drag her to the altar?"

"Right," Nash agrees with him, not even caring if the comment was sarcastic. "So I did."

"You two," Caine says, pointing at Nash and then me, "are out of your minds." He rolls his finger in a circle near his head. "And I'm going to be here for it. Just like he was when I was out of my mind for this one." He motions with his head toward Grace.

"Once he found out I sold feet pictures," Grace teases, putting her arms around his shoulders, "he was a goner."

The whole table bursts out laughing, and I look over at Nash, who is watching me instead of paying attention to what is going on at the table. He leans in and kisses my lips softly, his thumb rubbing my chin. "You okay?"

I nod. "I'm okay," I admit to him, "for now."

SIXTEEN

"NASH," SHE WHISPERS as she throws back her head.

"I can feel it, baby," I say, my hands at her hips as I help pull her up and then slam her back down on my cock. I watch her ride my cock with my back against the headboard. "I feel you all over me." I move my hands from her hips to her juicy fucking tits that are swaying in front of my mouth, twisting both of them at the same time. Her body jolts as she rides me faster. She woke me up with this mouth, swallowing my cock. I didn't want her to feel left out, so I dragged her up and set her right on my face, my tongue sliding straight into her pussy as she fell forward, taking my cock again in her mouth. I waited until she came on my face before I sat up and told her to ride me.

"Nash." She says my name again, this time her mouth against my lips as she slides her tongue into my mouth before arching her back. "I'm coming."

Her hands go from my forearms to my shoulders

where she holds on to me, fucking me faster. She rises all the way up to the tip of my cock before she slides back down. "Hold it off, baby," I urge her, and she shakes her head. "You come harder when you take your time." My hand lifts to the back of her head, fisting her hair in my hand and pulling it back. "Baby, don't make me take you off my cock."

"Don't you dare." Her words come out breathlessly. "I need you," she pleads.

"What do you need?" I ask, my mouth over hers. "You have my cock."

"I need your fingers," she says, slamming down on me and grinding her clit against me, "and your mouth."

"What my baby wants," I say, letting her hair go, "she gets." I move my hand between us, my thumb rubbing through her folds, her wetness on the tip now. "Damn, baby." I look down at her pussy swallowing my cock. "I thought my cock in your mouth was a good view." I rub her clit side to side, and her back arches. "But watching you ride my cock." I slide my tongue into her mouth. One hand reaches behind her, gripping my thigh, her nails scoring into the skin as the other hand comes up to hold my face. Her pussy gets so tight around my cock, I'm surprised she can even pull it off me.

Her forehead stays on mine as she pants, "I'm so close." Right before she sucks my tongue into her mouth like she was sucking my cock. "It's coming." My thumb moves even faster, matching her thrusts as my hips lift off the bed. "It's so good," she says right before she slams down on me, her back arching, her legs trembling, and my mouth absorbing her moans. "Nash." I close my eyes, feeling her pussy spasm around my cock and her wetness dripping all the way down my balls. "Nash." She says my name again, and because I'm sitting up, it makes it easier for me to wrap one arm around her waist and the other around her back before I flip her to her back mid-orgasm.

"Legs." I clench my teeth mid-thrust as she puts her legs over my shoulders so I can get deeper inside her. "Fuck," I curse as I drive into her harder than I have before. "You were fucking made for my cock."

"I think I'm going to"—her eyes roll in back of her head—"again."

"Tell me, baby." I slam into her. "Who were you made for?" I'm not going to last much longer. Being inside her is my fucking kryptonite. I'd give away everything I have to slide into her. "Whose pussy is this?"

"Yours, I was made for you." She barely has the words out of her mouth before my mouth crashes down on hers, and I come in the middle of the kiss. My thrusts slow down until I empty everything in her, and only then do I let her lips go. "How the hell does sex get even better?" she asks me as I slide out of her to the side. "Like for real." I look over at her as she looks over at me, lying naked on the bed. "Like I thought last night was over here." She puts her hand up. "But then now." She sits up. "Over the top."

"Better than the night we got married?" I ask, and she has to think about it.

"I mean, that is as high as last night, the day after,

however." She turns to get off the bed. "Now that is, I think, the highest."

She walks around the bed to the bathroom and stops by my side of the bed. "I will say on the record, your cock is the nicest cock I've ever seen"—she winks at me—"and used."

"I'm flattered." I fold one of my arms under my head as I watch her go to the bathroom. My eyes move from her to the open window, seeing the sun starting to come up. The sound of the water hitting the rocks is outside the open window.

"Nash." She sticks her head out of the bathroom with her toothbrush in her mouth. "Want to order room service?"

"If it means spending more time in bed with you"—I sit up and reach over to grab the phone—"I'm all over it."

The woman answers the phone after one ring, "Good morning, Mr. Griffin."

"Morning," I reply. "I'd like to order some pancakes, scrambled eggs, some sausage and bacon." I look back, hearing the shower turn on. "Also some coffee and orange juice."

"Sounds good," she says, "would you like some champagne?"

"Sure."

"It should be about twenty minutes," she informs me.

"Perfect," I say, hanging up the phone and walking into the shower in time to see her pinning her hair on top of her head. "Twenty minutes," I tell her. She looks over her shoulder, and I see a hickey on her ass cheek next to bite marks. My cock goes to half-mast. "You didn't tell me you were taking a shower."

She opens the glass shower door and steps in, laughing. "I didn't know I had to run it by you." Putting her head back and to the side, the water runs down her body. My cock is now fully hard as she turns around to make the water wash over her back. My hand goes to my cock. "You going to stand there and ogle me?" she asks before turning to face me. "Or are you going to come in here and wash my back?" She doesn't have to ask me twice. I take the four steps to the shower, pull open the door, and step in. My head bends to kiss her, and the taste of mint hits my tongue at the same time my hand finds her pussy and two fingers slide into her. "Hmm," she purrs, opening her legs more to give me access as she grips my cock in her hand.

"Turn around," I instruct her, and she turns so her back is against my chest as I kiss her neck. "Put your hands against the wall." She lays her palms flat against the tile wall, the water falling on the middle of her back. "Now, spread your legs and lift your ass for me." She doesn't make me wait long, and when she does, I squat down a little, grabbing my cock in my hand. "That's my good girl," I praise right before I push my legs up and slam my cock into her.

She comes three times before I come again. This time, it's not inside her. Nope, my girl drops to her knees when I tell her I'm close, and she swallows all of me. I'm slipping on the hotel robe when I hear a knock on the door as she walks out behind me. "I'll get it," I say, walking to the door and letting the room service guy in. He wheels in the cart. "I'll put it outside when we're done," I tell him, and he nods, turning and walking out.

"Where do you want to eat?" Zoey asks me once I wheel the cart into the bedroom, standing here wearing a matching robe.

"The only reason I ordered this was to get you back into bed," I tell her, and she gets on the bed. I grab the big tray in the middle of the cart and put it in the center of the bed. "I got you stuff for your taco shit."

She shakes her head and laughs. "Don't you even try to pretend you don't like it. You ate two yesterday."

Her skin looks sun-kissed, and her freckles are even darker than they were before, and every single day I have to pinch myself. I watch her make a taco and then hand me the plate. "Here, don't say your wife never made you breakfast." She smiles big, and I laugh. "We need to talk about things."

"I have never been married before," I start, reaching for the plate, "but I think it's never a good thing when your wife says we need to talk about things." Holding the pancake close, I take a bite. I've never had this before her, but I have to say, I will never eat pancakes any other way again.

"You might be right on that." She fixes her own plate, folding one foot while she stretches the other one out.

"Before we start," I say, holding up my hand, "happy anniversary." I smile at her. "I got you a gift, and it's waiting for you at home."

"Anniversary?" she asks.

"We've been married one week." I hold up my hand.

"Oh," she replies, not sure what to say. "Um, happy anniversary," she mumbles.

"Now, what did you want to talk about?" I ask nervously.

"I know I said I would give you ninety days," she says, and I drop my plate, the food that's in my mouth suddenly tasting like shit. "And I will," she quickly adds, "but where are we going to live?"

"I have a house." I don't know why I have to tell her this. "So we are going to live in my house."

"But I live in New York," she retorts. "Like, my house is in New York. My things are there in the house."

"Yeah, I assumed that when you said you live in New York." I wink at her, earning me a sneer. "Can I ask you something?" I take another bite of the taco. "Why do you call New York home?"

"What?" she asks, not sure of my question.

"Why is New York your home? Besides the fact you have a house there with things in it."

"I don't know. It's just home. I've always lived in New York."

"You grew up in Long Island," I point out.

"Yes, but I went to school in the city. It's my home." She motions with her hands going around in a circle.

"But what I'm saying is, there isn't anything but your things in your house that keeps you there. Your office is there, but your office is in your home, correct?"

"Correct."

"And you have no children that I know of." She just stares at me. "So, technically, you can move into my home."

"I can't move to LA," she gasps.

"Why not? It's almost like New York. Overpopulated, traffic is horrible, and they have matcha at every single corner." I grin. "It's not like I live in Fargo. It's LA."

"Yes, but—" she says.

"Okay, how is this?" I look at her. "Move in with me for a month, and if you don't like it, I'll see about moving to the New York office."

"That's…" She shakes her head. "That's crazy."

"It's the only solution to this talk, so if you don't like LA, I'll see about switching. If that can't happen, I'll commute."

"You'll commute from New York to LA?" She rolls her eyes. "It's not like you work in Manhattan, and we live in Brooklyn. It's a six-hour flight."

"Zoey." I take a deep inhale. "If I have to do it, I'll do it. I won't like not being with you, and maybe you can come with me a couple of times."

"You would fucking do that?" she questions, astounded. "Just like that, you would move to New York or commute?"

"Um, yeah," I reply, not even sure it's possible but knowing I'll do what I need to do for my wife. If that's either me switching offices or me fucking commuting, then that is what I'll have to do. We may have only been together for one week, but it's just cemented that she's the one for me. And I'll do what I need to do to make her happy. "You're my wife. Happy wife, happy life."

SEVENTEEN

"I CAN'T BELIEVE it's the last day of the vacation," I mumble from my side of the daybed, turning to Zara, who sits up. "Where are you going?"

"In the water." She points at the ocean. "The kids are finally out." She looks over to see the little kids all in the sand, building something or another. "Let's go."

"Okay." I get up, looking around to see if I spot Nash. He went off with Caine not long ago, and now I see him sitting with my father. I have to wonder if he's there because he wants to be there or because he has no choice.

I follow Zara, the soft waves hitting my legs as I walk deeper into the water. "I'm going to miss this."

"You've been drunk for two weeks," I remind her, and she shakes her head.

"I've not once gone to bed drunk." She holds up her hand, smiling. "It's called day drinking, and it's about moderation, Zoey."

I laugh and duck myself into the warm water. "Why

didn't Daniel come?" I ask about her fiancé.

"He couldn't get off work," she says. "He's been working on this huge deal for two months now." I look at her. "Anyway, let's talk about something more interesting than me. Let's talk about the hubby." She avoids talking about Daniel this time, and I let it go. Since she is wearing her glasses, I can't even see if something is bothering her. "What's going on with that?"

"Nothing." I extend my hands to the sides, moving them in the water. "I'm going to move in with him for thirty days and see how I like it."

"But how are things at this minute? Like, do you like him?"

"We're on vacation," I point out.

She throws her head back and laughs. "It's your honeymoon."

"Whatever it is. Of course things are good. Everything is chill. We drink, we eat, we laugh."

"You have amazing sex. Best sex in your whole—" she adds to my list, and I splash her with water.

"I told you that in confidence," I hiss at her, and she just laughs it off.

"But that's the thing." My voice comes out softly. "It's almost too perfect. Like he's saying the right things, doing the right things."

"You mean doing you the right way."

"That, like it can't be all good all the time."

"Why not?" she asks, and I just look at her.

"I mean, look at our parents or anyone from our family. They pretty much have the best relationships.

I'm sure they argue, but it's meaningless. I think most of them argue just to have makeup sex."

"Can we never put our parents and sex in the same sentence?" I fake gag. "Please."

"What I'm saying is, maybe he's that perfect. Maybe everything is going fine because he's your person. Maybe, just maybe, you've found someone who is all that and a big dick." She smirks and stands up. "Maybe you should be thanking your past drunken self for your present and future sore-vagina self."

It's my turn to laugh, and while I'm laughing, I spot Nash walking into the water. "Hey, you two." He comes right to me, bending to kiss my lips. "What are you talking about?"

"Your big dick and her moving to LA." If I could kill her, I think I would. I look at Nash to see if he's going to be pissed about what she just said, but instead, he shakes his head and wraps his arms around my waist before bending his legs and pulling me onto his lap.

"Sounds like I missed a good conversation, then," he replies as I wrap an arm around his shoulders.

"I mean, she did say you're selfish and always come before her," Zara deadpans, and I splash her with water.

"What? I'm trying to help you. He's probably going to go all caveman on you and make sure you have all the orgasms you can handle. We'll probably have to wheel you to the plane tomorrow." She gets up out of the water, turning to walk to the shore. "You're welcome. Now I have two hours before day drinking ends, so if you two lovebirds will excuse me, I have a drink to find."

We both watch her walk out of the water and hold up her hand for a drink. "Your cousin is a nut," Nash says. "Did you really talk about my big dick?"

I look at him. "Yes, and also your selfish ways. Funny how you didn't bring that up." He turns me so I'm straddling him.

"Baby," he murmurs, kissing my neck, "we both know it's almost three to one with us."

"Yes, because you're selfish and won't let me come when I want to come." I avoid looking at him, not even telling him that since we've been together—and he's been pushing me to hold out longer—my orgasms have been earth-shattering. There are things he needs to know and that is not one of them. "See? Selfish."

"I'll take it," he says, nuzzling my neck.

"What were you talking about with my father?" I ask him, and he stops nuzzling.

"You know, just the regular. The weather, the stock market, and if I break your heart, he's going to break my face." I gasp. "I mean, he didn't say it in those words." He laughs. "Actually, he said it exactly in those words."

"What did you tell him?" I ask, holding my breath.

"I told him that if anyone is going to break anyone's heart, it'll be you breaking mine." I don't know why, but the way he says it makes my heart hurt. "Then he laughed and said probably, but he's okay with that."

"That sounds about right." I try not to let his words get to me, nor do I want to think about how his words have hit me right where it hurts. Instead, I wrap my arms around him and lay my head on his shoulder as we sit in the warm water.

～

I walk up the steps to the plane, smiling at the flight attendant waiting for us. "Good afternoon, Mrs. Griffin," he greets, and it always shocks me when I'm called that.

"Good afternoon," I say, walking in and putting my bag in one of the seats, turning to see Nash enter the plane and give the man a chin up before walking and dumping his own bag in the same seat as mine.

"We will be off as soon as the bags are stowed," he says.

"Where do you want to sit?" Nash asks me as he pulls me to his side. My hands go on his blue button-down shirt that is again open at the top of his chest. "I'm going to go to the bathroom before we take off," he states and then leans in to whisper in my ear. "Do you want to come with me?"

"Yes, wait for me in there." I kiss the hinge of his jaw before he laughs and walks away.

I sit in the chair, knowing once he comes back, he will sit in the chair right next to me instead of sitting in the one in front of me. I take out my phone and open my Instagram, showing me I was tagged in a couple of pictures from Grace. One of them is the four of us last night. Nash stands behind me with his one arm wrapped around the top of my chest. My arm is folded up and linked with his dangling fingers, while his other hand is around my waist, trying to grab my other hand. My head is turned to the side, smiling at him, while he grins back at me. It was right before he leaned in and kissed me. My eyes only look at the two of us before I double tap it and write a heart comment.

"I knew you weren't coming," Nash huffs when he slides into the seat beside me. "I even waited."

I look over at him. "Too bad you didn't hold your breath. It would have been a very bad flight." I turn the phone toward him. "Did you see this picture?"

"I did." He takes out his own phone, and I see our wedding picture is his screen saver, and then shows me his Instagram where I see he's cropped Caine and Grace out. "Caine even wrote a comment," he says, and I grab his phone to read it. "You forgot to tag my hand that's cut off, dick." That makes me laugh. "I want to get it framed."

"Okay," I tell him as the plane takes off. It takes us ten minutes before he gets up and pulls me out of the chair to go sit on the couch. I go through my emails quickly when he lunges, putting his head in my lap. "Comfy?"

"I'd be more comfy if you took off your shirt and I could sleep on your tits, but this will do." My hand comes down to play with his hair as I scroll through my to-do list and add a couple of things. When I look down, he's asleep, and I refuse to move to wake him up. He wakes up three hours later, looking up at me. "What are you doing?"

"Nothing," I tell him.

"Are you watching cat videos?" he questions, annoying me that he knows what I'm doing.

"No." I turn the phone off. "We are landing any second," I tell him.

He reaches around my head, pulling me down to him. "Kiss me, baby." Here in the middle of the private plane, while we are landing, I kiss him.

I'm exhausted by the time we get in the car and are on the way to his house. "Tired?" he asks, and I nod. "We'll get you home and fed and then you can go to bed." He looks over at me. "Are you okay?"

"Yeah, why?" I ask.

"I was just thinking that maybe you might miss your family." I turn my head to look at this fucking man. Never, and I mean never, in my life has someone taken the time to think about how I feel. I mean, sure, my family, but not a man in this universe has gone to that extent.

"Yeah," I say, clearing my voice when I feel it fill with a golf ball, "but I'm okay."

"Maybe we can invite Zara to come out here for a week," he suggests. I look out the window instead of to him, the tears filling my eyes, making it hard to see. "See if she's free."

"Okay," I reply, hoping like fuck my voice doesn't crack. He doesn't say anything else as we make our way over to his house. We go through a wrought-iron gate when he puts in a code and then turns down the street toward his house.

He slows down and turns into a driveway, and I finally get a look at his house. The lights from inside illuminate the outside. He stops the car, and I get out to take a better look. There are two double-car garage doors. He opens the trunk and takes the bags to the front door. The house looks like it's all windows in the front, but you can't see in. You can only see the illumination from the lights. Even the front door looks like it's all glass all the way to the roof.

"Shall we?" He holds out his hand, smiling at me, and I know he's probably nervous I won't like his house. I walk with him up the driveway to the front door, going up the three steps. He stops at the door and enters the code before turning to me, grabbing me around my waist, and picking me up.

"What the hell are you doing?" I ask, wrapping my arms around his shoulders.

"I'm carrying you over the threshold," he declares, kicking open the door with his foot. I can't help but laugh as he takes a step into his house. "Welcome home, Zoey."

EIGHTEEN

NASH

HER LAUGHTER AS I carry her over the threshold goes from my chest to my stomach, and then straight to my dick. I kick the door closed with my foot as we stand in the foyer. "Um, Nash?" She looks up at me. "Our bags are still outside."

"I'll get them after I give you a tour, and you can settle in." I lean down to kiss her lips.

"Are you going to carry me for the whole tour?" she asks.

"If you want," I answer her without even caring. If she wants me to carry her through the house for the tour, then that is what I will do.

"I think I'm good to walk."

"Fine," I pout, reluctant to let her out of my arms but making a mental note to carry her to the bedroom, even if it's over my shoulder or on my back. I make sure she has her balance before I let her go. "This is the foyer," I tell her, and her eyebrows rise at the square staircase in the middle of the open-concept house. "That's the formal living room." I point at the room on my right-hand side. "And the dining room."

"Do you even use these rooms?" she asks as she steps into the living room, looking around and stopping when she spots a mirrored frame on one of the coffee tables. "Wait." She walks over and picks it up. "How did you do this?" She looks at the picture of her right before she walked down the aisle. She's looking at the camera with her hip cocked to the side, one hand on her hip and the other hand by her side, holding the bouquet. She looks sexy as fuck but also fucking beautiful.

"The photographer emailed me the link for the pictures," I tell her, "and I got a couple to put around the house so you would feel sort of at home." She puts the frame down. "Since you'll be in every room."

"That's very sweet, Nash." She walks over to me and gets on her tippy-toes. "I would also very much like to see the pictures of our wedding."

"I'll send you the link after," I tell her, slipping my hand in hers. "Now, come so I can show you the rest of the house." I pull her toward the stairs. "This is the mudroom." I point at the little room on my left-hand side, and she looks up at the hanging ceiling light that shows you the railing for upstairs.

"I love how open this is," she states, turning but never letting go of my hand.

"Good," I say as I continue walking. "Now this is the kitchen, obviously." I point to the right where there is a huge gray marble island right in front of a U-shaped kitchen. "That must be your gift." I point at the white box on the island next to what is a replica of her bouquet when we got married.

She lets my hand go to walk over to the island. "Is this from that day?" She points at the vase of flowers, and I shake my head.

"No, but I remembered so—"

"Can I open the gift?" she asks, her eyes lighting up even more. I see she likes gifts. I make another mental note. "It's big."

"Not as big as my dick, though." I point at her, making her laugh. "Don't forget that."

"How could you ever let me forget that," she deadpans, pulling the white ribbon off the white box. She lays it flat on the counter before she pulls the top off and moves the tissue paper off the frame that is in the box. "Nash," she whispers, "this is…" She looks into the box, her finger trailing over the glass. Inside is a frame I had made with three hearts in the middle of it. Under each heart is a different saying and the date of when the event happened. The first heart is the day we met and the location we met, with the word "Hello." The second heart says "Will You?" And the third has "I Do."

"It's a map of our story. A controversial one, but a map nonetheless," I explain, and she turns to look at me. I see she has tears in her eyes that she's ferociously blinking away. "I wanted you to put it where you wanted to."

"This is…" She looks down at the frame in the box. "I can't believe," she says and then laughs, "the Will You and the I Do have the same date and almost the same location.”

“Yeah, the man who did it messaged me twice to make sure I didn’t fuck it up. I was going to put it up on the wall.” I point at the wall we just walked past that faces the staircase. “That way, everyone sees it when they walk in. We can put family pictures around it, but it’ll be like the wall’s foundation. Sort of like our family tree.”

“That sounds like a great idea.” Her voice is soft as she looks back down at the picture in the box.

“Do you want something to drink?” I ask her, walking over to the stainless-steel fridge. “I had them stock the coconut water you like as well as the sparkling water.”

She shakes her head as she walks over to the family room. “This room”—her hand goes in a circle from the kitchen that leads to the family room—“it’s very much like the house I grew up in.” She clears her throat. “I can’t tell you all the time I spent at the island doing homework and then sitting on the couch while my mother was in the kitchen making or trying to make food.” She laughs as she remembers. “It is what I always wanted in the house I was going to live in.”

“Well, I guess we can say one for LA, then.” I put my hands in my back pockets as she walks into the family room and gasps, looking at the wall. “Our wedding picture,” I say when she points at the portrait hung up on the wall facing the couch.

“I’ve never seen this picture,” she tells me. It’s similar to the one we posted, but this one has her leaning forward a bit, and her mouth is open as she laughs. Her face beams with happiness, which is why I chose it.

"We can change it if you like. It's just that I love your smile in that one, and I swear I can hear your laughter through the picture.

"We do look happy, don't we?" I ask as she walks over and puts her hands on my hips.

"We do," she admits. "Now, are you going to show me upstairs?"

"Is that code for you want to see my dick?" I push the hair over her shoulders so I can kiss her neck. "Because the answer is always yes."

I stroll over to the stairs as we walk up and head straight to my bedroom. "How many bedrooms are in this house?" She looks around when we get to the top of the stairs.

"Five bedrooms and a media room. The master bedroom is on that side." I point over to the other side of the staircase.

"Where the magic happens." She holds one of my hands in both of hers.

"I can tell you there will be magic there tonight," I confirm before she's the one pulling me toward the bedroom. "Of course we can change anything you don't like," I tell her when she steps into the bedroom, and she stops in her tracks at the door. I had the bedroom changed to everything she has in her house in New York. The same covers and pillows, even the same throw blankets.

"What?" she says, looking at me. "How?"

"I asked Zara," I tell her, shrugging, "before she started her day drinking. Whatever she didn't remember, your mom did." She walks over to the bed with a white robe folded on the top. "I noticed you wore the white robe all the time on vacation. It just has your initials on the front and not the name of the hotel. I'd prefer you naked, but this one is similar."

"I'll try my best to be as naked as I can be, just to make you feel more at home, that is. I'm going to start now." She peels her T-shirt over her head. "I'm going to get in the shower while you go get my bag."

"But then you'll have clothes to wear," I counter, and she laughs.

"I promise not to wear any clothes for the rest of the night." She turns and walks to the bathroom. "That is until we leave to go to work tomorrow."

"Fine." I give in. "I'll get the bags and meet you in the shower."

"So what you're saying is you are giving me a full two minutes to wash myself before you come and fuck me?"

"No." I shake my head, walking to her and pulling her to me for her to feel my cock is ready to join her. "I'm giving you a minute and maybe a half. I'm bringing the bags in. I don't have to bring them up." She puts her head back and laughs. "Go get naked and wet for me."

"Nash." She puts her hand on my cheek. "Not sure you've been paying attention, but I'm always wet for you." She kisses my jaw. "Just thinking about this"— she palms my cock over my pants—"and it's like I'm instantly ready for you."

"How bad do you need the bags?" I ask, gripping her hips harder in my hands as she wraps her arms around my neck. "I have a Ring cam." I pick her up and carry her into the bathroom, her feet never touching the floor. "If anything happens, I'll replace everything in there and then some." I turn on the water in the shower. I don't give her a chance to answer because my tongue slides into her mouth, and that's all it takes. Our hands frantically try to get the other one naked like we haven't been together in weeks instead of hours, and when she walks out of the shower before me, I can still see my fingerprints on her ass cheeks.

I'm slipping on a pair of shorts when she storms back into the bathroom wearing the robe that was on the bed. "Um, what the fuck is in the master closet?" She puts her hands on her hips. "Seriously, Nash, what the fuck?" I stand here, my hands still in the elastic of my boxers. "There's women's clothing hanging in the closet." Her voice rises even higher. "Is there something you should have told me before I moved in here?" She folds her hands over her chest, and I can see her chest rising and falling, and her eyes look like she could kill me. I start to open my mouth. "I can't believe you." She throws her hands up. "A woman was living in this house, and she still has clothes here, and you didn't even have the decency to tell me before." She shakes her head. "Unbelievable. I knew you were too good to be true," she hisses, and I fold my hands over my chest, pissed. "Don't you give me that fucking look, Nash. You fucking lied to me." She jabs her finger in my direction. "Un-fucking-believable."

"Are you done?" I ask, and she just glares at me. I can say at this moment we are glaring at each other. "For your information, those clothes are yours. I told your mother you were moving in with me, and she set it up so you would have a wardrobe ready for you here in case you were missing anything. She—" Her face goes soft. "I don't know what she did, but she had everything delivered here and ready for you. Those are your fucking clothes." I point at the closet. "I can't believe you would think I would have a woman living here and not tell you." I shake my head before I walk out of the bathroom and say something I can't take back. I get our luggage from the front door before turning off all the lights and bringing the suitcases upstairs with me. When I walk into the room, she's in the middle of the bed, sitting on the back of her feet, waiting for me.

"I'm sorry," she states softly, "I should have—"

"Yeah," I say, wheeling our bags into the closet and seeing her mother did not mess around. It's like she's been living here for a while. I hear her walk into the closet and then feel her hands wrap around my waist as she kisses my back. "I wanted you to have some things." I put my hand on hers. "I didn't think she would…"

"I'm sorry I jumped to conclusions." She presses her naked chest into my back. "I should have known better."

"I think we just had our first fight." I turn in her arms. "Which means we get to have makeup sex." I pick her up, carrying her to the bed. "Regular sex is amazing, and shower sex I've never come so hard in my life, but makeup sex might be out of this world."

"You know what might be better?" she says to me. "Angry sex."

"That might break my dick." Both our mouths attack each other, swallowing the laughter, before we have makeup sex. I was right. It was out of this world.

The following morning, my eyes fly open at four thirty as if they know I'm back from vacation. I look over to see Zoey on her stomach, facing the other way. I slide out of bed, grab my workout gear, and head to the gym I have set up in the backyard pool house.

I run on the treadmill for an hour before I lift weights for another hour. When I slide back into the house, the sun is already peeking out by the time I walk into the kitchen. I'm shocked when I see Zoey walking down the steps. "Morning," I greet her as she walks my way. She is rubbing the sleep out of her eyes.

"Morning," she replies, pulling a stool out from under the island. "What time did you get up?"

"Four thirty." I kiss the back of her neck as I walk into the kitchen and start making my protein shake.

"I didn't hear the alarm."

"Didn't set one," I tell her as I walk over to the fridge and grab her oat milk. "Guess my body knew it was back to work."

I pull out the black kettle that is on the counter, something I also ordered when we were away. "You want a matcha?" I ask, and she smirks.

"Why, you going to make me one?" she asks, and I nod.

"While you've been watching cat videos, I've been watching matcha videos," I inform her, grabbing the bag of green matcha tea. "Prepare to drop to your knees." I wink at her. "In the shower."

I make her green tea, and even after making it from scratch, I will never, ever drink this shit again. I swear it's like I was mushing grass clippings. "This tastes amazing," Zoey praises while she takes a sip, and I take a gulp of my shake. "We should set some boundaries now that we are going to be working and living together." I put my shake down in front of me.

"Such as?" I lean my hip against the counter as she puts her matcha down and walks over to the fridge.

"Well, and this is non-negotiable." My eyes just stare at her. "There is no funny business at the office. It's where I work, and I want to be respected because of my work and not because I'm going to suck the boss's dick in the shower in thirty minutes." She takes the eggs out and places them on the counter.

"And when we get home and right before bed," I add the other two times I want her mouth on my dick. "But I will agree to that. I've never mixed my personal life with my work life." She gives me a yeah-right look as she goes in search of a frying pan, finding it, and putting it on the stove. "In the office, I mean. What else?"

"Well." She takes another sip before going over to get a mixing bowl. "I really didn't think of anything else. I don't want favoritism or special treatment." She cracks some eggs into the bowl before adding a splash of milk and moving on to get the butter.

"Baby," I say her nickname, and she glares at me and points. "In this house, you are baby to me, but at work, I will call you Zoey," I correct myself. "You know we work together, and you don't work for me, right? We're working together on this, but I'm not your boss, and you are not my employee." I take a sip of the protein shake as she prepares the eggs before grabbing a pack of bacon and another pan. "What about copping a feel?" I ask. "Like, can I grab your ass in secret?"

"No, the minute you touch my ass, you have to go and grab my boobs, and then we're somehow having sex." I try to argue with her, but she isn't wrong. That is exactly how it happens.

"Somehow having sex," I repeat her words, laughing as she puts bread in the toaster. "Meanwhile, you were the one copping all kinds of feels when we were on vacation."

"We were on our honeymoon." She walks over to grab a plate, piles the fluffy eggs on them, and adds the two slices of bacon before the toast pops up. She butters the toast, cuts it in half, then places it on the edge of the plate before handing it to me. "Eat your breakfast."

"You made me breakfast?" I ask, shocked when I see she hasn't even made herself anything.

"Yes." She nods, picking up her matcha. "Now, I have to go get ready for work."

"And my blow job." I put the plate down and follow her up the stairs, grabbing her ass, and then sliding my hand into the robe and pinching her nipple.

"I just slaved over the stove to make you breakfast," she moans.

"You have to eat your breakfast first, and then I'll go down and nuke the one you made me." I kiss her neck.

"See? Working together is going to be perfect."

Forty-five minutes later, I've showered, nuked my breakfast, and I'm slipping on my suit jacket when she comes walking into the closet to get her shoes. She's wearing a tight light pink skirt with a high-neck, sleeveless white shirt. Her hair is down. But all I can stare at are my rings on her finger. She only takes them off when she has to put her cream on her body or when she applies sunscreen. Other than that, she's had them on the whole time. Even when she takes them off, you can see the tan line from where they were. "You know what's great about going to work with you?" I pull out the cuffs on each arm. "I know what you look like naked. I don't have to sit there and imagine it."

"You imagined me naked?" She slides her feet into her mile-high nude heels.

"Do I have a dick?" I ask. "Sorry, a big dick?"

"We should get going." She ignores my question, walking out of the closet but stopping close to me and putting her left hand on my chest. "Also, I might have pictured you naked once or twice." Her hand moves down, and she cups my package. "So much better than what I imagined."

"You can't do that and have me not want to fuck you," I scold her, and she throws her head back. "What about lunch sex?"

"I have back-to-back meetings with everyone in the company today, including your parents," she says, "so that should be fun."

She pretends it doesn't bother her, but I see her hands

tremble as she walks out of the bedroom. I take my phone out and text my family group chat.

Me: *Meeting with Zoey today. If I'm not on the call, I expect you all to remain professional.*

Caine answers right away.

Caine: *We are ALL going to be professional.*

I know I have him to back me up, which makes me feel better, but my parents were not thrilled with the news I got married to someone they didn't know. They were especially not thrilled I did it in the way I did. They let me know it, in all the ways a parent can tell you, even to the point where they asked if I had lost my ever-loving fucking mind.

"Nash," she shouts my name, "are you coming?"

"I wish." I put the phone in the inside pocket of my suit when I walk out and see she made the bed. I hear the sound of her heels going down the stairs, and five minutes later, we're walking out of the house hand in hand.

"I'm so nervous," she admits when we park the car and she gets out. "Do you think they know?"

"Zoey, I left for two weeks, and the whole time, I've been posting us on my Instagram. They know."

I open the door for her as she steps in. "Good morning, Nash," Lulu says, smiling big. "Good morning, Zoey."

"Morning, Lulu," Zoey returns, walking toward the conference room. I see her setting up her workstation as I make my way into my own office to deal with a couple of things I put off while I was away.

The phone beeps from inside my pocket, and I expect

it to be my parents, but instead, I see it's from Zoey.

Zoey: *Have a great first day back at the office.*

I smile when the next one comes in.

Zoey: *Picturing you naked right now.*

I can't help but throw my head back and laugh.

Me: *Should we go home for lunch? And by lunch, I mean should we go home and not come back?*

Zoey: *We were gone for two weeks. You can last until tonight.*

I make a few phone calls, and it's almost after lunch when I look around. I walk out of my office and see Zoey talking to Cecelia and Becky, who deal with the client portfolios. They are getting up when I walk into the conference room. "Hey," I say as they walk out, and they both smile at me. "Did you have lunch?" I ask when I get next to her chair and prop myself on the table as she puts her hand on her stomach and leans back in the chair. "How is your day?"

She doesn't have a chance to answer me before I hear a male voice. "There he is." Zoey looks over at the door. "The groom himself." He laughs, coming around the table. I stand to greet him as he walks to me and slaps me on the shoulder before he squeezes it.

"Hey, man." I look over at Zoey, who is watching the exchange. "Zoey, this is Derek," I say of the man, "one of my closest friends."

"Zoey." He extends his hand to shake hers. "It's nice to meet you."

"Derek works in the merger department," I explain, putting my hands in my pockets instead of around her waist, knowing she would kill me.

"Mrs. Griffin." He laughs. "Never thought I would see the day that you settle down." He claps his hands like it's a joke. "Especially since I know you like to play the field and keep all options open."

The minute he says the words, I can see Zoey's shield come up. "Well, when you find the one—" I start to say.

"Maybe when he's out of town," Derek says to Zoey, "we can go out and get to know each other." If we weren't in the office, I think I would punch him in the face.

"That sounds good," she replies, but even by her tone, I know it's never, ever going to happen. I also know that as soon as Derek is out of this office, we will be having words. "I'll let you know." She looks at him and then at me, and I don't have a chance to do that because Lulu comes in with a brown take-out bag, and then Kailyn walks in, telling me I have a call with my parents in thirty minutes.

Derek and Kailyn start to chat when the phone rings from beside Zoey's computer, and I look down in time to see it's Josh. His name is on the top of the screen with a red heart beside it and the picture of the two of them together. Zoey steps forward and presses the side of the phone and turns it over, pissing me off. The whole thing from the time Derek opened his mouth to now seeing Josh call her and she turned it over, not sure if she was hiding it or not, I don't even know. I'm feeling like I'm at the edge of the cliff, and someone just pushed me off.

"Everyone out." My voice is tight and louder than I want it to be. "Out"—I motion with my hand—"except you." I point at Zoey. "You stay here." They all look at us with big eyes before they walk out and close the door behind them. I walk out to the middle of the tables and grab the remote that is there, pressing the button that frosts the windows to give you privacy.

"What are you doing?" Zoey asks as I walk to her without saying a word. Instead of saying anything, I take her face in both my hands, and I kiss her. Wet, long, and hard, not giving a shit if this is not allowed on her list. I need her to know she's mine, and I especially need for me to feel like she's mine.

NINETEEN

I PUT MY hands on his hips as he slides his tongue around and around in my mouth. My tongue fights with his even though I'm pissed he's kissing me at work. I savor it, trying to drown out Derek's words: "he likes to keep his options open."

He lets my lips go, and my eyes flutter open a bit. "Don't say it," he warns. "I don't want to hear it."

"What is it you don't want to hear?" I ask as he drops his hands from my face, but I keep my hands on his hips. "No kissing you at work and all that? The windows are tinted.

"I don't think we'll need to draw everyone a picture of what we are doing in here," I tell him when my phone buzzes once and then stops. Both of our eyes go to the phone, and he steps out of my touch to grab the remote and press the button, making the privacy go away, and everyone can see in.

"That's your lunch." I point at the bag. "I ordered it

this morning when I got in." He just looks at me, not sure what to say. "I hope you eat what I got you."

He looks at the bag, stopping in his tracks. "I'll be back in fifteen for the call with my family." He walks out as if he's not leaving me here breathless from a fucking kiss. A kiss I didn't even know I needed but then suddenly wanted.

I sit down in the chair, my legs shaky, when the phone buzzes yet again. I turn it over and see I have a missed call from Josh with a voicemail, which is weird since he's never left me a voicemail before. If I didn't answer his call, he would send me a text.

I press the voicemail and the woman asks, "Who's calling?" I enter my code zero-two-five-seven, and she tells me I have one new message.

I press one to hear it, and then his voice comes through, "Hey, Zoey, just calling to see how your day is going. I miss you. Call me when you get off work." His voice stops, and I think he's hung up, but he didn't. "I love you, Zoey."

To replay this message press one, to delete press two, to save press three. I press two, deleting the message from my phone. My stomach sinks when I look up and see Nash standing next to the receptionist's desk, talking to Derek. I know Nash saw he called, and with that, I pull up his contact and change his name to just Josh without the heart beside his name. I also change the picture out, opting to leave it blank, before I text Zara.

Me: ***Josh just called me again and left me a voicemail, asking me how my day was going and to call***

him when I got off work.

I know she's by her phone all day long, so it's not a surprise when she answers right away.

Zara: *Did you say you're doing amazing and then send him a picture of Nash's big dick?*

I snort, thinking it might be something she would do if she actually got burned by a guy.

Me: *No, I deleted the message.*

Zara: *Are you going to tell Nash?*

Me: *He was here when he called, so I turned over the phone.*

Zara: **The tea is piping hot… What did he say?**

Me: *Nothing, he kicked everyone out of the room so he could make out with me.*

Zara: *Did you block Josh's number?*

Me: *No.*

Zara: *Dumb, dumb, and dumb.*

Me: *I've never blocked someone in my life.*

Zara: *Super easy, go to the contact and press block this number.*

Me: *Isn't that childish?*

Zara: *He knows you're a married woman, and he's calling you. That's childish. Someone stole your toy that you had been playing with for a year and now you want it back.*

Me: *Two years.*

Zara: *And after two years, he couldn't commit. Time to cut the line. Block him.*

I'm about to answer her when Nash returns to the room, holding a folder in his hand. I look at him and I try not to let what Derek said get to me. I mean, I was assuming he was a serial dater, but we've never sat down to discuss it. I don't really think I'd want to know, if that makes sense. I said I would give him a chance and I meant it. I mean, yesterday when I saw those women's clothes in his closet, I wanted to set it all on fire, but instead I tried to have a semi-rational conversation about it. Which ended up with me riding his cock before he came on my stomach and then ate me out after. Basically, up there on the list with one of the best days I've had.

Nash pulls out the chair beside me sitting down. "Are you going to eat?" I ask him softly, wondering if he's going to ask me about Josh. The anticipation of him asking about it or bringing it up is making me so nervous, as if I'm hiding something from him. I know I sort of am, but there isn't anything I can tell him. He called, and he obviously saw I didn't speak to him.

"I am," he says, grabbing the brown bag in the corner. "Did you eat?" He looks over at me, and I shake my head. He pulls the sandwich out of the bag, then grabs the salad at the bottom of the bag, handing it to me.

I take the salad from him to keep my hands busy. "This looks good."

"I'm really not hungry." I have to look at him as he takes a bite of the sandwich. "For food anyway." His eyes stare into mine, and I know exactly what he means. "All I know is I'm going to be famished tonight." The minute he says that, I have to cross my legs to stop the throbbing because now all I'm picturing is him with his head buried between my legs. "I really wish we didn't have this meeting." He moves his chair from side to side, as if we aren't having a sex talk in the conference room. "I'd take you home." He looks around. "I don't even think we'd make it into the house." He grins. "The hood of my car is really sturdy."

"Nash," I say, not sure if I'm warning him to shut the fuck up or asking him to take me home and do whatever it is that he was thinking about doing to me.

"Did you get the email I sent with the pictures?" he asks, changing the topic as I take the top of the salad off, mix in the dressing, and shake it before grabbing a fork and eating some.

"I did. They are all so good." I smile. "I don't even remember half the pictures, or better yet, I don't even remember him snapping all those pictures."

"He was even there when we had our first dance," Nash shares, pulling up the picture on his phone. It's of him looking down at me with me facing the camera. The huge smile on my face was in every single shot. My arm around his shoulders with the bouquet hanging in my hand, my left hand on his arm, showing off my ring. "I ordered this for the living room downstairs." He shocks me. "Let me know if you want to order any."

"Surprise me," I say, and he smirks, but his smirk stops when the ringing starts from his computer. "Here we go," I say, putting down my salad and bracing for the meeting with his parents, trying not to freak myself out too much. The screen opens, and I see Caine pop up first, joined quickly by Grace, who I think is doing it to show support for me, I hope. Then his parents pop up on the screen, my in-laws. The thought brings me a mix of emotions.

"Hey, before we start, Mom, Dad, I'd like you to officially meet Zoey," he says, looking over at me and giving me a smile.

"Mr. and Mrs. Griffin," I say, clearing my throat when it sounds like it's going to crack, "it's nice to finally meet you. Nash has told me so many wonderful things about you." I lie, and even Caine knows I'm lying when his eyebrows pinch together.

"It's nice to meet you too," Mrs. Griffin replies. "I was hoping our first meeting would be in person."

I try not to think about whether that's a dig at me or not. "That's okay," I say, my hand shaking. Nash moves his hand out of the way to put it on my leg and squeeze softly.

There is nothing but awkward silence for a moment before Caine cuts in, "I have fifteen minutes before we have to leave. Zoey, why don't you tell us what you have been doing and what you think the next step should be." This I can do, this is my job, this is why I'm so good. I forget they are my in-laws and get down to business. By the end of the call, I've gotten a couple of smiles from his father, and his mother claps her hands and said it was all wonderful.

When he clicks the hang-up on the Zoom, I let out a huge sigh of relief. "That wasn't so bad." He leans back in his chair.

"I think it went as expected," I answer. He looks like he's about to say something when Kailyn comes into the room to get him for his next phone call.

"I should be done by five." He gets up. "I had to reschedule everything from the past two weeks."

"That's okay, I have stuff to do," I tell him as he nods and walks out without kissing me, which is what I wanted, but now makes me twinge a bit. He and Kailyn walk side by side, and he laughs at something she says before they disappear into his office.

I tap the pad with my finger before grabbing my phone and texting him.

Me: *Lunch was good, but something tells me that I'll be famished for dinner.*

I put the phone down while I answer my own emails and make notes for some of my other clients. I don't even see the time go by until Kailyn sticks her head in the conference room. "Nash told me to tell you he'll be done in five." She smiles. "He's going to be swamped all week doing double duty." Her tone is accusatory. "But you know Nash, act now think later."

"I don't know about that." I put my pen down. "Looks like he knows what he's doing."

"Most of the time." She tries to joke with me, but there is no laughter there. "Have a good night, Zoey."

"You too," I reply, watching her walk away and head back into his office. I close down my computer and see Josh has called me twice more.

I close my computer and put it in my bag before making sure I clean up the conference room, deciding to work in one of the work spaces he has set up tomorrow. I'm pushing in my chair when Nash comes out of his office carrying his jacket in one arm, and I see his rolled-up sleeves. "Hey," he says, meeting me at the conference door, "you ready?"

"Yeah." He reaches for my bag, carrying it with his empty hand as we leave the office. Lulu waves at us as we walk out, and the heat outside hits me right away. "It's so nice out."

"We could eat outside, if you want," he offers, opening the trunk and tossing my bag and his jacket in there. "Pick up a couple of steaks and grill."

"Umm." I shake my head. "I hate steak."

"What?" he asks, shocked.

"Yeah, I know, but I just don't like steak. Maybe it's because I ate it so much as a kid, but I just—"

"We could grill some salmon, then," he suggests without skipping a beat, "or some shrimp."

"Ohh, that we could do." He opens the door for me but blocks me from getting in with his arm. "You need something?" I ask, my pulse picking up from him being close to me now.

"Yeah," he says, tilting his head to the side and kissing my lips. His tongue comes into my mouth for a bit before he lets me go. "You." He bends to kiss my neck before moving his hand so I can get into the car. "I was hard most of the day because of your text," he tells me. "I'm having dessert before we eat."

He slams the door, and I try to get my heartbeat back to normal as he gets in. We go to the supermarket, grabbing things to throw on the grill, and when we get home, I walk upstairs to get changed first.

The phone rings in my hand the minute I step into the bedroom, and turning, I see it's Josh. I finally answer his call, "Hello."

"Hey," he coos all sweet, "I was wondering if I'd catch you. I've called you all day." I roll my eyes.

"Calling me three times is not calling me all day." I sit on the bed, not adding in *dumbass.*

"How was your day?" he asks, not even correcting me. "I know how busy you are when you get back from vacation."

"Yeah," I agree. "Listen, Josh—" I start to say but he interrupts me.

"I'm coming down to visit this weekend." His declaration shocks me.

"For what?" I about gasp.

"I got us dinner reservations at seven thirty." His voice is cheerful. "I figured we can have drinks before. There are some things we need to talk about."

I look at the phone to make sure I'm not dreaming this up. He's never made a reservation for dinner in the whole two years we were dating. Not even on my birthday. "Um, what?"

"I have to go," he quickly says. "I'll see you on Saturday. I love you, Zoey."

The phone disconnects and I don't have time to think things through before Nash comes in. "Who was on the phone?" he asks me, leaning against the doorjamb.

"That was Josh." I'm not going to lie to him. That's not the person I am. "He called me today. You saw it, and now he called me again a couple of times."

"What did he want?" He folds his arms over his chest, his jaw getting tight.

"He's coming to town and wants to go out on Saturday."

"You're not going on a date with him," he snaps, standing up.

"I think I have to just to shut it down," I say. "Closure for both of us."

"Closure for both of you? I thought you had your closure when you asked him to commit to you, and he didn't." His words are truthful and also sting at the same time.

"You're right," I admit to him, "but I need to see him face-to-face to tell him it's over."

"He's playing a game with you." He walks into the room, pulling me up from the bed. "Trust me, I know the game he's playing." The words confuse me even more. "Little does he know that the game he's playing"—he pulls me to him—"I'm going to fucking win it," he says right before his lips crash onto mine. He spends the whole night making me say his name over and over again.

TWENTY

I WALK UP the steps with her matcha in one hand and my protein shake in the other. The sun was slowly peeking out of the clouds when I walked back into the house twenty minutes ago because it was only a little after six. Stepping into the darkened room, I make my way to her side of the bed. She's lying on her stomach, one leg cocked to the side with one arm under the pillow, the other one stretched out. The covers are at her naked shoulder, her hair draped across the pillow. I put the two drinks down before I sit on the bed softly, trying not to wake her just yet.

I take a minute just to look at her. The feelings I'm feeling for her are ones I've never felt before. I knew she was the one, but I wasn't sure how that feeling would go with that sentiment. Without being able to stop myself, I reach one hand around her hip and bend to kiss her neck. She moans under my touch, and my cock goes to half-mast. I kiss her again and again until she finally stirs and calls my name, "Nash." Last night after her motherfucker of an ex called her, I made it a point to make her say my name all night long.

"Good morning, baby." I move my kisses from her neck to her shoulder and then back up again. "I made you a matcha," I say as she turns to her side facing me, tucking the cover under her arm. "I'm going to head into the shower."

"What time is it?" she asks, trying to open her eyes and keep them open.

"Just a little after six." I bend to kiss her lips. "You have time."

I go to move, and her hand grabs my wrist, pulling me back to her. "Give me a hug." Her voice is grumbled and soft.

"I'm all sweaty," I warn her, looking at my shirt that is a little wet from me working out for an hour and a half.

"Wouldn't be the first time you put your sweat on me." She leans up on her elbow, the cover falling off her to her waist. Her tits are on display, her nipples looking tight and pebbled, inviting me to suck on them. Tempting me, the little love bites around them make me smile. "I don't think it'll be your last either." Her hand moves up to wrap around the side of my neck as she tips her head back and up to kiss me on the lips. "Good morning," she finally says.

"You're beautiful." My hand that was at her hip comes up to rub her chin with my thumb. "So fucking beautiful." Her eyes get glossy from the words and then slowly go lighter. "You take my breath away." I kiss her quickly before getting up and maybe saying things I don't even know how to say. Saying things that might fuck it all up before we are both in that safe space where we can say things like that and have it be okay.

I pull off my T-shirt. "You can finish watching that show from last night," I tell her, and she sits up with her back against the headboard. "The man married to four women."

"One woman now," she corrects me, "and I would have finished if someone hadn't trailed his fingers down my body, followed by his mouth."

"I didn't hear you complain." I smirk at her as I toss the T-shirt in the laundry basket. "In fact, there was a lot of 'Nash, don't stop.'"

She reaches over to grab her matcha. "We remember different things, then."

"I remember everything," I assure her, and her cheeks get pink while she grabs the remote and turns on the television. At the same time, I walk into the bathroom, going straight for the shower. I pull open the glass door and set the water to just how I like it before taking off my shorts and boxers, and tossing them in the laundry basket in the corner. I undress everywhere in my bedroom, and I have four baskets around so I don't have clothes piling up. I pull open the door and step into the warm water, wetting my hair first and then running my hands through it before I grab my shampoo. I'm rinsing it out of my hair when I feel a draft and look over to see Zoey stepping into the shower. "Hey." I see her hair down and not pinned up like she usually has it when she gets in the shower.

"I need to wash my hair." She takes steps toward me until she's standing in front of me. Putting her head back and wetting her hair, she pushes it away from her face. "Plus, I have to take care of something." She moves under the water spray before her hand comes out to grip my cock that went from zero to a thousand the second she stepped through the shower door.

"What is that?" I watch her hand fist me. The water runs over her nipples, so I bend my head, sucking the nipple into my mouth, her hand gripping me even tighter.

"Morning blow job," she states and slowly drops to her knees. "Can't start the day without that, can we?" She looks at me as her tongue comes out, and she licks me all the way up from my balls to the tip of my cock. "Someone might be grumpy." She sucks the head into her warm mouth before letting it go and licking it back down to my balls.

"No one likes grumpy Nash." My voice is low as I try to focus on her face instead of the amazing feeling of her tongue. "Put your hands on the floor," I tell her, and she lets go of my cock, leaning forward, putting her palms on the floor. The water from the shower lands on her lower back, her perfectly shaped ass arched. "I'm going to fuck your face," I inform her, opening my legs more and then holding her head between my hands. "Nice and slow." I slide my cock as much as I can into her mouth before pulling out. "And then I'm going to set you on the counter"—I thrust back into her mouth—"and fuck your pussy." She nods when I pull out just until the tip, and she sucks me back into her mouth. Slow and steady,

I fuck her mouth. "My girl likes to suck my cock." She looks up at me as my cock goes to the back of her throat, my hips moving as if I'm fucking her pussy. "That's a good girl," I praise when she takes a bit more of me into her mouth. "Take it all." I move out, and she sucks me back in, and I can't help but put my head back and close my eyes. I take in the heat of her mouth, the wetness of her tongue. "I'm close," I warn her, and she sucks me stronger this time until I'm coming down her throat. She takes everything I have to give her. The minute I'm done, I pick her up from the floor, put her on the bench, and get down on my knees. "How much do you need to come right now?" I slide my tongue into her pussy, her juices invading my mouth before I lick up to her clit.

"Nash." She opens her legs wider. "I need you."

"What do you need?" I ask her as I suck her clit into my mouth and I ram two fingers inside her. Her hips lift off the bench.

"That," she pants out, "and more."

"Who do you need?" I curl my fingers inside her. "Tell me who you need."

"You, Nash," she moans, "I need you." I snap when she says that, slipping my fingers out of her before moving her off the bench, pushing her back to the shower wall, picking up one of her legs, and then slamming up into her. "Always you, Nash," she declares right before I pull out and slam back inside her.

The water is ice cold by the time we get out because after she's come on my cock twice, I pull out of her and soap up her whole body, finger-fucking her again until she almost comes. Over and over again. She trembles under my touch, the need to come so hard that she screams when I bring her to the edge again and then pull her away. "Need to show you who you belong to." The kiss I give her is as wet as she is. "My name will be the first thing on your lips in the morning." I tweak her clit. "And the last thing before you slide into bed." I turn her around, picking her up and slamming into her ruthlessly over and over again until she screams my name at the top of her lungs. "That's my girl." I plant myself inside her until I follow her off the cliff, leaning forward and kissing her shoulder.

"I'm not talking to you." She glares over her shoulder at me, my cock still buried inside her as she contracts her pussy. "That was too much, and the next time you do that"—she moves so my cock slips out of her—"I'm going to leave you and get my vibrator."

"Baby." I grab her chin in my hand. "That's going to be even more fun for me. Fuck you with it while you suck my cock." Her eyes hood just with the thought. "Make you choke on it while I fuck your pussy." I slap her ass. "Next time." I swallow her mouth with mine, and when she steps out of the shower, she's still glaring at me. "It's not my fault you drive me crazy."

"Oh, it's my fault?" She wraps the towel around her after twisting her hair up in one. "How is this my fault?"

"Should I show you?" I wrap my own towel around my waist.

"No," she snaps, "we are going to be late for work."

"We aren't going to work," I tell her. "I'm taking you

out on a date."

"During the day?" Her mouth hangs open.

"Yup, made all the arrangements." I smirk at her. "We're going for a drive in the clouds."

"I don't even know what that means, and you just got back from two weeks off." She follows me to the closet, where I look at her clothes hanging. "Kailyn said you are swamped."

"Don't worry about what Kailyn says." I grab a white sundress with little sleeves and small purple flowers all over it. "Wear this and comfy shoes."

"Nash." She shakes her head. "This isn't smart."

"Zoey." I say her name. "I'm thirty-two years old." I drop the towel from around my waist and grab a pair of boxers. "I work hard, I make a lot of money, and if I want to spend the day taking my wife on a date"—I pick the towel up off the floor—"I'm going to take my wife on a fucking date."

"But—" she starts and stops when I put my finger in front of her mouth.

"Comfy shoes. We leave in an hour," I tell her and then walk out of the room without giving her a chance to say anything else.

One hour later, she's walking down the steps wearing the dress I picked out for her with her hair in a ponytail on top of her head and white Converse sneakers. "I'm going to go on the record and say two things," she says, standing in front of me. "One, I don't think this is a good idea."

"Noted." I smile at her.

"And two, I'm very excited about driving in the clouds, if that is a real thing, and not us having sex in the car." I can't help but laugh at that. "Either way, I think I win."

I shake my head. "If you think you win in all of this, Zoey"—I slide my hand in hers—"you would be wrong. Waking beside you every single morning, sharing most of the day with you, sharing all of the nights with you, I'm the one who wins." I kiss her fingers as I walk out of the house with her and get into the car.

Stopping at the little bakery I know, I buy stuff for a picnic before I grab her an iced matcha and get back in the car.

"Do you know what?" she says, taking a sip of her matcha.

"Matcha is gross?" I ask, pulling away from the curb.

"No." She laughs. "I don't think I've ever played hooky before." Her face is so fucking beautiful when she smiles. "I also have never had a picnic before."

"You live in New York." I drive away from the city toward the hills. "You have Bryant Park, Central Park." I laugh. "Lots of parks."

"I know, I've just never done it." I shake my head as I reach over for her hand, putting it in my lap. "Now that I think of it, it's just sad that I didn't pack a blanket and have a picnic, even with myself."

"Well, I'm glad I'm going to take you on your first," I tell her as she smiles and looks out the window.

"I'm glad also." She watches the scenery as we drive toward the hills. On my side, it's the mountains, and on her side, it's the coast. "It's so pretty," she admires as I go up and around the hills.

The higher I get, the cloudier it gets. "This is what I mean," I say, pointing out the window. "A drive in the clouds."

"Nash," she gasps and looks all around us, "it's magical." She takes out her phone and starts snapping pictures. "You can barely see." She looks over at my side. "It's like we are in another world." Her smile is everything. We finally make it out of the clouds when I pull over at one of the clearings. "Are we there?" she asks, and I look around.

"I'm hoping," I admit, "I've never really been here before, so I'm not sure. If anything, we can eat at that table." I point over at the picnic table that has seen better days. "From what I found online this morning, there are trails."

"You don't even know where we are?" she gasps but opens the car door anyway and gets out. "You could be up here feeding me to the wolves."

I meet her at her side of the car, gripping her hips in my hands. "Baby, the only wolf you have to worry about"—I kiss her lips—"is me."

TWENTY-ONE

I GET OUT of the shower, the back of my neck tingling with nerves. As I walk over to my closet, my stomach is filled with knots. The whole week has been strange, to say the very least. After our picnic, Nash has been very in my face, showing me how amazing he is, but I know he's thinking of tonight. He hasn't brought it up, but he also hasn't made any plans for tonight. Usually, by the afternoon, he's already asking me what I want for dinner. But not today.

Today, we woke up like we always do, him bringing me my matcha, followed by us having sex before he took off to go to the gym, leaving me alone to my thoughts, I guess. Even when he got back inside and I had his breakfast ready for him like every single morning, we sat on the stools side by side eating, but he didn't really say much, which made my heart hurt. After tonight, things with Josh will be officially over, and we can go on to the next stage.

What that stage is, I have no idea, none whatsoever. All I know is that since I've been with Nash, it's been the most amazing time I've ever had. At first, I thought it was because we were on vacation, but then working side by side with him, seeing how much he's done with his company in such a short period. I'm in awe of him. Which makes me going out to talk to Josh that much more difficult. I walk into the closet, grabbing a pair of jeans and a white bodysuit. The jeans are loose all the way down and just tight around my hips. I swear, even getting dressed I feel like I'm going to throw up, and it has nothing to do with Josh and everything to do with Nash.

I pick up my phone when it beeps, hoping it's Nash, which is stupid since he's downstairs on the couch, working on his laptop.

**Josh*: Where do you want me to pick you up?*
Me: *I'll meet you there. See you at seven thirty.*
Josh: *See you then, Zoey.*

I don't even answer him, and when I walk out of the closet, Nash sits on the bed. "Hey." I stop in my tracks.

"Hey," he replies as he looks at me from head to toe, taking my outfit in. He gets up and walks over to me. My heart beats so fast that I can't hear anything else. "You know he doesn't deserve you, right?" He puts one of his hands on the side of my neck, making my mouth dry, before he bends to kiss my neck.

He turns and walks out of the room, and I have to walk over to the bed to sit on it. "You go and say what you need to say, and then you leave," I tell myself, walking into the bathroom and not even putting makeup on. I finish getting dressed and walk down to say goodbye to Nash. I find him in his home office. "I'm going to head out," I tell his back, and he looks over his shoulder, the look on his face gutting me.

"Take the car," he says. I stand here waiting for him to tell me not to go. Secretly wanting him to say "Stay with me." Secretly wishing he would say "You aren't going," and I wouldn't go because I don't want to go anymore. I wanted to go to close the chapter, but as time went on, I wanted to go less and less.

I get in the car, pulling out of the driveway, and look back at the door to see if he's there, but he's not. I try to blink away the tears that are coming, but one escapes, and I fight back the rest. The last thing I want to do is show up there and look like I've been crying and have Josh think it's for him.

I get to the restaurant, park the car, and then put the keys in my purse, along with my phone, before walking into the restaurant Josh booked. The restaurant is bursting with people. A couple of people wait by the hostess stand for their table. I smile at the hostess, who is standing at the podium, before spotting Josh right over her shoulder, waiting for me at the bar. He spots me, getting off his stool. His blond hair is pushed back to the side, his white button-down tucked into his blue chino pants. I walk around her toward him, and his face lights up with a smile, and I feel nothing for him. Actually, I'm more pissed at myself for coming than I am for him booking a trip to come and see me. "Zoey," he says my name, wrapping an arm around my waist and trying to kiss me on the lips, which is avoided when I turn my head to the side and the kiss lands on my cheek.

"Josh." I move one step to the side so his hand falls from my waist, and he's not touching me. "Shall we sit at the bar?" I ask him, hoping that it'll be even less time, but he shakes his head. I look at the only empty chair, hoping for the best.

"Our table is ready." He points at the table for two in the corner. "I was just waiting for you." He puts his hand out in front of him so I can walk. I hold my purse in both hands to stop him from trying to hold my hand. I zigzag my way to the table as he pulls out the chair for me and I sit down, watching him pull out his own chair before he sits in front of me.

Before either of us can say anything, someone pulls out a chair beside me, and when I look over, I see Nash sitting down. My eyes widen in shock as he smiles at me. He's wearing a T-shirt and jeans, exactly what he was wearing when I left him in his office. "Sorry I'm late, baby," he says, kissing me on the lips before turning his head toward Josh, who is staring at him with his own shocked expression. "You must be Josh." I'm assuming he holds out his hand with his wedding ring, just to spite him. "I'm Nash, her husband." Score one for Nash. Well, if you count the wedding ring in his face, that would be two.

Josh looks at Nash's extended hand and then looks at me. "This is a joke. You brought him with you?" He laughs nervously.

"She didn't bring me anywhere," Nash quickly informs him, and it's a good thing because I'm actually still in shock that he's here sitting next to me. He puts an arm around my chair. "So what are we going to talk about?" His hand that was extended is now on his leg.

"We," Josh says through clenched teeth, "were going to talk about what a mistake this is."

"What is?" Nash is the one having the conversation with him. My hand goes to Nash's knee now, to make sure I'm not dreaming he's here. His hand moves from around my chair to on top of my hand, linking his fingers with mine. Josh's eyes follow Nash's every move.

Josh puts his head back and laughs, but not a real laugh, a laugh that you know is fake and irritating. "Your wedding-slash-fake marriage, obviously." He shakes his head. "You have to know she did it because she wanted to make me jealous." Nash is the one who now throws his head back and laughs, but his is a full-on belly laugh, and it's so loud people around us look over. If you were looking at us, it would look like three people having a great time, but it is anything but that. "You can't think it's for real." Josh's head advances toward us. His tone is almost hissing, and I don't know why I find this funny.

"As real as it can be," Nash confirms to him and then looks over at me. "A man and a woman who will spend their lives together, in holy matrimony." He makes a joke, and that just pisses Josh off even more. But I can't help the smile that fills my face.

"She did it just to spite me," he spits, pissing me off, and again, before I'm able to talk, Nash is the one opening his mouth.

"You keep saying she did all this for *you,* but *you* have not once mentioned anything about her." My stomach soars when I hear that. Of course Nash would think about what I want instead of what he wants, because that's Nash. That is who he is, maybe who he always was and I was too blind and dumb to see it. "Maybe she did it to make herself happy, like she deserves to be." He leans back in his chair before turning his head to me. "From what I heard, you didn't really make her happy nor did you even ever try to make her happy." Okay, that part is a lie, more or less, because we've never even spoken about Josh, to be honest. Since we got married, we've never even brought up Josh unless he called or texted me.

The jab must sting Josh because he quickly defends himself. "I made her happy." He looks from Nash to me. "We were happy."

"Um," I say, unsure of what I'm supposed to say, and again, Nash doesn't even give me a chance.

"What was your plan?" he asks Josh. "How were you going to fix it all?" I can see the frustration grow on Josh's face because he probably doesn't even have the answers to these questions. "How were you going to build the trust with her? Do you know she hates fucking steak? And you booked a steakhouse to take her to." Nash shakes his head. "You had your chances, buddy. Why did you decide to step up now?" He waits for a beat, but literally just one. "Is it because someone else wants her? Because someone else would do anything to see her smile?" I squeeze his knee as I listen to his words.

"Because I would happily drink matcha if it meant she was in that kitchen with me. You couldn't make me walk away from her." He then turns to me. "Do you want to stay for dinner, or would you like to go home?"

I look at Josh, who is seething and, to be honest, hasn't even tried once to say what he was here for. He made this whole trip to plan this grand gesture, and what does he do? Books me a restaurant that I hate so he could tell me he missed me and wanted me back. It's literally been almost a month since we've gotten married, and he waited this long to come to me. I left Nash five minutes, if that, before he rushed out to chase me. The answer was written on the wall even before I walked in. "I'd like to go home."

"Zoey," Josh says to me when I'm getting up.

"I want to thank you," Nash says when he is standing next to Josh, looking down at him. "Thank you for fucking up with her because I will never forget how important and special she is." He reaches for my hand. "She will never, ever have to wonder if I'm committed to her. I'll show her every fucking day." He pulls me to his side, dropping my hand so he can wrap his around my waist. My hand comes up on his chest. "You ready, baby?"

I bend my head to silently laugh before looking over at Josh. "One month," I tell him. "Actually, it might be even longer since we had that last meal together where I gave you that ultimatum." He glares at me. "Then you saw my wedding picture on Instagram and what did you do?" I ask him, but like Nash I'm not waiting for him to answer. "You called and texted instead of getting on a fucking plane and coming to me. If you wanted me so bad, you would have moved heaven and earth to find me."

"I wasn't just going to show up in Vegas," he says, as if the thought alone was ridiculous.

"Yeah," Nash and I both answer at the same time.

"I mean, not that I would let you anywhere near my wife," Nash chimes in.

"Then I went on vacation, and I've been back in LA for a week. It took you a week to come and see me." I shake my head. "I was out of the house for five minutes before Nash chased me. That's someone who wants to be committed to me." I point at Nash. "Not this."

"Two and a half," he whispers in my ear. "Had to make sure you actually left."

"Not now," I hiss at him. "I hope that you get the point now, Josh. I'm not answering your phone calls anymore. I'm not going to meet you for anything else. It's over." I look at Nash. "Now, I'm ready to go." He nods at me, slides his hand from around my waist, and takes my hand. "Goodbye, Josh."

TWENTY-TWO

NASH

THE MINUTE SHE says, "Goodbye, Josh," I turn and walk out of the restaurant, pulling her with me. We walk past the hostess station, and I give her a quick nod. When I walked in, she smiled up at me and asked me if I had a reservation. It took me less than three seconds before my eyes found Zoey, and I ignored her, walking straight to the table. I don't even know which table I took the chair from; I just know it was in passing to their table.

"Have a great night," she says from behind me as I push the door open and step outside of the restaurant. My body feels like it's one big fucking nerve ready to fucking explode. I spot my car and make my way over to it. Stopping behind it, I wait for her to open the doors.

"Where is your car?" Zoey asks from behind me, and I look over at her, stopping and turning to face her.

"I took an Uber," I tell her, and she lifts her eyebrows at me.

"You were so sure I'd leave with you?" She folds her

arms over her chest.

I lean against the trunk of my car, putting one foot on the bumper. I didn't want to do this with her here, but it's been fucking brewing all fucking day long. "If you hadn't"—I try to keep my cool—"I would have carried you over my fucking shoulder, but only after I ordered the most expensive bottle of wine for that dickwad to pay for." I point at the restaurant. Not sure I want to point out that he still isn't fucking chasing her.

"He's not a dickwad," Zoey counters, and it's the wrong fucking thing to say right now.

"Who asks a married woman to go out on a date with them?" I hold up my two hands, waiting for her to give me an answer.

She tries to hide her smile, making me go from borderline Hulk pissed off to wanting to grab her face and kiss the ever-loving shit out of her. "A dickwad." She looks down. "Are we really having this discussion in a parking lot?" She looks around.

"No," I say but I don't move, "but we are going to address this."

I can see her eyes start to get irritated, and I know her annoyance is growing when she folds her arms over her chest as she cocks a hip. "What if one of my exes," I point at myself, and the minute I say exes, the irritated look goes to pissed off, "asked me to go out to dinner?"

"Which one?" She raises her eyebrows, definitely fucking pissed, and I'm happy she's pissed because I've been pissed since fucking Monday, and it's now Saturday. "Should we start at the letter A?"

"We can start wherever you want to start. Let's say Alabama."

"You went out with someone named Alabama?" she hisses at me.

"I didn't, I was picking an A name, and that's the first one that came to mind," I answer her honestly. "Would you be okay with it?" I put my palms on the back of the car, outstretched beside me.

"You never even said anything!" she shouts, throwing up her hands.

"If my ex asked me to dinner alone, how would you feel?" I look at her as she thinks, but I can quietly see she's struggling when she finally admits to me.

"I'd be jealous."

"Exactly." I try not to raise my voice. "You came here knowing he wanted you back, even though he doesn't deserve you." I remind myself I need to keep my cool. "It killed me to see him touch you. It took everything in me not to ruin my shirt with his blood on my fist." I push away from the car and go to stand in front of her. "You are my wife. He will never be the man to make you happy."

I grab her face in my hands and see her chest rising and falling. "Like you will?"

I grin at her before my mouth claims her. "Baby, I'm just getting started." I pull her to me and kiss her with all the anger and frustration I have had for this past week. I move my hands from her face to around her, pulling her closer to me. Her hand wraps around my waist and her other hand fists my shirt at the same time. "Get in the car."

"Nash," she pants.

"Car now," I tell her, "and when we get home, I want you fucking naked." Her eyes darken, and I know she wants that just as much as I do. "Is that okay, Zoey?"

"Yes." She steps away from me, opening her purse and tossing me the keys. "Drive fast."

I swear, she doesn't even wait for the car to stop before she's rushing out of the car and into the front door. She leaves the door open, and I can see a trail of clothes as I finally step in. I close the door behind me, taking two steps at a time, and there in the middle of my bed is Zoey, naked, exactly like I told her I wanted her. I rip my shirt off, kicking my shoes off at the same time. The jeans, boxers, and socks are off in one swoop. I fall into the bed on my side, and her mouth finds mine as I turn onto my back with her straddling me. My hands go to her ass and squeeze it as the kiss goes even more frantic. She bites my lower lip as I turn her onto her side, her leg hitched up over my hip. I palm her ass at the same time she bites my lower lip. My hand moves, sliding over her asshole to her pussy, where I slide two fingers into her.

"You going to meet him again?" I slide my tongue in her mouth, not giving her a chance to answer me. I bite her lower lip this time. "You going to go see him again?" I move my finger over her G-spot, knowing it drives her crazy. I pull my fingers out of her and slap her ass, the sound echoes. Her hips buck. "You going to see him again?" I slap her again and then rub her ass. "Or are you going to be my good girl?" I don't wait for her to answer me. Instead, I lie on my back. "Come and sit on my face and hold the headboard." She turns and lowers her pussy onto my face, my tongue coming out to slide into her. Her back arches. "You don't move," I tell her as she starts moving her hips back and forth. "You sit there and take what I'm going to give you." I slap her ass again. "And you think about your answer." I bite her clit hard, and she moans. Sliding my hand between us, I slip one finger inside her and then another. I finger-fuck her while I nibble on her clit.

"Nash, I'm going to—" she starts as if I don't feel it all through me when she's about to come.

"No, you're not." I pull my fingers out of her, and she groans, her head hanging back. "Not yet."

I push her down on the bed, throw one leg over my shoulder, and pull her onto my cock at the same time as I slam into her. "Good girls get rewards." I fuck her mercilessly, moving her hips with my hands and ramming her onto my cock each time. "Today, you weren't a good girl." I take my cock out of her and slap it on her clit twice before slamming it back into her. "You were a bad, bad girl."

"Nash, please," she pleads with me, her eyes rolling into the back of her head.

"You going to be a good girl from now on?" I put my hands beside her arms and thrust into her over and over again. Her pussy is so fucking wet it's dripping down my balls. She gets tighter and tighter. "Or are you going to be a bad girl?"

"I'll be your good girl," she vows. "Please, Nash, I'll

be—” The words stop when she moans, and I know she’s ready to explode on me. Before she does, I pull out of her, flip her onto her stomach, pull her hips up, and slam into her. “Fuck, Nash.”

“Ass up and face down,” I tell her. Her elbows lower, and her ass rises, one ass cheek redder than the other, so I rectify that. “Good girls get to come.” I fuck her harder than I’ve ever fucked anyone before. The frustration and anger from today coming out of me. “Bad girls don’t get to come.” She grips the sheets in front of her, holding on. The sound of skin slapping on skin fills the room. “Which one are you going to be?”

“Good,” she declares. “I’m going to be a good girl.” Her pussy contracts around my cock. Looking down, I see it coated in her juices.

“And whose good girl are you going to be?” I growl between clenched teeth, feeling my balls start to get tight.

“Yours. I’m always going to be your good girl,” she says, and this time, I move one hand to her clit, moving it back and forth before pinching it. Her hips shoot up, and she comes all over my cock. I have to hold her tight, or she’ll fly off my cock. She comes over and over again, and only after the second time do I decide it’s my turn.

I pull out of her and turn her over, taking her hair in my hand. Her mouth opens for my cock. “When you are a good girl, I’ll come in your pussy.” She sucks me all the way to the back of her throat. “Tonight, you were a bad girl, so you swallow my cum,” I scold as I finger-fuck her cunt that is open for me. She’s so fucking wet it’s oozing out of her. She comes at the same time I come down her throat. "Baby," I whisper when I stop fucking her face. My cock slides out of her mouth at the same time my fingers slip out of her. The bed is a wet mess from her as she throws herself back on the pillows.

Her chest is rising and falling. "That was—" She tries to get up on her elbows and look over at me collapsed on her other side. "That was—" Her elbows give out as she lies there, her legs still wide. "I might have to be bad if you are going to fuck me like that."

I can't help the chuckle that escapes me. "Zoey." I roll off the bed before reaching for her and grabbing her like a rag doll.

"Where are we going?" she asks me as I walk into the bathroom. "Oh, bath time."

I put her down while I start the bath and put in her salt things, and then put a couple of drops of her oil that she likes with some bubble bath.

She sits in the tub on one side, waiting for me to get in. I close my eyes and put my head back, waiting for the water to fill it up.

She moves between my legs, and when I open my eyes, she's kneeling in front of me. She puts her hand on my abs. "Nash," she says softly, "I'm sorry I went to meet him." She puts her forehead on mine. "I won't go and meet him again."

"You bet your fucking ass you won't," I snap at her, "never a-fucking-gain, Zoey."

She smiles the smile I've literally fallen in love with. The smile I crave to see all day. The smile I'll do whatever the fuck I need to do to see. "Never a-fucking-gain, Nash."

TWENTY-THREE

I TAKE A deep inhale as I turn my head from left to right on the pillow as my eyes flutter open, taking in the semi-darkened room. The thick drapes are pulled closed, but the middle is open just a little, letting a bit of sunshine into the room. I move my hands from the side of me to over my head and stretch out, blinking a few more times to get my eyes used to the light. I look over, seeing the bed beside me empty, which is nothing new. I don't think I've ever woken up and he's been beside me unless it's in the middle of the night when I go pee.

I hear sounds coming from downstairs, and when I grab my phone and check, I see it's a bit after eight. Tossing the covers off me, I slide my feet out of the bed before walking over to the bathroom. I finish brushing my teeth, grabbing my white plush robe before walking out and heading downstairs to catch up with Nash when I see him walking into the room with a tray in his hand and wearing just his boxers. "Why are you dressed and out of bed?" he asks me, his eyes going from big to a huge glare, making me laugh.

"I got up," I tell him, "and again, I was alone in bed." I point at the bed that looks like we spent the night wrestling in it instead of sleeping, which we sort of did. I mean, I think the last time I saw the clock, it was close to midnight when he gathered me in his arms, holding one breast in his hand as he spooned me. All I know is I looked over my shoulder to kiss his lips before falling asleep, and the next thing I knew, it was morning. "Alone in bed as a newlywed is not fun, Nash."

He rolls his eyes. "It's not my fault that your favorite drink is matcha and it takes me an hour to make."

Now it's my turn to roll my eyes. "Can you exaggerate a little more?" I wait for him to walk close to me, seeing he has a tray filled with a matcha for me and a coffee for himself. A plate is in the middle with some fresh fruit and two wrapped bagels.

"Good morning." He looks down at me when he is standing in front of me. "I see we are up in fighting form this morning." His head bends to kiss my lips.

"Why did you get breakfast?" I ask him. "It's like the only thing I get to do for you, and now you've taken it away from me." I try not to sound like I'm sulking.

"Baby, you were sleeping," he says softly, "and I wanted to keep you in bed all day long."

"I'm a lover, not a fighter," I joke with him before kissing him one last time and turning to get back into bed. I right the covers as he walks over to his side of the bed, placing the tray on his bedside table, right in front of the picture of me from our wedding and the picture of us on vacation in a smaller frame right next to it. He moves the covers off his side before getting in and tucking his pillows behind him, then grabbing the tray and putting it between us. "Breakfast in bed." I fix my own pillows before reaching for my matcha. "Does it get better than this?"

"Um," he says, looking over at me, "your lips on my dick." His face is not even cracking a smile. "That's the best wake-up I've ever had." He grabs his own coffee. "I mean, also you riding my dick."

I snort out as I take a sip of the matcha. "So as long as it has to do with your dick, it's a good morning."

He takes his own sip of coffee before reaching over to grab the remote. "Pretty much. Also, you sitting on my face while sucking my cock." His face doesn't even crack a smile. "That's a good morning too."

"How can you sit there and talk about sex without even looking remotely aroused?" I ask him.

"Baby," he murmurs, and I swear to God when he says that nickname the way he does, my pussy literally gets wet. "We work side by side, which means my dick is hard pretty much most of the day, so I have to go to great lengths to make sure it doesn't show just how bad I want to fuck you on or bend you over whatever surface is closest to us. At this point, I feel like James fucking Bond."

I shake my head. "It's not that bad."

"It's not that bad," he scoffs. "I watch you get dressed every single morning." His voice rises. "I know exactly what's under your clothes, or better yet, what little is under your clothes. So trust me, if I knew I wasn't sinking into you the minute we got home, I'd be beating my meat in the bathroom hourly."

"Well, good thing you aren't beating your meat hourly. That would get the office talking." We've been working side by side for the past two weeks. Two weeks that have been relatively quiet, aside from when Josh came down last week. After that, it's like we both turned the corner. I didn't block him on my phone because there is no need to. If he messages me again, I won't answer him. It's just that simple. He plays no role in my life anymore, and I am more than okay with moving on. Besides, Nash didn't give me time to wallow in the what-ifs. We had the fight in the parking lot, followed by the most incredible sex that we've had since getting married, and we've had a lot of it, except that night it was just over the top. We go to work together every single day, and when we get home, we cook side by side before sitting and either watching television, which can lead to us fucking on the couch, or we forgo watching anything and just go to bed, which then is hours, and I mean hours, of us touching and getting to know each other even better. "What do you want to watch?" I ask him as I reach for the remote from him and turn on the television.

"Don't care," he says, and I've realized Nash doesn't watch television, like ever. Which is shocking to me since I'm all about watching television. "Whatever you want to watch."

"Really?" I put my matcha down on my bedside table,

right in front of the picture of Nash I had done last week. It's from our wedding, and it was when he was watching me walk down the aisle. It's not like he didn't know what I was wearing because he saw me in the dress, but his expression is one of pure joy. His eyes are light because he is smiling, and it's not a full-face smile where his eyes crease at the corners. No, this smile is almost a smirk and a grin that says "That's all mine." He gives me a smile often when I walk in the room or he walks in and his eyes look for me. It is a smile that is on the top of the list of smiles he has given me.

"Really." He tries to hide the smile forming on his face with his coffee cup at his lips. "Besides, after I finish this and eat a bit, I'm going to have dessert." He takes a gulp of his coffee. "Then, hopefully, your mouth will be full of dick."

"I can't start my day without a mouth full of dick," I say sarcastically.

"Trust me, baby." He leans over and kisses my neck. "I know."

I don't answer him because he's not fucking wrong. "What do you want to do today?" I ask him as I scroll through the DVR to search for something to watch.

"I have something set up for tonight." He reaches for one of the wrapped sandwiches. "And I have someone coming in to cook for us."

"What?" I ask, shocked. "What do you have set up for tonight?"

"If I wanted to tell you, don't you think I would have told you?" He takes a bite of his bagel. "It's called a surprise for a reason." I grab the other wrapped sandwich, seeing it's a bagel with egg and sausage in an everything bagel. "You'll like it."

"I'm sure I will." I chew and put on my show, and even if he doesn't admit it, he's into it, at least for a little bit until he gets bored and slips my robe off me to rub my back, which ends with his dick in my mouth but with me also sitting on his face.

I'M AT THE sink fluffing my hair when he sticks his head into the bathroom. "You ready?" he asks me, and I look at him in the mirror.

"I wasn't the one banished to my bedroom and told 'don't come out until I come and get you.'" I smile at him. "How could I not be ready?" I turn as he walks in and I see he's wearing jeans and a button-down shirt, open until the middle of his chest. "Is this okay?" I ask him and see him do a sweep of my outfit. I went with a long, flowy yellow skirt that falls to my ankles but has three layers to the dress that sweep side to side when I walk.

He closes the distance to me, putting his hands on my hips. "I like this," he says of the white shirt that is more of a crop top, showing off my stomach. His fingers rub softly. "Are you wearing a bra?" he asks me of the double-layered shirt that has cute cap sleeves with little cutouts in it and is tight around under my breasts and kicks off just a bit.

"Nope," I say, seeing his eyes go right to my chest.

"So all I have to do is," he says, lowering the top of the shirt, "and then do this." He sucks a nipple into his mouth.

"Basically," I tell him, trying not to show him how much he always gets to me. "Show me my surprise," I urge him, and he slides his hand in mine as he walks out of our bedroom with me. "Wait." I stop him right before we walk out of the bedroom before rushing to the closet to get my own surprise.

"What's that?" He points at the white envelope I have in my hand. "This is a surprise," I tell him. "You aren't the only one who can make surprises." Slipping my hand in his, I pull him out of the bedroom.

When we come to the bottom of the stairs, the formal living room is transformed. The couches are pushed aside, and there is a long table with two chairs in front of it. White easels are set up in front of each chair. "What is this?" I turn to ask him, seeing the bucket of ice on the side holding two bottles of white wine.

"It's a sip and paint night. We are going to paint, and I have a chef preparing some of your favorite dishes so we can eat also," he explains at the same time as a woman comes into the room wearing a smock over her pants and shirt.

"Hi, Zoey," she says to me, extending her hand. "I'm Sammy, welcome to your very own sip and paint."

"Thank you, Sammy." I shake her hand before turning to Nash. "I can't believe you did this." I can't stop the excitement of my voice. "I've never done this before."

"Neither have I, but it looked like fun," he replies, walking over to a bottle of wine and pouring me a glass. "Time to start sipping." I take the glass from him, waiting for him to fill his own glass before holding it up to toast with him.

"To sip and paint," I say, clinking my glass with his before looking around to make sure it's just the two of us. "Also, just so you know"—I get up on my tippy-toes to whisper in his ear—"I'm not wearing any panties either." I kiss him right beside his ear, and he can't help but wrap his free hand around my waist, his hand moving down to palm my ass. "You can search, but you'll come up empty-handed."

He closes his eyes. "How excited are you for tonight?" His question surprises me. "Like on a scale of one to ten, if I kicked everyone out right now so I could fuck you on that table, would you be upset?"

I put my head back and laugh at him. "Very," I tell him the truth and then turn my head when I hear footsteps coming back into the room. Sammy walks in carrying two clear bins in front of her. "What are we going to be painting?" I ask Sammy as she puts down the two clear bins.

"Cherry blossom trees," she answers with a smile. "Take a seat whenever you are ready."

I look over at Nash. "You can't be trusted with anything I say." I told him a couple of weeks ago that I saw a picture of the cherry blossom trees they have in the spring in China.

"That's not true." He pulls me even closer, and I melt

into him. "You just have to know that once you say it, chances are I'll do whatever it is in my power to make it come to life."

"Well, with that said," I say, handing him the envelope, "this isn't anything you said, and it's probably silly." I suddenly get nervous when he grins at me, grabbing the envelope. I watch his hands turn over the envelope holding my breath as he opens it, pulling the little booklet out that I spent the past week doing in secret.

His eyes go big when he reads the front of it: Nash's Naughty Coupon Book. "What?" He chuckles before flipping the front to see the next one. "Oh, I like this one," he says. "Redeem for a day of your personal nude maid service." He winks at me and flips the page. "Forget it, I like this one better, thirty full minutes of oral." I roll my eyes.

"You get that anyway." I pick up my glass of wine to take a sip as he flips to the next one.

"One lap dance!" He nods. "Yes, please." He grins before turning to the next one. "Use for a naughty free wish. I have a wish right now, and it's with you under this table." He flips again. "Playtime in just heels." He puts his head back. "I've never been so hard in my life. One new position every night (https://www.yourtango. com/2013176621/7-fun-sex-positions-try-tonight)   for a week!" He looks over at me. "I'm going to get very creative for this one." I have to cross my legs because he's not the only one getting turned on by this. "One sex session. Anytime, anywhere. Right now, right here." He makes me laugh. "I will do anything you ask for an entire day!" He closes his eyes and groans. "I am literally going to have to go to the bathroom and jerk off," he says, and I can feel my cheeks getting hot. I didn't think he would read them all aloud. "One erotic movie night. Would we recreate what is on the screen?" he asks, and I shrug because at this moment right here, I would agree to anything. "You choose the toy tonight.'" He shakes his head. "Baby, baby, baby." I'm about to snatch it out of his hand. "A sexy all-nighter." He looks at me. "I might have to redeem this tonight," he says before reading the last one. "You pick the hole." He tosses the booklet on the table before he pushes his chair away.

"What are you doing?" I ask him, grabbing his wrist.

"I'm going to kick everyone out of our house so I can use some of those coupons," he says, his eyes filled with lust, and I roll my lips.

"Nash," I hiss at him. "I have to enjoy my gift, and then you can enjoy your gift," I tell him, and he looks up at the ceiling as if he's saying a secret prayer.

"Fine," he grumbles, "but just so you know, I'm going to redeem some of those tonight."

I lean over. "Be careful, because once they are redeemed, they won't come around again."

He pulls me to him, smashing his lips down on mine. "I think it's safe to say that I'll take my chances." He kisses me softly. "Thank you for the gift, baby."

TWENTY-FOUR

I HEAR THE car pull up in the driveway and put down my laptop, walking to the front door. I look outside to see Zoey get out of the car and walk over to the trunk, grabbing two big canvas bags in her hands. I unlock the door, and when she's on the last step, I open the door. "Hey, baby," I greet her, reaching out for the bags she's carrying. "What is all this?" I look down at the bags in my hands.

"Well," she starts, stepping into the house after me and shutting the door behind her, "since you surprised me yesterday." I make my way from the front door to the kitchen. "I thought I would surprise you today." I pass the wall where I hung both our paintings from last night. I did it the first thing this morning when I got up and out of bed. While she made us breakfast tacos, naked. She told me not to because she said the trees looked sad, but I refused to be talked out of it. She shook her head and told me she was heading out.

"But you gave me the best present I've ever gotten in my whole life." I wink at her, mentioning the coupon book I might have to lock in the safe to make sure it doesn't go missing.

"That was something I made as a joke." She laughs.

"Pick any hole is not a joke and will never be." I put my hands on my hips, my voice tight.

I peek in the bags. "Ooh, did you get some crotchless panties?" I ask over my shoulder.

"Of course, it was the first thing on my list," she deadpans, and I stop in my tracks. "I'm joking."

"One never jokes about crotchless panties, Zoey." I put the bags on the counter, then look in them. "What is all this?"

"This is a game." She walks around the counter to stand next to me. "It's called get to know your partner." She reaches into the bag and takes out the two small whiteboards she got. "We each ask each other questions and write them down to see how well we know each other."

"Oh, you know what would make this even better?" I ask, reaching into one of the bags and taking the dry-erase markers out of it. "Doing it naked-style. If you get the wrong answer, you lose a piece of clothing."

"So strip get to know your partner?"

"Yes." I nod as if I just invented a new game. "We should play right now." I grab the two whiteboards in my hands and walk toward the living room. "Grab the markers and let's get this game going." She laughs as she follows me. "Should we move the table out of the way and play on the floor?" I wonder if we need more space to spread out once I get her naked.

"We don't need all that room." She sits in one corner of the couch. "Actually, I'll sit in this corner, and you sit in that corner." She points at the other side of the couch, and I glare at her as I hand her a whiteboard and walk over to the other side.

"And the more naked you get, the closer you get to the other person." I make up the rule as she tosses me the markers. "I like this game already."

"You can't cheat," she warns me, and I gasp. "Like you have to answer truthfully."

"Baby." I chuckle. "You should know I play to win"—I wink at her—"at every-fucking-thing."

"Good. I'll go first." I grab a marker out of the pack. "What's your partner's favorite color?" I look down at the board and write purple on it. "Okay, what did you answer?" When I tell her the answer, she's shocked that I knew this. "Yours is blue."

"Shit," I swear when it's right. "I mean, technically, my new favorite color is nude."

"Next question." She ignores me. "How do they take their coffee?"

"That's easy," I say, "she likes to drink grass." She also gets it right. "Can we get to the naked part yet?"

"This should get you to lose a piece of clothing." She smirks. "What's your favorite book?"

"I don't have a favorite book," I tell her. "So how about, what's your favorite genre of book."

"Fine," she concedes. "What did you answer?"

"Romance." I look at her and see she's shocked. "You?"

"Sex stories," she replies, and I can't help but laugh out loud.

"You aren't wrong, but I'm more of a mysteries type of guy," I tell her, and she turns the whiteboard over for me to see that she wrote mysteries. "How did you—"

"Nash, you have Dan Brown right there." She points over at the bookshelf.

"At this point, are we ever going to get naked?" I groan.

"What's your favorite movie?" she asks with a huge grin on her face, and I just laugh because I know she's not going to get this one, so she'll be losing one scrap of clothing. "Okay, what did you put?"

"*Pride and Prejudice*, but the one with Keira Knightley," I gloat and turn my board around to face her, "because that's just the way it is." I repeat her words that she told her cousin while on the trip. "Now what did you put?" I smile so big.

"*Mission Impossible* and not James Bond." My mouth gapes open. "I heard you chat with one of the guys in Vegas."

"That's cheating." I point at her and belly laugh. "What's the next question?"

"What's their favorite nickname to be called?" She asks the question and then quickly writes down her answer. "What did you write?"

"Baby." I turn around to show her. "You love it when I call you that." Her eyes get softer. "What did you write?"

"Well, I don't really have a nickname for you," she says, "but you do love when I moan out your name." She turns it around to show me her answer, and now I'm the one who is laughing.

"We're exceptionally good at this game." I scowl. "I don't like it. "What's your honey's favorite dessert?" She can't help but hide her smile. "What did you put?"

"Dick." I turn my board around, showing her the picture I drew of a dick.

"That looks like a spaceship." She laughs. "I put pussy on yours."

"That's my favorite meal and dessert," I tell her, and she wipes away her answer.

"Does your partner prefer FaceTiming, texting, or calling?" she quizzes, and I write down my answer. "What did you write?"

"There is more than one answer. You love FaceTiming your family, but everyone else you like to text, and you only take calls from clients."

"You know that you're annoying"—she points at me—"and you watch me way too much."

"Score one for me." I hold up my hand. "What did you write?"

"I sort of wrote the same thing for you. You love FaceTiming your niece, Meadow," she answers, and I just watch her, "and you FaceTime Caine every morning."

"And I watch you too much?" I use her words against her. "You know what I don't like about this game?" I don't wait for her to answer me. "That you aren't naked."

"What is your partner's favorite animal?" she

continues, and I don't even write it down.

"If you don't say cat, you're a fucking liar." I point at her, and she throws her head back and laughs. "You spend at least one hour a day watching cat videos."

"It helps clear my head. I put cat for you also since you spend most of the time watching them with me," she snaps. "What's the best place you've ever traveled to?"

"Hmmm," I say, "I have no idea on this one. Is it Europe?"

"Nope," she replies, so I toss the whiteboard to the side and slide my T-shirt off.

"Now this is fun. What about you? What did you write?"

"Mexico." She shows me her answer, and I smile.

"Take it off," I instruct her, and her mouth opens. "It was Mexico, but now it's Vegas."

"That's not fair."

"Take it off, baby." She pulls her shirt over her head, leaving her in her lace bra. "The bra also, it's part of the shirt." She wants to fight me on it, but instead, she just takes it off and tosses it my way.

"Happy?"

"I'm getting there." I grin when she asks me her next question.

"How does your partner de-stress?" She giggles. "Should I even write it?"

"Are you going to write sinking into his wife's pussy or mouth?" I ask. "Because that's the only answer to that."

"I was going with sex or blow job." She shrugs. "So

I'm right."

"You would be right," I admit. "For you, I wrote sucking my dick or riding me." Her mouth opens in shock. "But then I also wrote watching stupid cat videos."

"What's your partner's favorite holiday?" she asks, and I erase my previous answer and write down my answer, then show it to her.

"Christmas," I say, and she nods. "What is mine?"

"Your birthday," she declares, and I smile big.

"Nope, I'd like to see you take off your pants."

"What's your favorite holiday?" She refuses to take off her pants.

"Our anniversary," I state. She throws her marker at me, and I move to the side as it zooms by my head. "Take it off, Mrs. Griffin." I wink at her as she tosses the whiteboard in front of her, standing up and taking her pants off. "And the panties."

"No fucking way," she fires back. "If you take off your pants, you still have your boxers."

"Not if I'm not wearing any," I tell her, "which I'm not, so it would leave me naked."

"That would be a you problem"—she sits down in her lace thong—"and not a me problem." She winks at me, "Does your partner apologize?" She picks up her board.

"Nope, I don't think she knows how to say she's sorry."

"Um," she snaps, "I said I was sorry the last time." I raise my eyebrows. "In the parking lot, I said I was sorry I went to meet him."

"I seem to remember it differently." Her eyes are on

me. "It was when we got home, after I fucked it out of you." I point at her, and she just glares at me. "Let's call that a draw."

"Fine," she huffs. "How often would your partner like to have sex?"

"The only answer is all day, every day." I lean my head to the side. "So twenty-four seven."

"The only answer, of course," she mocks me. "Does your partner like using sex toys, and if so, which one is their favorite?" She tilts her head to the side. "Looks like someone is going to be naked in about two minutes."

"Yeah." I look at her. "Is that someone going to be you?

"What's your answer?" I ask, and she turns her whiteboard over, and I read what she wrote, *cock ring*. I laugh. "When have I ever mentioned wanting to use a cock ring?"

"It's the only thing I could think of." She throws her hands up in the air. "It's not like you would use a silicone vagina." She folds her arms over her chest, pushing her naked tits in the air. "Anyway, what did you write?" she asks. "Whatever it is, you're wrong."

"I wrote the rabbit vibrator." I turn my board around to show her.

"Wrong," she says proudly, and I smirk. "It's my rose toy vibrator."

"Really?" I ask. "Explain this vibrator to me. Because I still have a coupon that I need to redeem."

"There is a little piece that you put inside me," she explains, "and then the rose part sucks on my clit."

"It's basically the same thing," I huff.

"But it's not," she tells me. "Take off the pants, big man." I toss the board to the side, stand and unbutton my pants, my cock springing free once I push them off my hips.

"Happy?" I ask. "Now, take off that thong, baby."

"Fine." She gets up and shimmies her way out of them as she tosses them to the side.

"Well, I think we both won," I tease, and she shakes her head. "We're both naked."

"There is one more question." She stands in front of me naked. "What is your partner's favorite sex position?" she asks, and I clap my hands together. "Yours is with my legs over your shoulders."

"Wrong." I storm toward her. "It's going to be this one right here." I grab her around her waist and lift her off the floor. "I like any position as long as my cock is inside you."

TWENTY-FIVE

ZOEY

ME: *I HOPE you are having a great day.*

I press send on the text, smiling to myself. I always send him a text in the morning when I get to my desk, telling him to have the best day, like we didn't arrive in the car with each other. Then I always surprise him by having lunch delivered to him, knowing he's got a busy day ahead of him. Which always earns me a text telling me I'm the best in the world.

Then I always send him a midday text when I think of him or look over and catch a glimpse of him.

Nash: *It'll be better when I get to kiss your face, among other places.*

Me: *See you soon, then.*

I open the phone app and go to my favorites, going down the list to my mother, pressing her name, and then putting it to my ear.

"Well, well, well, if it isn't my favorite daughter," she answers, laughing, making me laugh.

"I'm your only daughter," I point out. "You should have answered 'if it isn't my favorite child.' That would have been better."

"I'll know for next time. How are you doing?"

"I'm good." I look around the office and see Nash is sitting in the conference room on a video call with his brother. "I'm calling because I'll be in New York next week," I tell her of the plans I made less than five minutes ago when one of my clients reached out to me. "Are you going to be home?"

"I will be." I can hear the smile in her voice. "We should do a dinner."

"I'll probably be home for a week, so we can do all the dinners."

"So living in LA is agreeing with you?" she asks, and I take a deep inhale.

"So far, so good," I answer her honestly.

"What's that sigh about?" Of course she picked up on that.

"The weather is amazing." I start with that. "Work is thriving. I've even gotten a couple more clients since I started here because of the show I went to in Vegas."

"Um, Zoey…" She trails off. "How is Nash?"

I look down at my yellow pad in front of me. "He's," I start strong, and then my voice dips a bit, "amazing. He's funny and smart and"—I smile—"thoughtful."

"Why does it sound like you're going to say but?" She laughs, and I lean back in my chair, my stomach flipping over back and forth, and my hands starting to get clammy.

"There is no but, that's the thing." I look over at Nash, seeing him laugh at something his brother says. "Like, I can't pinpoint one thing that he has wrong with him."

My mother bursts out laughing. "That's a good thing," she tries to tell me. "It's more than good. It's a great thing."

"It's weird, Mom," I finally huff. "Like nothing, and I mean nothing, bothers me about him. Even if I want it to. He doesn't leave his stuff lying around. He makes me matcha every single morning even though he fucking hates it. He's considerate of me and always asks me what I want to do before telling me what he wants to do." I hear how silly I sound.

"What is really bothering you?" she asks me the million-dollar question.

"He asked me to give him ninety days to fall in love with him." My mother gasps at my confession. "I know, I know, but we had just gotten married." I close my eyes and even I groan for how it sounds.

"And you've fallen in love with him in less than a month," she points out.

"Well, no," I counter, "but the fact is, when the ninety days is over, then what?" My stomach gets tight. "He hasn't even brought it up. Like, what if I fall in love with him, and then he decides he's not in love with me after the ninety days? Then what?"

"Zoey," she says softly, "think about what you just said. Do you really think he would be doing all of this if he wasn't in love with you already?"

"I don't know," I answer her honestly. "I know he

must like me, and the sex is—"

"Too much," she quickly says. "I don't need to know that part." I laugh because I'm in my thirties, so she knows I have sex. Now that I'm married, I'm more than allowed to have all the sex, and trust me, I do.

"Mom, what happens after ninety days?" I ask her what I've been wanting to ask Nash for the past week. Ever since it dawned on me that I've fallen in love with him. Which makes no sense. Who falls in love with someone after a month?

"Why are you even putting a time limit on it if he's not brought it up again?" she asks. "If in ninety days he doesn't say anything, you don't either."

"So it'll be the big elephant in the room no one talks about," I say, shocked. "Immediately fucking no, Mom."

"Then ask him where he is?" I gasp even more.

"And be the one who is like, so do you like me?" I shake my head. "That's not an option either."

"Heaven forbid your generation learns how to communicate without blowing everything out of proportion."

I laugh loudly. "Oh, like my mother who tweeted my father to crash her ex's wedding?"

"That wasn't blowing anything out of proportion," she fights back. "Anyway, I married him, so what does it matter how it started?"

I'm about to say something to her when a hand moves my hair over and then slides around the back of my neck. "We leave in ten." Nash looks down at me with his bright blue eyes, mouthing it to me because I'm on the phone.

"It's my mother," I tell him, and he bends forward to talk into the phone.

"Hi, Zara," he says into the phone.

"Tell him I say hello and ask him how he feels about you." My mother laughs at herself.

"She says hello." I leave out the rest of it. "Okay, Mom, got to go. I'll see you next week. Give Dad a kiss for me."

"Love you," she says before hanging up, and I put my phone down.

"Is she coming here next week?" Nash asks, leaning back on the desk, and I shake my head.

"I'm going to New York." I can see the surprise on his face. "Got a couple of meetings I have to have with clients, so I called and let her know."

"Okay." He stands up. "I'll call my parents, and we can have a family dinner."

"Wait, what?" I look up at him. "You're going to come with me?"

"I'm not letting you go by yourself," he replies, putting his hands in his pockets. "I have to go close my stuff. We have that dinner tonight." I nod at him as he bends, and I raise my eyebrows.

"No kissing at the office." I hold up my hand.

"You know they see me sucking your face the minute we leave this office." He shakes his head and chuckles. "Be back." I watch him walk away from me and go into his office before I turn and start to put away my own things. Ten minutes later, we walk out of the office, and sure enough, the minute we are outside, he pushes me against his car and proceeds to suck my face, and I love every single second of it.

～

I'M TUCKING MY hair behind my ear when I watch him walk into the closet. "Damn," he swears, looking at my reflection, "you look hot." I take him in wearing one of his many black suits.

"You don't look so bad yourself." I smile at him in the mirror as his eyes move from mine and then down to my ass. "You done ogling me?" I turn to face him. "Is this okay?" I ask him, looking down at the sleeveless black dress with a low dip in the front, which has a lace underlay that matches the lace on the bottom part of the skirt with a deep slit. His eyes roam all the way up to the top, then all the way to the black slingbacks I paired with it.

"More than okay." He doesn't move from the door. "I would come over there, but if I do, I'm going to end up fucking you, and we aren't going to this dinner." I grin.

I look down, chuckling. "Then let's go." I slide my hand in his as we make our way over to the dinner.

Pulling up to the restaurant, the valet opens my door, and I step out, waiting for Nash to round the car. He stops beside me, kissing me chastely before sliding his hand in mine and walking into the event. "Try not to make everyone fall in love with you here," he says over his shoulder. I want to say there is only one person I want to be in love with me, but I don't because the minute he steps in, someone comes over to say hello to him. He introduces me as his wife to everyone, and even though he sees people he knows across the room, he never, ever leaves my side.

We're walking across when a blond woman turns around from talking to a man. Her blond hair is perfectly curled to the side, and her red dress molds her body. Her eyes go big when she sees Nash beside me. Her face quickly goes from shock to a smirk. "Nash," she purrs his name and I look over to see he smiles tightly. "I was hoping to see you here." She comes over to him and leans in to kiss his cheek, but it's too close to his mouth to be an accident. Staying glued to his side, she looks at him.

"Emmy," he says her name and nothing else as he tries to step away from her. Her hand falls from his shoulder, but she makes sure to rub his arm all the way down to his hand that he quickly puts in his pocket.

"And who must this be?" she asks, looking over at me and smirking, taking me in from head to toe.

"This is my wife," he states, pulling me closer to him, his hand slipping out of mine so he can wrap it around my waist. "Zoey." I look over at him and smile, while Emmy's eyes go straight to my hand to see my ring. "This is Emmy. We used to work together."

I extend my hand to her. "Emmy, it's a pleasure," I say, and she shakes my hand.

"Nice to meet you," she says, then ignores me. "Nash, call me. We obviously need to catch up." It's at that moment I realize what real jealousy really fucking feels like.

Nash doesn't answer her. Instead, he nods and turns us away. "Should I guess that you guys dated?"

I stop and turn to him. "We went out a couple of times." I nod at him. "Would you like something to drink?" he asks, not giving me more, and it's not like I want to ask all the questions.

"I'm good, thank you." I hold my purse in both hands as he leads me to our table. He pulls out the chair for me, and I sit. The meal is uneventful. Nash includes me in all the discussions, as always. His arm is around my chair as he rubs my arm with his thumb. "I'm going to go to the bar to get myself something to drink."

"I'll go for you." He gets up halfway, and I put my hand on his cheek.

"No, this is your thing. Be the superstar you are." I kiss his lips and turn to walk to the bar.

I zigzag through people until I'm standing in line, waiting for a drink. "So you're the one," someone says beside me and I look over to see Emmy standing there, a wineglass in her hand.

"Excuse me?" I pretend I didn't hear her comment.

"The one who think she's going to change him." She shakes her head from side to side and then takes a drink of the wine. "You won't be the first to try."

Her words get to me, even though I pretend they don't when I laugh at her remarks. "Maybe that's where everyone else failed." I raise my eyebrows. "I don't want to change him."

She stares at me, and if her eyes had daggers, I would be lying on the ground dead. "He's going to get bored soon enough." She tilts her head to the side, goading me.

"Is he?" I ask. She's going to say something else, but she stops when she sees Nash put his arm around my waist.

"Hey, baby," he says softly before he gives me a soft kiss, "can I have this dance?" His eyes never leave mine. He ignores Emmy, who is standing right there and acts like it's just the two of us.

"Yes." I put my hand in his as he leads me to the dance floor. He wraps his arm around my waist, pulling me closer, and my hand goes on his lapel.

"This is fun, isn't it?" He just looks at me. "Your ex, my ex."

He laughs. "Fun, fun, fun." He turns me in a circle on the floor. "But none of them matter when I have you right where I want you."

"Yeah, and where is that?" I ask him softly.

"Here." He bends his head a bit. "Right here in my arms," he declares right before he kisses me, and it's not just a little soft kiss. No, it's a wet, hard kiss, making no one mistake that I'm his, and more importantly, he's mine. At least for one more night.

TWENTY-SIX

NASH

I GRAB MY protein shake in one hand and the matcha in the other, walking up the steps toward the bedroom. The room's still dark, so I know she's probably still sleeping. Last night was not ideal for us both. I should have told her there was a possibility Emmy was going to be there, but to be honest, she was the furthest thing from my mind. The only time she crossed my mind was when I saw her, and the only thing then on my mind was making sure Zoey knew she was a thing of the past. Fuck, if anyone knew how she felt, it was me. Seeing her with her dickhead ex made me feel things I never wanted to feel again. Emmy was an afterthought, and I spent the whole night making sure Zoey knew that. Even when we got home, I wanted to make sure she knew how I felt about her. I secretly told her I was in love with her while staring into her eyes. It was the coward's way out, but I didn't want to push it on her.

When I get to the top of the stairs, I find her sitting up

in bed with her phone in her hand, the top sheet across her chest, and I know she's naked underneath it. "Good morning, baby." I grin as I walk to her side of the bed, and she sits up even more, the sheet dropping and exposing her tits. I moan my appreciation, handing her the cup of matcha before bending down to kiss her lips at the same time, using my free hand to pinch her nipple.

"You're going to make me spill my matcha." She pretends to be irritated, but I can see her smirk trying not to come out.

"We don't want you to spill your matcha." I sit on the side of the bed and take a sip of my protein shake. "All that green shit in the bed, eww." I shake my head as she giggles. "Why are you up?"

"Not sure. I just got up," she answers, and I stare at her, knowing she is not sure of something, but always wondering if she's going to bring it up. "I tried to doze back but figured it would mess me up more."

"So you got up to watch more cat videos?" I put one hand over her legs and lean into her.

"No," she lies to me, but I look down at her phone in her lap and see that I'm right. I raise my eyebrows as she flips over the phone. "Why don't you go shower?" she says, and I nod at her and get up.

"Do you want to join me in the shower?" I ask, and she puts down her matcha tea.

"I wouldn't mind a shower, but I don't want to get my hair wet."

I shake my head. "If you come in the shower, chances are your hair will get wet, even if I go down on you."

"How is that?" She tosses the covers to the side and swings her legs off the bed, and my cock goes suddenly hard, like it always does for her. I've never been more attracted and in sync with a woman in my life. In. My. Life. For the rest of my life, I know sex with her will never, and I mean never, be dull.

"Well." I wrap my hand around her waist, pulling her to me as she gets on her tippy-toes. "After I make you come with my tongue and my fingers, I usually like you to finish coming on my cock."

"Okay."

"And when I fuck you, it's usually either against the wall or you riding me, which you then put your head back and your hair gets wet."

She rolls her eyes. "Not every time." I pick her up, not even bothering to have this fight with her. "There was that one time," she counters as I carry her to the bathroom and place her down on the counter as I turn on the water in the shower, "that you bent me over, and only my back got wet." She watches me peel my shirt off and then pull my boxers and gym shorts down as I kick off my shoes. Her eyes slowly go up and down, taking me all in. "I might get my hair wet," she mumbles before I pick her up and take her in the shower with me. "I'll give it a quick blow-dry."

"I'd like you to give me a quick blow." I wink at her as I bend and kiss her lips, my tongue sliding into her mouth at the same time as our hands reach out for each other. Her hand grabs my cock at the same time I slide my fingers through her slit and slip inside her.

"Then I guess it's time to get on my knees," she says as she moves down to suck my neck, the warm water running down my back.

Her fist pumps my cock. "Don't let me stop you." I watch her make her way down, kissing my chest, then her tongue comes out to slide down to my stomach, my abs contracting with her touch. My eyes never move from her until she swallows my cock, and my eyes shut. "Fuck, that's good." That's the last thing I think I say until I come down her throat and return the favor. She gets out of the shower before me because her hair did, in fact, get wet, but not while I fucked her. It happened when she took my cock to the back of her throat.

"I'm not going to have time to make you breakfast," she says as she blow-dries her hair.

"Unless you are okay with me toasting you a bagel?" I smile at her. I might wake her up in bed every single day with a matcha, but she makes me breakfast every single day.

"We can order something," I tell her, and she turns off the blow-dryer to go and get her phone, handing it to me.

"What is this for?" I ask, leaning against the counter.

"For you to order breakfast," she informs me, turning the blow-dryer back on, and I pfft out.

"I'm not using your phone." I get my own phone, ordering us both something and her another matcha instead of making it for her again, as I pick a suit and get dressed. When we step out of the house, her matcha is there waiting for her, so I bend to pick it up.

"This is only because I let you wet my hair." She

grabs it in her hand, stepping out of the house and walking down the steps. The clicking of her nude sky-high heels makes me stop to take her all in. Today she's wearing a skirt that goes to her mid-calf, except it's tight as fuck and hugs every single curve, plus shows off her incredible ass. "Stop staring at my ass," she retorts, still looking ahead, and I have to laugh.

"Stop wearing things that make me stare at your ass, and I'll stop doing it." I make my way over to the car, opening the door for her. "It's like right in my face." She turns, and I look down at her flowy, floral shirt. "And the shirt is all 'look at my tits.'"

She laughs, looking down at her shirt. "That's all in your head. This shirt doesn't give anything away."

"Well, I know you're wearing a lace bra under it," I tell her, and she shakes her head, pulling the door handle open.

"That's because you watched me get dressed." She slips into the car. "Maybe I should move my stuff to the spare closet."

"Yeah?" I glare at her. "Try it." I slam the door, but her laughter is heard from outside the car.

I get into the car, and she leans over and kisses my cheek. "Don't be cranky," she soothes before reaching for her seat belt. "No one likes a cranky Nash."

I put on my sunglasses before making my way to the office. Ever since we got married, I start my day at eight o'clock, getting in with everyone else. When we arrive at the office, she gets out, holding her bag in one hand and her matcha in the other. I kiss her as soon as we get to the door and I pull it open for her to walk in. "Good morning, you two," Lulu greets with a smile.

"Good morning," Zoey says to her and then walks away from me. "Have a good day."

I watch her walk toward the shared office space before walking into my own office. I get my computer started when a text comes in, and I smile because I know it's from her.

Zoey: *Have a great day at work*.

It's little things like this that make me smile throughout the day.

Me: *Thank you, baby.*

I send her the text before I get to work. I'm getting up a couple of hours later, going to find Zoey to see if she's hungry, when I hear Lulu paging her to the front. A bouquet is on the desk. I put my hands in my pockets, trying to calm the burn in my stomach. "You rang?" Zoey asks when she comes closer to the door, looking at Lulu and then at me. "Did you have me paged so I can come to you?" She puts her hands on her hips.

"I did not," I reply, my voice tighter than I want it to be.

"He didn't, but I think in a way he did." She smiles at her. "These were delivered for you."

She points at the flowers on the desk in front of her.

Zoey looks at me with a smile, and I make a note to send her flowers more often. "Why did you do this?" she asks, reaching for the card.

"I didn't," I say at the same time she opens the card and reads the message on it. Her face turns a touch red as she looks at me and then at Lulu, who is now just looking at us, not sure what to say.

"So who are they from?" My mouth asks the question before my brain can stop it.

"I'm going to go and make coffee." Lulu gets up to give us a private moment. I watch her walk to the back, and I'm about to say something else when Kailyn walks from the kitchen.

"Hey, you have a Zoom meeting in five," she says, looking at the flowers and then looking at Zoey. "Isn't he the sweetest?" She looks at me and then walks to her desk.

"Those are nice flowers," I note, waiting for her to say something. "They from Jarod?" I do it on purpose, getting his name wrong.

"It doesn't matter who they're from." She avoids looking in my eyes. "I'm going to put them in the kitchen." She grabs the glass vase, still avoiding my eyes.

"What did the card say?" I ask, and she stops and looks at me.

"What difference does it make?" Her shoulders go back. "At least with me, it's not right in my face every single day. It's in waves."

"What the hell are you talking about?" I snap, trying to keep my voice low.

"I'm talking about not only having to go one-on-one with Emmy last night," she replies, her voice low, "but having to watch Kailyn fawn all over you all day long. 'Oh, Nash, you have a call in five minutes.'" Her voice is high. "'Oh, Nash, you look so good in that suit.'" She glares at me. "News flash, it's the same suit every day, just a different color." I'm literally speechless. I have no idea what the hell she's talking about. "'Oh, Nash, I'd love nothing more than for you to do me on your desk.'" She rolls her eyes.

"She's my assistant," I say, looking around trying to keep my voice down, but I'm shocked she's even saying these things.

"Who wants you to do her on your desk," she repeats.

"I would never, ever cross that line with her or anyone else who works for me," I declare between clenched teeth.

"Not for you but with you. That's a big difference," she says sarcastically as she walks away from me.

"How the fuck did this turn around on me?" I mumble as she walks through the office to the back.

"If anyone wants to take home these flowers," she offers to a couple of people who must be in there, "you are more than happy to have them." She comes out of the kitchen and looks at me still standing here, glaring at me before she makes her way over to the desk, stopping. "Don't forget your call." She uses that voice again before she rolls her eyes and disappears, leaving me with my mouth hanging open.

TWENTY-SEVEN

ZOEY

I PULL OUT my chair and sit down, forcing myself not to look at his office because I know he's still staring at me. My leg moves up and down with all the nerves going through me. When I got paged to go to the front, I thought it was for Nash to ask me what I wanted for lunch. What I wasn't expecting was the big, beautiful flower bouquet. I looked over at Nash, thinking he sent it to me, but when I opened the card and read the words, I wanted to take the flowers and throw them across the room.

I was standing in front of Lulu, who thought Nash sent me the flowers. I was so embarrassed I wanted the earth to eat me up, and then he asked the loaded question. Who sent me the flowers? I should have lied and said it was my parents. I should have told myself I did nothing wrong, and it wasn't my fault. But I felt like people would doubt me, or us for that matter. What married woman gets flowers from her ex-boyfriend? Or better yet, what married woman wanted to get flowers from her ex-boyfriend? I can tell you I'm not that person. I knew Nash was angry about it. I could feel the tension in the air after Lulu excused herself to not be in the middle of our argument.

I should have taken the time to calm down, but instead, I was pushed over the edge. Already feeling the way I felt, Nash's tone sounded accusatory or at least that is what I thought it sounded like. So instead of making a joke of it, I threw last night in his face and even the shit with Kailyn. The minute the words came out of my mouth, I knew they shocked him. He looked like a deer in the headlights.

I look back down at the white envelope in my hands, pulling the card out and reading the fucking words again.

Zoey,

I miss you so much, it's hard to comprehend.

Let's fix this.

J.

I rip the card in half and then in half again until it is in tiny little pieces. Should I text him and tell him it's never going to happen? Probably. Should I call him and tell him to fuck off? Yes. Will I give him the time of day? No. Because he's a non-factor to my day. If I call him or text him, he wins. He will get what he wants, which puts me right back where it did when we were dating, where he got what he wanted, and now I see that I didn't. I kept giving and giving and got nothing back. So I was not going to give him another thought more than he deserved.

I don't have any more time to think of things when I

get a call from one of my clients. Which lasts more than two hours as we go through everything he wants to focus on in the next quarter. Only when I hang up the phone, I see Nash sent me a text.

Nash: *Have to run an errand. Not sure what time I'll be back. Let me know, and I'll send a car for you.*

I look over at his office door, seeing it open, and then look down to see it's almost after four anyway. I try not to be pissed that he sent me a fucking text instead of coming to see me. But well, it doesn't work. Instead, I open my Uber app and order my own car, packing up my stuff.

When I get a notification my ride is there in a minute, I grab my bag and head toward the door. "Good night, Lulu," I say, smiling at her.

"See you tomorrow," she replies, and I avoid looking at her eyes, wondering what the hell she must be thinking.

I get in the car and don't even bother texting Nash back. I'm a grown-ass woman. I don't need him to send a car for me. I sit in the back of the car stewing, which makes it even worse. Even getting into the house, I make my way upstairs and change out of my clothes, putting on shorts and a shirt. I avoid my phone the whole time. Instead, I go downstairs to watch television. I think about maybe calling Zara, but I'm not ready to let anyone in on what is going on, or better yet, what is not going on.

When six o'clock rolls around, and he's not called nor texted, I'm past the point of being pissed. Like, what the actual fuck? I walk over to the kitchen and open the fridge. "He wants to play this game," I say to myself, taking out the salmon we were going to eat for dinner. "He's going to play this game by himself," I mumble as I prepare the salmon, putting it in the oven before starting on the rice and then making a quick little salad. As the time ticks by, instead of me relaxing and going with it, I get angrier and angrier. I literally want to go upstairs, pack my shit, and take off, but that would be immature of me.

I'm taking the salmon out of the oven when I hear the front door slam, making me jump. I listen to his steps getting closer and closer to the kitchen. His face is hard and tight when he sees me. "You didn't call me." He puts his hands on his hips.

"I didn't think I had to call you." I place the salmon down, taking off the baking mitt. "I finished work and got a cab." I try not to let my voice show how pissed I am. I have to wonder if I'm this pissed off because so many things haven't been said out loud. Like, for example, how he's feeling toward me. How do I feel toward him? I'm in love with him, but does he know this? Does he feel it? The elephant in the room is getting bigger and bigger, and it looks like neither of us is going to take the leap and bring it up.

"I waited and waited for you to call me." He doesn't move from where he is, which is weird, since every single time he comes into the house to find me, he comes right to me to kiss me. Today is not like that, and I have to wonder if today is the day everything changes. I notice he isn't even wearing his suit jacket. Instead, his white dress shirt is rolled up to the elbows.

"Well, as you can see, I made it home." I extend my hands beside me on the counter. "And I made dinner. Have you eaten already?"

His eyebrows push together at the question. "Of course not. Why would you think that?"

"I have no idea." I shrug. "All I know is you went to run an errand at three, and it's almost seven."

"Yeah, and I've been on the road the whole time," he retorts. "They called me, and I rushed out of there."

"Who?" I ask, the curiosity getting the better of me as he holds up his finger, turning and walking back out of the house.

It doesn't take him long to walk back out of the house, the door slamming, and then maybe a couple of seconds later it slams again. I walk around the counter toward the hallway and see him walking in, holding a little crate in his hand. "What is that?" I ask him. My heart speeds up a million miles a minute, and it feels like it's going to come out of my chest.

"This is..." he says softly, opening the front of the cage and taking out the most beautiful kitten I've ever seen in my life. It's all white, and he holds it gently against his chest. "Whatever you want to name her." I look at the little ball in his hand, her blue eyes looking around as she shivers in his arms. "I ordered her the minute we got home, but she wasn't ready until today. They called me at the last minute. I rushed over there to pick her up, but I had to go and get all the things she needed. It's all in the car."

"You got me a cat?" I whisper, my hands itching to

hold her but standing here in shock. "A real cat?"

"Well, she's not fake. I can tell you that." He takes a couple of steps and holds the cat out for me. I gently take her in my arms and hold her like a baby as she looks up at me. "I'm going to go get the things out of the car." He points at the door, turns, and walks out as the cat looks around at the house.

"You are the most beautiful little cat I've ever seen in my life," I tell her as she squirms a little in my arms until I rub her head. "Like the most beautiful."

I hear a thud and look to see he was not kidding. "I bought whatever they suggested," he says. "I even got two cat trees that need to be put together."

"Nash, you got me a cat."

"Yeah," he confirms as if it's nothing. I'm trying not to freak out, but I'm looking at a cat I'm probably going to fall in love with. "You are always watching those cat videos, so I thought this would be perfect."

We should have perhaps spoken about this," I start to say, and everything with today just snowballs. "Like what the fuck happens if this doesn't work out, and now we have to figure out custody of the cat?" I ramble a bit.

He stands there confused. "Excuse me?" His head tilts to the side.

"After ninety days, we could be divorced," I remind him, thinking I'm being honest with him about the situation. What happens if he gets bored with this life we are creating and suddenly wants his old life back? "What if you, or we, decide this isn't what either of us wants?"

The minute I say the words, I see something flash on

his face. His eyes change a different color, and his jaw gets tighter than I've ever seen it get before. I even see his shoulders slump just a bit as I take a step toward him. "Nash." I say his name, not sure what else to say when his phone rings from his pocket.

He grabs his phone, and I blink away the tears in my eyes. "Hey," he says, clearing his voice like something is in his throat. "Yeah, I have it right here. Give me a second," he adds. "I have to take care of something that I was supposed to handle this afternoon before I had to leave."

"Of course," I say as I watch him walk away from me and head toward the office.

I look down at the cat, who now is really squirming to get out of my arms. "We should get your litter done, I think," I murmur as I place her on her feet in the middle of the kitchen, and she looks around. "But I don't know where to put it." I suddenly feel uncomfortable being here. "Should we wait for Nash to see where he wants to set you up?" I put my hand on my stomach as I breathe in and out, and I sit down on the floor next to the cat. "What should we call you?" I ask her as I pet her, looking toward the office where I hear him talking. "I think I know what I want to call you," I say softly. "Lovey-dovey." My voice cracks as I look back down the hallway, hoping I didn't ruin it.

TWENTY-EIGHT

I LEAN BACK in the chair and listen to Caine and my father talk about the merger they want to do. A meeting that was supposed to be this afternoon, but I got a call a week early to go and pick up the cat. My head is half in this phone call, half on Zoey and her words.

"After ninety days, we could be divorced. What if you, or we, decide this isn't what either of us wants?"

I close my eyes, trying not to focus on the words and the fact my heart has never felt such pain as when she said we could be divorced. It was as if she kicked me in the balls, and I went down on the floor to my back, and then they came and stomped right on my chest. It left me so winded I had no idea what to say. The words were all stuck in my brain, but the only thing I could think is she already has one foot out the door. Is she doing this just to say she did it for ninety days and then just leave me, leave us?

"What do you think, Nash?" My father's voice brings

me back to the conversation.

"Um…" I clear my throat. "I agree with everything Caine said." It's my go-to, always has been because out of the two of us, he has his shit together, always has. Minus the part where he met his horrible, wretched ex-wife before meeting Grace.

Caine's laughter fills the phone. "That means he hasn't heard a thing we've said for the past hour because his head is elsewhere."

"It is, actually," I admit. "It's almost eight here, and it's past Caine's bedtime." I try to make a joke to get off this call. "How about we reconvene tomorrow morning at eight my time?"

"Sounds good. Have a good night, boys," my father says right before he hangs up, and I laugh because we are both in our thirties, but we are still boys to him.

"Later," I say.

At the same time, Caine says, "Good night."

I put my phone down, seeing the emails that have come in since this afternoon when I left, knowing I have to answer a couple of them before I head to bed. I get up and walk out into the kitchen, seeing Zoey sitting on the floor trying to assemble one of the cat trees while the cat sits between her legs. "We are almost finished," she tells the cat, and I see she put out the white water bowl I bought for her and right beside her the white bowl for food, "and then we are going to set up the litter box. I just don't know where to put it." I can't help but feel centered and at peace when I hear her voice or know she's around. "I was thinking the laundry room upstairs, but we'll see once Nash gets off the phone."

"I don't care where you put it," I cut in on their private conversation. "You can put it wherever you want it."

She looks up at me, and all I can do is stare at her. "Oh, you're off the phone," she says softly.

"I am, but I need to answer a couple of emails," I tell her, looking at the food on the counter that she was taking out when I got here. "Did you eat?"

"No." She shakes her head. "I was waiting to see if you ate or not."

"I'm not that hungry."

"Oh," she says, looking down at the cat, who is now sitting up, looking at me until she puts a paw on one of Zoey's legs. "Okay, I'll set up the cat and then grab something to eat." I put my hands in my pockets, itching to go and touch her or kiss her. I don't think we've gone more than eight hours without kissing each other, and that's only because we are either sleeping or at work.

"I'll leave you a plate on the stove in case you get hungry after your emails," she offers and gets up off the floor. "If you don't eat it, just put it in the fridge." She bends to pick up the cat in her arms, who leans forward and looks up at her with the biggest eyes.

"Will do," I reply before I turn and walk out of the room, instead of asking her what the hell she meant by us getting a divorce. Instead, I go into the office and grab my phone.

I see Caine texted me.

Caine: *What's up with you?*

I look at the phone and then at the door to see if she's

going to follow me to ask me if everything is okay, but she doesn't.

Me: *Not sure.*

Caine: *Want to call me?*

I know that it's past eleven his time, and he has a wife and daughter he has to take care of, so I push him off.

Me: *No, it's late, we'll talk tomorrow.*

Caine: *You sure?*

Me*: Yup, it's nothing that urgent.*

Caine*: Okay, call me tomorrow.*

I put the phone down before dropping my head back and looking at the ceiling as I drag my hands over my face. *Ninety days, we could be divorced,* the words make my hands ball into fists.

I turn in my chair and do what I know I do best, I get to work. I answer the emails that need to be answered, and before I know it, it's past eleven. "Fuck," I curse, turning off the computer and grabbing my phone.

I walk out, seeing the house mostly dark with just the light over the stove on. I walk over and put the plate of food on the top in the fridge before turning the light off and making my way up to the bedroom.

I look over to the right and see the light is on in the laundry room, so I walk over and see she set up the litter box with another bowl of water and food for the cat. I don't turn off the light, but I close the door enough for it not to shine in the hallway. I walk over to the bedroom, where I see Zoey on her side with the cat curled up in a ball by her stomach. Both of them are sleeping. I quietly tiptoe to the bathroom, taking off my clothes before sliding into bed. Her back is to me, and even though I want to wrap my arms around her and pull her into my chest, I don't. Instead, I lie on my back, looking up at the ceiling most of the night.

The cat gets up a couple of times, jumping off the bed and waking Zoey, who looks over at me, but I fake sleep, watching her get out of bed and follow the cat around the house. She climbs into bed a couple of minutes later, again turning her back to me. When I open my eyes a bit after five o'clock, I look over at her and see she's turning toward me with the cat still sleeping next to her.

I slide out of bed slowly, so as not to wake them, before going out to the gym where I just run on the treadmill, trying to run the nerves out of me, along with everything else. When I walk into the house, I'm shocked to see her in the kitchen. "Good morning," I greet her, and she looks over at me as she stirs the eggs in the pan in front of her.

"Hey," she says softly.

"What are you doing up?" I ask, and she shrugs.

"Cat thought it would be a good idea to see if my eye would open if she stuck her paw in it." She laughs before bringing her cup to her mouth. First time since we've been home that I haven't made her matcha. "News flash, I opened it and then scared the shit out of her." She looks around. "I haven't seen her since." She plates me breakfast, putting it on the counter where I always eat.

"I'm sure she'll come out eventually," I mumble to her as I make my protein shake.

"Are you okay?" she asks, and I turn to look at her

standing there in my kitchen wearing shorts and a tank top. One foot on top of the other, her hair wild and free around her face, and I have to think she's never looked more beautiful since I've met her.

"You tell me," I ask, "are you okay?"

She picks up her cup, brings it to her lips, turning to the side and nodding her head. "Then I'm okay," I answer, but the truth is I'm far from okay. I hate this. I also know I'm not ready to push her to have this conversation because what if she says things I don't want to hear? What if she is ready to throw in the towel on this marriage, and I'm not ready to hear the words? What if she's making plans to move back to her life in New York? What if dickhead is in the wings waiting for her? The what-ifs are making me fucking sick. I barely mix my protein shake. Unlike yesterday, when I took it upstairs and then we fucked in the shower, when I walk upstairs, she's in the bathroom with the door closed, which is also a first.

I turn around and head over to the spare bathroom, turning on the shower and then seeing her cat has followed me in here. She looks up at me and meows. "She's in the other room." I point at the door. "Go find her." I bend down and pet her. "I thought she would be so happy to have you," I tell the little cat, who I'm sure has no fucking idea what the fuck I'm saying. I pick her up and take her back to the bedroom, seeing Zoey walk back out of the bathroom. "I found her, or more like she found me. She followed me into the other bathroom."

"The other bathroom?" she asks, confused.

"Yeah, the door was closed, and I didn't want to

bother you, so I was going to shower in the other one."

"Oh. Well, I'm done. You can have the bathroom." I stare at her and see her nose is a touch red. I don't say a word. Instead, I nod at her and walk into the bathroom, not closing the door, and starting the water, hoping like fuck she comes and joins me. She doesn't. When I come out of the shower, the bed is made, and she's not in the closet. I get dressed with dread, and when I head downstairs, I hear her.

"We have to leave to go to work, but you have a couple of toys to keep you busy, and I'm going to leave food and water out, and even leave the faucet in the sink on, just in case." I smile at her voice and see her wearing pants and a shirt as she holds the cat in her arms.

"Ready?" I ask when I walk into the kitchen. She nods before kissing the cat and putting her in the basket of the cat tree she built.

I wait for her to walk out of the house, like I do every single morning. "I think I'm going to come home at lunch and check and make sure she's okay," she tells me as I get into the car.

"You can even work from home in the afternoon." I start the car, and the rest of the ride to the office is done in stone-cold silence. The tension in the car is so thick my chest feels like it's being constricted. When we get to the office, she walks ahead of me for the first time, barely holding the door open for me.

Lulu greets us with a smile as Zoey smiles at her with a fake smile before walking over to her side of the office. Lulu just looks at me confused, and I'm pretty sure everyone is going to think we're fighting.

I walk into my office and close the door, something I've not done often, so if Lulu didn't know we were fighting before, she will definitely know now. Pulling out my phone, I call the one person who will sort of help me make sense of this or maybe not.

He answers after one ring. "Caine Griffin," he says, and I roll my eyes.

"How you still do not look at the call display is still a mystery." I put the phone to my ear, leaning back.

"It's a force of habit," he says, "you should try it. Sometimes it is better than yo or 'sup."

I chuckle before I hear his voice go low. "You okay?"

I look at the closed door before I answer him, "I have no idea."

"What happened?"

"I wish I fucking knew," I answer him honestly. "It was going so good until her ex sent her flowers, and then she got defensive about being surrounded by women who want me," I hiss. "Then I got her a kitten, and she got pissed at me because in ninety days, we could be divorced."

"You bought her a cat?" he asks, the shock in his voice so apparent. "Like a small living pet?"

"She likes to watch cat videos, so I thought, let me buy her a cat," I explain, thinking perhaps it was a little too much. "That is beside the point."

"Okay, when she said you could be divorced in ninety days, what did you say?"

"I didn't fucking say anything. I was in shock like,

what the fuck?"

"Did you tell her how you felt?" he asks, and I don't answer the question. "You've told her how you felt, haven't you?"

"Not in so many words," I admit to him, "and maybe it's a good thing since she obviously doesn't feel the same way."

"What do you mean, not in so many words? You've either told her how you feel, or you haven't."

"I've shown her how I feel every single fucking day."

"But you've never said 'Zoey, I'm in love with you'?" I tap the top of my desk. "Dude, you can't be that dumb." He laughs. "You can show her a million different ways, but it doesn't replace the words."

"Yeah," I say, not sure I agree with him, "it's just that—"

"Stop being a chickenshit and just fucking tell her how you feel." I look at the door. "Just tell her." I take a deep breath in. "Might not solve all your problems, but at least she'll know how you feel."

"Yeah, maybe you're right," I tell him. "Thanks." The knock on the door makes me look over. "I'll call you back." I hang up the phone before I yell, "Come in!"

The door opens, and Zoey sticks her head in, and my heart speeds up. "You busy?"

"For you, never," I reply as she comes into the room. "I was just coming to find you anyway." I smile at her. "What's up?"

"I was just on the phone with Gabriella," she mentions her cousin, "and she's in LA, but she's leaving this afternoon to go to New York, so I was thinking of hitching a ride with her." I stare at her. "Unless you want me to stay?"

I think about laying my heart out to her, but at this moment, she might reject it, and I just can't do it. Instead, I tell her the words I don't even want to say, yet say them anyway. "If you want to go early, you should go."

TWENTY-NINE

ZOEY

I STAND HERE in front of him asking, begging him, to tell me to stay. To give me something, anything. My heart beats erratically in my chest, my breathing feels like I'm panting, my stomach feels like it's in my throat forming a huge ball.

"If you want to go early, you should go." The words come out of his mouth, and it feels like I'm being crushed. The only thing I can think of is, this is what it's like to have your heart broken. This is that feeling I've never felt before. Either that or I'm having a heart attack.

I straighten my shoulders. "Good," I say, trying to keep my shit together. "I'll tell her that I'll go with her." I nod, turning and hoping like fuck he calls my name. Every single step I get closer to the door is one step I get farther and farther away from him. I grab the handle of the door, shutting it behind me without looking over to see him.

"Is he free?" Kailyn says to me, and I look at her.

"He's all yours," I answer before walking back to my side of the office, where I grab my phone and text Gabriella.

Me*: I'm good to go when you are. Even if you want to leave early.*

I put my phone down and look at my computer screen, wondering if I'm even going to get any work done. I'm pretty sure the whole office can feel we are fighting, or it might be in my head. Either way, I feel the need to get the fuck out of here, and I'm saved when Gabriella answers me back.

Gabriella: *Oh, that's even better. Romeo just got a plane for noon. Is that too early? Can you make it work? We should land in New York by six thirty, max seven.*

Me: *That works perfectly for me. I'll meet you at the airport in about an hour and a half.*

Gabriella: *Want us to come and get you?*

Me*: No, I have to swing by home and grab some things, so I'll just meet you there.*

I have never lied to my cousin in my life, except for this moment right here. I'm not going home. I'm going straight to the airport from here because going home will just make it harder for me to leave. Every single minute that goes by I look at his office door, waiting for it to open. Every single time it does, I hold my breath, but then I see it's always Kailyn coming out to get something at her desk and then going back inside.

I order myself a car, and when it's five minutes before, I get up and head toward his office. I'm about to knock when Kailyn comes out again. "Hey," I say, and she closes the door behind her, "is he busy?"

"He just got on the phone with his father and brother," she replies, her body shielding the door. "He asked not to be disturbed." I smile at her, and she must think I'm going to turn around and walk away, but I'm pissed at all the things today, so I fold my arms over my chest.

"I'll take my chances." I reach over her shoulder and knock on the door. "If you'll excuse me." I wait for her to move away from the door, and she just smirks at me as she saunters away.

I turn the door handle, suddenly nervous he'll be pissed I'm interrupting him, so I just stick my head in. He looks up from his computer. "Sorry, I know you told Kailyn you don't want to be disturbed"—his eyebrows pinch together—"but I'm heading out and just wanted you to know."

"I'll call you back," he says immediately to the screen and closes the top of the computer before getting up. "What do you mean you're heading out now?" He walks around the desk.

I walk into the room. "Gabriella got an earlier flight so—" I stop when I'm standing in front of him. "And the car will be here in a couple of minutes."

"You ordered yourself a car?" he asks, looking out the window at the parking lot.

"I didn't want to inconvenience you," I explain nervously. "You have a busy day, and you worked late last night." I try to make it sound like it's no big deal. "I'll call you once I land," I say softly and take a step to him, leaning in for a kiss. I kiss him softly on the lips as my heart crushes even more when his phone rings, and he looks back at his desk to where the phone is ringing. "I'll let you get back to work." I smile at him or at least I hope it is seen as a smile and not as a broken fucking smile.

Again, when I walk out of the room, I'm expecting him to call my name. Even when I grab my bag and start heading for the door, I look into his office as he's on the phone at the same time typing frantically on his laptop. I hold up my hand one last time before walking out.

My head is down as I make my way to the car. I give myself a minute to let one tear fall out of the corner of my eye before I hold my thumb to it to stop it from falling down my face, as I quickly blink my eyes and take a deep inhale. "Hi," I tell the driver, putting my bag to the side of me. "How are you doing?" The driver tells me he's doing fine as he pulls away from the building.

My head is scrambling around and around, wondering when it all fucking fell apart. Maybe it was always going to fall apart. Maybe there were signs I didn't see. I have no idea. I know I can't take long to dwell on it because Gabriella will see right through my bullshit, and I'm still trying to figure it out myself and don't need the outside noise.

When I get to the airport, I see I'm right behind Gabriella and Romeo. I open the door and step out. "Well, fancy meeting you here," I tease, grabbing my bag before thanking the driver.

"You didn't change at home?" Gabriella asks me

when I walk toward her.

"Stuff came up last minute, so I came straight from the office." I avoid looking at her, instead walking over to Romeo to kiss him on the cheek. "Hey, Mr. Royalty," I tease him, and he rolls his eyes.

"That's my father," he jokes back, "I'm Jr. Royalty." He grabs Gabriella's hand as we walk toward the plane.

"I'm surprised Nash didn't join us," Gabriella says.

"He had two huge meetings. He might come down next week." Another fucking lie, and I make a mental note to remember it. There is a reason one shouldn't lie, and that's because it's hard to fucking keep track of them.

Romeo stands by the stairs of the plane, letting Gabriella go up first and then holding out his hand to tell me to go ahead of him. I smile at him, walking into the plane and heading to the left side where there is only one chair, instead of the seat next to Gabriella.

As soon as the plane takes off, Gabriella turns toward me in her seat. "So how is married life treating you?"

I put my eyes to the corner and pretend I'm in wedded bliss. I mean it's not a lie since I was in fucking wedded bliss. "Amazing. I didn't think I could just slide into it, but it's been so much fun. And he bought me a cat."

"He bought you a car?" Romeo asks me, thinking he heard wrong.

"No." I shake my head. "A cat with a t." I take out my phone and turn it toward them so they can see her. I was with her for a day, and I took about fifty pictures of her.

"She looks like a snowball," Gabriella notes, and I smile, looking down at the picture, swiping left until I get to the last picture we took right before we left for the dinner. Standing in front of the mirror in the closet, he pulled me to him as he kissed my temple, right before he told me he was going to fuck the shit out of me when we got back home. Which made me burst out laughing.

"I guess it's not all amazing, then." Gabriella shocks me with her words. "Your face went from fake smile to sad in the matter of ten seconds." I shrug. "So you're hiding something."

"Not hiding anything," I tell her honestly. "I'm just working something out in my head."

"Do you need to talk it out?" she asks me.

"Gabriella, leave her alone. If she wanted to talk it out, she would have talked it out," Romeo says to her while he's typing away on his phone.

"Did I ask you to join this conversation, Romeo?" She glares at him as she hisses, "I don't think I did, so why don't you mind your business and leave this conversation"—she points at her and me—"to us."

Romeo turns in his seat, and I have to bite my lip not to laugh at the way he's unfazed by her warning. "Did it sound like I wanted you to join the conversation?"

"Who's hungry?" I ask, trying to cut through the tension. "I'm starving. I didn't eat anything."

"Don't think I don't know what you're doing," Gabriella scolds me. "I'm the queen of hiding how I feel." I don't have a chance to answer her because the flight attendant comes over with bottles of water for us. "So what do you think is going on with Zara?" she asks me, and I look over at her. "Is she ever getting married?"

"I asked her the same thing." I'm thankful to change the subject, and by the time we land, I'm so tired I feel like I could fall asleep on my feet.

Two cars are there, and when I kiss them goodbye, I get into my car and head toward my house. I look out the window at the familiar sights before me, expecting to feel glad that I'm home. Even when I spot the brownstone, and I get out carrying my bag, I'm expecting to feel relief that I'm here. This is my home, after all. Walking into the house, it feels so stuffy from being closed up.

I put my bag on the side table before kicking off my heels and walking toward the kitchen. I see a stack of mail on the counter before grabbing a bottle of water and walking upstairs to change. Even when I walk into my bedroom, it feels cold and not homey like it once did. I slip on a pair of shorts and a T-shirt before going back downstairs to figure out dinner.

Grabbing my phone at the front door, I call Nash even though I have to wonder if he even cares that I've landed. It rings four times before going to voicemail, and instead of leaving a message, I just hang up.

I pull up his name and text him.

Me: *Landed.*

But before I press send, I delete it and close it. I open the fridge, seeing that all there is are things to drink, so I pull up the order app. I'm scrolling to see what to order when the phone rings in my hand, and I see it's Nash.

"Hey," I answer the phone, pretending I'm fine and that everything is okay.

"Hey," he says and I hear a door shut on his side, and

I wonder if he's just getting home. "You just got in?"

"Yeah, not too long ago. I was going to order something to eat." Even this conversation feels forced. "What are you going to do?" I close my eyes, trying to pretend I don't miss him, but not being able to hug and kiss him has pushed me to the edge, and I'm about to jump fucking over.

"Not sure yet," he replies.

"I think we need to talk when I come back," I say the words I've wanted to say since last night after I said the words I've regretted since.

"I think we need to talk also," he finally agrees. "There are things that need to be said."

"I agree," I say, nervous and wishing we could just hash it out now instead of prolonging this shit.

"Do you know when you're coming back?" he asks me, his voice soft.

I'm about to answer him when the doorbell rings. I get off my stool, walking over to the door. "I think I'll be back by next week, just not sure of the date yet." I don't even bring up we were supposed to have dinner with his parents on Monday, wondering if he told them I came without him. "I will know more by Tuesday." I unlock the door and open it and stand here staring in shock.

I see him standing there, looking like he's run his hand through his hair for hours, wearing exactly what he was wearing at the office. His phone is in one hand and a green case in the other hand. "You forgot your cat."

THIRTY

HER MOUTH IS open in shock, the phone still to her ear as she takes me in. I probably look disheveled because it took me a lot longer than I thought it would. I had already booked a plane when she came and told me she was leaving. Then when she came back and said she was leaving right then, it threw all my plans out the window. I watched her walk out while calling the plane and pushing it up, rushing to get the fuck out of my office before going to get the cat.

I hold up the green-and-brown carrier in my hand. "You forgot your cat," I say, knowing it's the stupidest excuse known to humankind.

I don't know how long it takes her to answer me. It could have been seconds, but it felt like hours. "Nash," she whispers.

"Do you know how hard it is to travel with a kitten?" I ask, trying to make her smile, something I haven't done in the last couple of days. "She cried for a good thirty minutes until I let her out, and then she climbed everywhere for a good two hours before napping the rest of the way." I stand here on her stoop, holding her menace cat in my hand, hoping she lets me in. "Can I come in?" I finally ask her, and she snaps out of the shock and moves away.

"Of course you can," she says, moving away but holding out her hand for the carrier. "Hi, my girl," she says to the cat. "Did you go on an adventure?" She looks from the cat to me, putting the carrier on the floor and then opening it to take her out. "I don't have anything for the cat here."

"I called Zara before I got on the plane," I tell her, and again, she just stares at me. "She said she left everything in the laundry room, and you owe her for going into a pet store."

She gets up and walks over to the laundry room, opening the door and seeing everything there. "She got her a water fountain." She smiles over her shoulder as she kisses the kitten's neck and then puts her down in the litter box, before coming back out to join me.

"I can't believe you're here," she states, and I can see her bottom lip tremble. She looks down and I see her hand come up, shaking a bit as she wipes away what looks like a tear.

"How could you think I wouldn't be here?" I ask her, and she just looks at me. I see the big tears welling at the bottom of her eyes. It's more than I can take, so I walk two steps toward her and hold her face in my hands. "We need to talk," I repeat, my own hands shaking now. "You are going to have to bear with me because I've never done this before," I tell her honestly. "I fucked up," I start with that because it's the first thing that comes to my mind, "and I'm sorry."

"Nash." She wraps her hands around my wrists that hold her face, my thumbs sweeping her cheeks, brushing away the tears. "Before you start, I want to say one thing." She holds up her hand to stop me from talking, and I don't think I even take a fucking breath as I wait for her to say what she so urgently has to say. "I'm so sorry about what I said." I see her nervously twist her hands together. "It was so uncalled for, and I wanted to take back the words the minute I said them—"

I shake my head, trying not to get my hopes up high as I say what I came here to say. "Just let me say what I have to say." I quickly cut her off. "I'm in love with you." I finally say the words, not caring how vulnerable it makes me. "I'm so fucking in love with you I can't see fucking straight." I bend to kiss her lips. "I know we have a lot to work out, but I don't want a divorce. I didn't want a divorce before I fell in love with you, and now, I definitely don't want a divorce." My eyes search hers. "When you mentioned divorce, it threw me off. I mean, I knew I asked you to give me ninety days, but I didn't think it was hanging over our head. I was hoping you could see how much I was falling for you. I was hoping you saw how much I love you." I bring her closer to me. "You had to know. You have to know how much I love you."

"I was hoping," she finally replies, a smile forming

on her lips. "I was really fucking hoping. That's why I brought up the divorce, to see where you were at. I didn't want it. I never, ever wanted it. You have to have known also." Her eyes turn red with tears. "But I needed to hear the words. I needed you to tell me you love me so I could know I wasn't in this alone."

"Fuck, baby, you had to know you weren't in this alone," I reinforce as my lips find hers, my tongue sliding with hers. "I know there is more to say, but I've missed you so fucking much." I drop my hands from her face, wrapping one arm around her waist to pull her to me. "You had to have known." I kiss her jaw. "You had to have known how much you own me." I kiss her neck. "How I live for you." I suck on her neck. "How I breathe for you." I rub my nose along the vein in her neck, where I can feel her heart beating. "You had to have known how my heart beats for you." I pick her up and start walking toward the stairs. "You fucking own me, baby. Every single fiber of my being is yours." I walk up the steps toward her bedroom. I've been without her for two days, and it feels like I haven't touched her in years.

I walk over to her bed, her arms wrapped around my neck. "I love you," she says when her knees hit the bed. "I thought I loved Josh. I thought he was the one." She holds my face. "I was wrong. I've never felt what I feel for you, ever."

I smirk at her. "Good, at least I know I'm not the only one. I've never told someone I love them before. I mean, my family, but I've never put myself out there. I knew, I knew the minute I met you that you were different." I put my knee on the bed, and she unwraps her legs from my waist. "I knew the minute we kissed you were out of my league, and you had the power to destroy me, and I was not fucking wrong." I pull her shirt off over her head. "I'm fucking jealous of anyone who makes you smile because I want to be the only one who makes you smile," I admit to her. "I want to throat punch anyone who makes you laugh because, again, I want it to be just for me."

"You have to know also"—she pulls my shirt out of my pants and unbuttons them—"that if I smile, it's nothing like the smile I give you." She gets to the last button. "No one makes me laugh like you do. No one makes me feel the way you do, ever." She pushes the shirt over my chest. "I'm sorry I overreacted about Kailyn and threw it in your face."

"She's fired," I fill her in, and her eyes go big. "She was fired two minutes after you walked out the door."

"Nash, are you insane?"

I shake my head. "Nope, never thought clearer in my life. She told you not to disturb me?" I remind her. "You're my wife. For you, I'm to be interrupted every single time. I don't give a fuck who I'm on the phone with. She went over a line, and she found out it was the wrong one."

"Nash." She puts her hand on my chest, palm flat against where my heart is beating. "I love you."

"Fuck, I've never thought three words could make me so happy." I kiss her neck, and I'm about to move my head lower when we both feel the bed dip, and I turn to the side to see the cat walking toward us. "You need to beat it," I tell the cat at the same time Zoey picks the cat up.

"Mommy and Daddy are having playtime." She gets off the bed with the cat. "After, I promise I'll come and play with you."

"Tomorrow," I add, and Zoey looks back at me. "Okay, fine, later, like in an hour." She puts her down and turns to walk back into the room and close the door, but the cat beats her to it, and she just laughs. "Mommy really needs to play with Daddy," she explains to the cat, then looks over at me. "We should play in the shower." She motions with her head toward her bathroom. "I don't think cats like water."

"I'm really rethinking getting you that fucking cat." I get off the bed and walk toward the bathroom. "Did you see the scratches on my hands? Fucker does not like to be placed in the carrier." I hold out my hands for her to see the little scratches.

"Did you hurt Daddy?" she asks the cat, who looks angelic, but I'm pretty sure isn't. "Now Mommy has to kiss and make it all better."

"I have something Mommy can kiss and make all better." I grab the cat and toss it on the bed when she gasps out my name. "It's a cat. It lands on its paws." I look back over to see the cat on its side, lying down. "See, she's fine." I grab her hand, bringing it to my cock. "But he's not, and he needs your attention."

She squeezes me through my pants, and I think I'm going to literally come the minute she puts her hands or mouth on me. "Let's go and see what I can do about this."

She walks backward to the bathroom, going straight to the shower and letting me go just to start the water. "You need to show me what's got you all hot and bothered." She reaches around her back, unsnapping her bra and letting her tits spring free. My mouth waters. "You know the good thing about us being here?" She looks at me. "Besides all the makeup sex?"

"And you sucking my cock because it missed you."

She rolls her eyes. "Yes, obviously, I need to make sure he knows I missed him too." She unbuckles my belt. "We can play with all my toys."

If I wasn't as hard as steel before, my cock gets even harder. "Do not joke like that," I scold her, grabbing her ass cheeks in my palms and squeezing them, pulling her to me. "My cock just got ten times harder."

She gets on her tippy-toes. "Just imagine how hard you can get when you watch me play with myself." She kisses my neck. "I love you, Nash." I look down when her voice goes soft. "And I don't want to not say it anymore."

"Baby, there will never be a time in your life when you will doubt how I feel for you. There will never be a time when you will go a day without me telling you how I feel for you. I love you," I say before I kiss her lips.

THIRTY-ONE

HIS HAND ROAMS down my back toward my ass, his fingertips trailing along the way. I'm on my stomach turned away from him, one leg cocked out, giving him direct access to me. The coldness hits me right away when he throws the covers off me. My eyes flutter open for a second and then close back again. "Morning, baby," Nash says softly into my neck, giving me little kisses while his finger runs through my slit to my clit and then back again.

"Morning." I turn on my side, my hand wrapping around his neck, sliding my tongue into his mouth. His hand moves from my pussy up my side to cup my tit, and I can't help but moan when he rolls my nipple between his fingers. "Nash." I fall onto my back, which is half on him, throwing my leg over his. "I missed you," I admit even though we went at each other like wild rabbits last night. I think we have slept a total of two hours.

He wastes no time moving his hand down, sliding two

fingers through my slit and right into me. "Fuck, I just had you, and my cock is hard for you again."

"You sound like that's a bad thing," I tease, moving my hips to the speed of his fingers. "I thought I would be sore this morning after all night. But all I want is more." He takes his fingers out of me, moving them to my clit as he rubs it in circles. "I want your cock." My hand moves the covers off him as I search for the hard cock I felt under me.

I grip it in my hand and move up and down with it. "Looks like you found it," he groans, sliding his fingers down and into me, but I move, the need to have him in my mouth bigger than the need for him to make me come. I get on my hands and knees and swallow his cock as far as I can take him in my mouth. "Baby." He puts his feet on the bed and grips my head with his hand. "That's my girl." I look up at him, something I've noticed he loves. "Eating my cock like I want it." His hips move up to fuck my mouth, my hand gripping the base of his cock as I lick around his head and stroke it. I suck him back into my mouth, my pussy getting wet from seeing how his eyes go hungry for me. "Going to coat your throat with my cum," he growls, and I can't help but moan into his cock, wanting him to give me everything he has.

One second, his cock is in my mouth, and the next, he's on his knees in front of me. I don't even have time to ask him anything because his hands are on my hips, twisting me to my knees before he shoves my head into the bed and then slams into me. "Nash," I moan his name, gripping the covers, holding on as his balls hit my clit. His hands grip my hips as he drives into me over and over again. He hits my sweet spot every single time he slams into me.

"So wet for me," he praises between clenched teeth and my head almost falls to the bed, but it stops once he takes one of his hands off my hips and grips my hair with it, pulling back and making my back arch. That's all I need before I'm crying out his name over and over again. My pussy convulses on his cock. "That's my fucking girl."

"More," I egg him on, "give me more." Did he ever give me more. He releases my hair to grab my hips again. He slams into me a couple more times before I'm coming again, but then so is he. His thrusts don't give up. He fucks me just as hard until there is nothing left inside him. His body falls on top of mine, his cock still buried inside me as he kisses my shoulder. "Now that is how everyone should wake up in the morning," I say after my breathing returns to a normal pace.

"I'm going to go downstairs and start coffee," Nash says, slipping out of me. "You want to have coffee in bed or downstairs?"

I watch him stand by the side of my bed, his cock at half-mast. "If you come back to bed, we'll end up fucking again."

"It's called makeup sex for a reason." He walks to the bathroom.

"It's makeup sex, not whole-night sex." I get out of bed and follow him to the bathroom.

"We've never actually been in this big of a fight

before. Like we've had makeup sex before, but this was makeup, makeup sex." He turns on the water before going over to grab a facecloth. "How was I supposed to know it was one time and not one night?" He kisses my shoulder before cleaning himself and sliding into a pair of boxers and going downstairs.

"That makes no sense at all." I shake my head. "But somehow, I understood everything you said." Reaching for my own rag, I clean myself off. I walk back into the room, grabbing one of his T-shirts to put on, and walking out of the room. The cat sits right in front of the door. "Good morning, princess." I bend to pick up the cat. "Did we have fun exploring the house last night?" I ask her, walking down the steps to the kitchen where I hear cupboards being slammed. "Sounds like Daddy doesn't know where anything is." I kiss her neck, putting her down before walking into the laundry room to grab her water bowl, emptying it into the sink, and then giving her fresh water before putting some food into her bowl. "There you go," I say before walking out of the room, and she follows me to the kitchen.

"There is nothing to make for breakfast," he says over his shoulder, "so I ordered your favorite bagels."

I walk beside him as he makes my matcha, going to grab a cup to make his coffee. We finish at the same time, and when I hand him his and he hands me mine, we smile at each other before he bends to kiss my lips. "I love you," he whispers, and my stomach gets little butterflies.

"I love you back," I say, bringing the cup to my mouth at the same time the doorbell rings. I don't have a chance to ask him if he wants me to get it when he puts his cup on the counter and walks to the door, returning with a brown paper bag. I pull out a stool, and he does the same before handing me my bagel and opening his own. "We should talk a bit," I suggest before I take a bite of my bagel.

"We should," he agrees. "Now that we got the whole, we love each other thing out of the way, I feel better."

"Same." I smile at him. "But I'm going to start by saying we are scrapping the ninety-day thing." He nods. "We should discuss where we're going to live."

"If you want to move to New York, I'll see what I can do." I look over at him, and this is one of the reasons I love him.

"No." I shake my head. "I like California, and besides, I can always travel back here if I miss it."

"So that's decided. What else do you want to talk about?" he asks, sipping his coffee.

"Kailyn." I say her name, and he side-eyes me.

"I'm not discussing her with you." His tone is tight. "She crossed the line, and nothing, and I mean nothing, you can say will change my mind."

"Maybe I misunderstood." I try to see if I might have been wrong. "I was already going through so much, I wasn't really—"

"Did you ask her to come into my office?" He asks me an innocent question, so I just nod. "And did she say no?"

"I mean, maybe she thought—" He holds up his hand to stop me from talking.

"I made it perfectly clear to her when we came back from our honeymoon, if at any time you called or needed me, I was to be interrupted. On that I will not go back. I've already spoken with a placement company, and I have a couple of interviews lined up on Monday via Zoom." I know that nothing I say will change his mind. "I would like if you have time to sit in with me."

"Okay, I have lunch with my mother and cousin," I tell him, "in about two hours."

"Do you want to have dinner with my parents tonight?" he asks, and I nod. "I'll call my father." He leans over, and I lean in and kiss him. "Love you, Zoey." I smirk at him.

"I don't think I'll ever get tired of hearing you say it," I admit to him.

"Good, because I'm never going to stop saying it." He puts his bagel down. "Are you ready to go take a shower?"

"Is that another code word for 'do you want to suck my cock?'" I laugh as I wrap up the little bit of bagel I have left. "Because if it is, the answer is yes." I wink at him and watch him push away from the counter before grabbing me.

"Mommy and Daddy are going to play." He looks at the cat. "We'll be back." I don't have a chance to say anything because my legs wrap around his waist, and my laughter is swallowed by his mouth on mine.

Two hours later, I'm rushing into the restaurant, spotting my mother, Aunt Zoe, and my cousin Zara all sitting at the table waiting for me. "Hi," I greet them, walking to my mother to kiss her cheek before going over to my aunt and hugging her from the back, kissing her cheek before kissing Zara on the top of her head. "Sorry I'm a bit late."

"You're four minutes late," Zara confirms, picking up her mimosa. "We started without you."

I laugh as I slide into the empty seat. "Imagine if I was later?" I look at her, putting the linen napkin on my lap.

"You're glowing," my mother says, and I look over at her and see tears in her eyes. "I've seen you on FaceTime, and I saw you were happy, but now seeing you in person."

"She might be faking it," Zara goads, and our mothers gasp at the same time. "What? Gabriella called me yesterday to give me the rundown on her not being herself."

I take a deep inhale. "She was right," I admit to them, "but since then, things have changed."

"It's been less than twenty-four hours," Zara blurts, shocked.

"Nash followed me here," I explain, putting my hand on the table.

"What do you mean 'followed you here'?" my aunt asks.

"We got into a little bit of a tiff," I start and tell them the whole story. It takes me a lot longer than I thought it would take.

"So wait a second." Zara holds up her hand. "He bought you a cat?"

"Why is everyone so fixated on the cat thing?" I huff

and hold up my hand to get the server's attention and point at Zara's drink.

"It's a living fucking thing, Zoey," Zara states as her eyes get even bigger. "Like, it's alive."

"That has to be the most thoughtful gift you've ever gotten," my mother says, putting her hand on mine. "I would kill your father, but it's so thoughtful."

"Remember when Auntie Vivienne got a fish from Uncle Markos?" my aunt says. "It was literally a world war." They both laugh.

"Anyway, I'm officially moving to LA," I inform them right as the server drops off my drink. "I love him." I look down at my ring. "Like for real, real. He's—" I look up and see my mother and aunt with tears in their eyes. "He's literally everything I could ever want in a man and more." I blink away my own tears of happiness. "I can't imagine my life without him."

Zara fake vomits from beside me, and when I look over, she smiles big at me with her own tears in her eyes. "I'm just kidding. I'm so, so happy for you. No one deserves it more."

"So what about you?" I turn the tables on her. "What's the scoop with the wedding?"

She lifts her hand. "We're in the middle of narrowing down the date." She avoids looking at us. "But it looks like this time next year, I'll be married."

"We have to go dress shopping now," my mother tells her, and she shakes her head. "You need time."

"I have no doubt, Auntie Za," she uses her nickname, "you'll find me a dress."

"Come hell or high water." She smiles at her.

"Shall we toast?" my aunt Zoe says, picking up her glass. "To love and finally seeing the girls fall in love."

"I'll drink to that," my mother agrees, picking up her glass.

"Hear, hear!" I join in, putting my glass in the middle.

"Hear three," Zara says, her smile not reaching her eyes. "One down, one to go." She clicks her glass to mine before bringing it to her lips. "To love."

THIRTY–TWO

Nash

I LOOK OUT the window at the city below us as the plane descends into the private airport. My back is to the couch as Zoey lies with her head in my lap and the cat curled up at her stomach, sleeping peacefully. A lot different from when I took her to New York. I also think she fucking hates me. Every time I get close to her, she glares at me.

The plane finally touches down and jolts both of them awake. "Are we here already?" Zoey looks up at me as she blinks the sleep out of her eyes, reaching her hands over her head and stretching.

"We are, baby," I confirm, bending to kiss her lips. The cat gets up and puts her two paws in front of her as she also stretches. "You need to get the cat in the carrier." I motion to the carrier on the seat. It is very much different from when I took her to New York. I had thrown a towel in there and put the cat in. Not Zoey. She placed a plush little cat bed with a couple of toys for her if she got bored.

"Let's go, my princess." She picks her up in her arms, kissing her neck that now has a pink collar with bling on it. "We're home," she says, and the way my chest settles when she says that is something I will never take for granted. This whole week we've spent in New York is something I think will always be at the top of my list of best times in my life. I told my wife I loved her and was happy she loved me back. The stupid ninety-day clock watch hanging over our heads is now out the window. My parents are madly and deeply in love with Zoey like I knew they would be. Evan sort of, kind of, likes me. His glare is now down to just a side-eye. Which to me is winning.

The plane comes to a stop as I grab our bags in one hand and her hand in my other. She spent the whole week packing up the house, which we shipped out yesterday, and it should be at our place in four days. I can't wait for her to unpack it and finally be home. "Do you have everything?" I ask her as she looks around, grabs her purse, then picks up the carrier.

"I think so." She smiles at me. "Are you ready, Mr. Griffin?" She stands in front of me as the plane doors open.

"I am now, Mrs. Griffin," I say as she walks ahead of me down the stairs and waits for me at the bottom.

We walk hand in hand to my parked car. I open the door for a bit letting the hot air out, before getting in. "Okay, do you trust me?" I ask her when I slam the trunk closed, turning to walk to her.

"Um," she says, "obviously."

"Good." I reach into my back pocket and take out the black satin blindfold. "Because I have a surprise for you."

"Nash." She smirks, looking at the blindfold. "You have to have me naked and tied to the bed before you bring that out." She winks at me, and my cock stirs at the thought.

"Next time, that's exactly when I'll use this." I swing it around my finger. "Get some clamps." Her eyes close a little as I wrap an arm around her waist, pulling her to me. "Tease you until you beg for me." Her chest starts moving faster and faster. "But until then, do you trust me?"

"Always." She doesn't even hesitate, my Zoey.

"Good. Can you put this on for me?" I ask her, handing it to her. "I have a little surprise for you."

"The things I do for you," she huffs, putting the cat in the back seat, then getting into her own seat before turning to me and putting it on her head. "There."

"You look so fucking sexy right now." I bend and kiss her lips before closing the door and jogging over to my side. I get in and enter the address in the GPS before pulling away.

"Can I have clues about this surprise?" She looks over at me. "Like, is it your dick in my face because I had it down my throat this morning, so it's not really a surprise."

I can't help but laugh out loud. "Not my dick," I tell her as I make my way to the destination.

"Is it something I can hold in my hand?" she asks, and I think about it.

"You can hold a piece of it in your hand, yes," I confirm.

"Can I eat it?"

"No," I say, "but you can eat in it."

"Can I get served in it?"

"You can." I pull up to the surprise and stop the car. "And you will.

"We have arrived," I announce. "Now, I'm going to grab the cat first," I tell her, "and then I'll come back and get you."

"Okay," she says.

"No peeking," I tease, getting out and grabbing the cat in the back seat and taking the cat inside before rushing outside to get Zoey, the door slamming shut behind me and automatically locking. I open her door and reach down to put my hand in hers. "Okay." I lead her away from the car to the front door. I look around and see the big trees in the front and kids playing in the street riding their bikes. "You can take off your blindfold," I instruct her, holding my breath as she takes it off slowly, blinking her eyes a couple of times before she looks around.

"Where are we?" she asks softly, her eyes going to the trees in the front and then off to the side. She smiles at the kids playing.

I pull out the key from my pocket. "This is our house," I announce, holding the key in my hand. Her gasp is louder than even she thought it would be. "You sat in front of me not too long ago and gave me a list,"

I remind her, "of what you wanted from the man you marry and the life you wanted." I smile at her. "You wanted someone who has your back and supports your career." I hold up my finger. "No one will have your back more than me and be your biggest cheerleader." She puts her hand to her mouth. "A man who is proud of you and who you are proud of." I hold up a second finger as I take a step toward her. "I couldn't be prouder of the badass woman you are, and I hope you are as proud of me." She shakes her head and tries to say something, but her mouth opens, then closes. "And you wanted a house with a white picket fence." I hold up my third finger. "I didn't bring you home to a house with a white picket fence," I tell her, "and I'm sorry for that." A tear falls out of her eye. "So I decided to rectify that." I look at the white picket fence that is around the property.

"But what about your house?" she asks, and I smile.

"It's being rented as we speak." I inform her of everything that went down this week. "That house isn't a house you can raise two point five kids in." I repeat more words she told me, and she laughs through the tears. "It's a bachelor pad." I shrug. "And I'm far from a bachelor." I look up at the white house with black window trim and doors. "This is a house your kids grow up in. This is the front yard filled with baseballs and soccer balls. It's a yard filled with little strollers and dolls. It's a yard where you hang a tire and make memories with your kids," I say, hoping she loves it just as much as I do. "This is a home where I want to have my kids with you. It's a house I want to come home to at the end of the day and hear screaming because someone touched the other person. It's the house I want to wake up to every single morning and make my wife the most disgusting drink ever known to humankind." I grimace. "It's a place that together we make it a home."

"Nash." She puts her hand on my cheek. "I'm going to need you to stop being so fucking perfect." She gets on her tippy-toes to kiss my lips.

"Do you want to see inside?" I ask, and she nods excitedly. "Then use your key." I drop it in her hand, and she looks at the key ring with the first letters of our names linked together. She puts the key in the door and slowly opens it once it's unlocked. She's about to take a step in when I stop her. "Not so fast, Mrs. Griffin," I say before I scoop her up into my arms. "I have to carry you over the threshold."

"You did that already," she reminds me.

"And I'll do it every single time." I walk into the house with her in my arms. "Welcome home, Mrs. Griffin."

Four months later...

The front door slams shut, and I look up from my computer. I hear the clatter of her shoes hitting the floor before I hear her voice. "Oh, Mr. Griffin." She sings my name, and I quickly shut down the laptop. "Where are you, Mr. Griffin?" she calls, and I can hear the little hiccup giggle come out of her, and I know she's probably tipsy. I get up from the bed and walk out of the bedroom, going into the living room that faces the front door. "There you are, Mr. Griffin." The smile on her face beams.

"Hey, baby." I meet her halfway. "How was dress

shopping?"

"It was so much fun," she says. "There were so many dresses." Her finger taps my chest. "But the good news is, Zara found her dress."

"So fast?" I ask, shocked. We are back in New York for the weekend so she could go wedding dress shopping with Zara.

"I know," she replies, putting her hand on my chest, "but she found the one." She looks up at me. "It was the first one she tried on. Then she tried on about a dozen more but came back out in the first one, so we knew." She smiles up at me. "She's going to be a beautiful bride."

"Not as beautiful as mine." I bend to kiss her as she jumps in my arms, wrapping her legs around my waist. "Definitely not as beautiful as mine."

"You're just saying that to get into my pants." She laughs at me as her phone rings from the front door. We ignore it the first time, but it rings again right after. "That must be important." She slips her legs off me before walking to her phone, which has stopped ringing.

She comes back in with the phone to her ear and a smile. "I left you literally in front of your house twenty minutes ago." The smile quickly fades from her face, and I take a step forward. "Zara, I don't understand you," she murmurs softly. "Breathe." She looks at me, and I walk to her, grabbing her phone from her and putting it on speaker.

The sound of Zara's soft cries comes out. "It's over," she sobs softly. "The wedding is off."

EPILOGUE ONE

ZOEY

One year later

I WALK PAST Lulu's desk and straight to my husband's office, knocking on the doorframe before looking in. He's sitting behind the desk with his assistant, Steven, in front of him taking notes. Both of them look my way. "Hey, am I interrupting?" I ask, and Steven smiles and gets up.

"I'll be back in a few," he says. "Can I get you guys anything from the kitchen?"

"I'm good. I'll be leaving in a bit," I tell him, and he walks out as I walk in.

Nash has already walked around his desk, and he grabs my hips and pulls me to him. "Hey, baby," he says softly, kissing my lips. Something we compromised on was showing some affection at work, and by compromised on, it means he gets to kiss me when he wants, and I don't bust his balls. It's the little things. "Where are you going?"

"I'm meeting with a client." I lie to him, hoping he doesn't press and ask me too many more questions. "I think it's frowned upon to bring a husband, just in case."

He laughs. "Okay, fine." He pretends to give in. "I'll meet you at home, then." He bends to kiss my lips. "I love you."

I nod. "I love you too." I disengage from his arms, walking out and quickly leaving before he asks any more questions. Then I'll have to confess there is no fucking client, and I'm on my way to the doctor.

I quickly wave at Lulu before waving at my husband and trying to act as cool as I can, except I'm about to throw up with all the nerves that are running through my body. I quickly make it to the doctor and check in, nervously sitting down and waiting to be called. I try to go through my social media but quickly close it as I look around. The door opens, and the lady calls my name. "Zoey Griffin." I get up and walk over, smiling at her. "Hi," she greets me with a smile. "I'm Cathy. How are you doing today?"

"Good," I reply. "Anxious, nervous, all of that, I guess." She smiles as she opens the door and steps in with me following her. The desk is in the corner, and the exam table is in the middle of the room at an angle. "I'm going to ask you a couple of questions." She sits at the desk and motions for me to sit down in the chair beside her. She asks me routine questions, and when she asks me when my last period was, I quickly smile and tell her, "About two and a half months ago."

"Have you taken a pregnancy test?" she asks, and I nod.

"What form of birth control are you on?"

"I was on the pill, but I stopped it six months ago," I tell her.

"Is this the first time you've been late?" she asks, and I nod.

"Perfect, let's do a urine sample first, and then the doctor will come in and examine you." She wheels her chair to the back, grabbing a small plastic container. "This is for you." She then points at the bathroom in the corner.

I quickly go into the bathroom and will myself to pee, even turning on the tap water. "Come on, come on, come on." I look down, chanting to my vagina, and then it trickles out. I fill it halfway, then close the lid on it before I rinse off the container and wash my hands. Stepping out with the container in my hand, I give it to the nurse, who is wearing blue surgical gloves now. She walks over to the other corner of the room, grabbing a little strip before opening it and dipping it in.

I wait a second as she looks at it. "Well, you are pregnant," she confirms, making my heart jump. Even though the five pregnancy tests I took said the same thing, I shouldn't be surprised I am. "If you can take off your bottoms, there is a sheet on the exam table." She points at the square white sheet that doesn't really cover anything. "The doctor will be right in with you."

It takes over forty-five minutes, but I'm leaving with a little black-and-white picture of what looks like a blob.

It's the most beautiful blob I've ever seen in my life. The tears are flowing the whole way, and even when I make it home and put it in the frame, I can't stop the tears from coming. Nash arrives literally five minutes after I've changed out of my work clothes and I walk down the stairs. Pictures of our beautiful life are scattered throughout the house. I walk down, carrying the white box in my hand with a pink-and-blue ribbon on top. "Hey," I say, walking in the room, and he turns from the fridge with a bottle of iced tea to his lips. He takes one look at me and stops drinking.

"What the fuck happened?" He tosses the bottle in the sink before turning to walk to me. "Why are you crying?"

He stops when I take a step back from him, his face filled with worry and confusion. "I lied to you," I say softly, and his hands shake in front of him. "I didn't have an appointment with a client today."

"I knew it," he whispers. "You were acting all weird this morning."

I try to laugh, but I'm so nervous that it comes out as a sob. "This is for you." I hold out the box, and he takes it. Walking over to the counter, he puts it down. His hand unties the satin ribbons. The white tissue paper creaks when he opens it and sees the white frame in the middle. "Almost two years ago, I sat in a bar in the middle of a crowded casino and told this hot beautiful man what my ideal life would be, never thinking by the end of the night I would be married to him." I smile. "From that day on, he's spent every single day showing me how much he loves me. He supports me and is proud of me. He bought me the most amazing house with a white picket fence, and now he's given me the final thing I had on my list," I say as he looks at me and then back at the picture. "It might not be two point five kids, but it's a point five."

"Are you?" He looks at the picture, then at me, and then at my stomach. "How?" He runs his hand through his hair when I raise my eyebrows at the question. "When?" Again, I raise my eyebrows.

"It can be literally any day of the week, and let's not talk about the weekend and the occasional Sunday naked fuck day."

He looks back down at the pictures. "This is our baby."

I walk to him and put my hand on his back, and he looks at me with tears in his eyes. "That is our baby," I state proudly. "Thank you," I tell him when he slides one hand around my waist while still holding the frame in the other hand. He looks down at me as I lift my hand to touch his face. "Thank you for making all of my dreams come true."

EPILOGUE TWO

NASH

Six years later

I GET IN the car and call her right away. The phone rings four times before she picks up. "Hey," she answers breathlessly, sounding like she's running, "are you on your way?"

"I am," I say, pulling out of the parking lot. "I should be home in about twenty minutes."

"Sounds good," she says. "Love you, got to go."

"Love you more," I say right before she hangs up, and I have to smile. She's been on the go since we had our first son, Easton, five years ago. She was so calm with him, and he was calm in return. Then we had our second son, Evander, two years later, and it has been nonstop. Whatever Easton does, Evander does tenfold.

When I pull up to the house, I see a tricycle that looks like it was thrown to the side, and a couple of plastic hockey sticks are on the front lawn right next to a soccer ball. Our sons are all-in with every single sport they try. Do they excel in hockey more than the others? Unfortunately, it's like they were born to skate, which irritates me since soon they will be better than I am. I open the front door at the same time I hear Zoey. "Easton, if you don't eat your dinner, there is no soccer," she warns, and I hear him whine.

"But, Mom, my stomach is full." I walk from the front door toward the kitchen, seeing the pictures on the wall showing how far we've come in six years. Pictures of us on our first anniversary. Pictures of when we did the gender reveal for Easton and then for Evander. The life Zoey and I have created over the past six years is everything I could have wished for and more.

"Really, your stomach is full?" she asks as I round the corner. "So I should toss away the cake pop we got for after dinner?"

"I have enough room for that but not for both," he barters, looking at Evander, who doesn't even pay attention to him as he eats his food. "So I have to choose one."

Zoey looks at him, trying to think of something to come back with. "Hey," I greet them, coming into the room and shrugging off my jacket.

"Daddeeee!" Evander shrieks, his face filled with a smile that is exactly like his mother's, just with my eyes and hair. He holds a fork in one hand while he eats with the other. His mouth, actually, his whole face, is filled with food.

"Daddy," Easton says but doesn't smile at me,

"Mommy says I can't have a surprise." I ignore that since I heard what was going on, and instead, I change the subject.

"How are my boys?" I walk to them, kissing Easton on his temple before I turn to kiss Evander on the top of his head because he's literally covered in tomato sauce. "How is my girl?" I walk around the counter to her. Her hair is piled on her head, and she wears cutoffs and a tank top, showing off her tanned legs. She spends most of the time in the pool with the boys or at the park.

"I'm good." She looks up at me as I bend to kiss her lips. "We had to have an early dinner," she explains. "They were starving."

I look over at the stove and see my covered plate waiting for me. "That's good. I had a late lunch."

"Good," she replies, "because we need to talk when the kids get to bed." She avoids looking at me as she glances over at the kids. "And since we've been out all day long, and they woke up at the ass crack of dawn, they should go down early."

"Mommy says ass," Easton says, pointing at her. "That's a bad word." I roll my lips while she closes her eyes.

"How about you go upstairs and take a nice bath, and I'll handle them?" I suggest, and she shakes her head.

"And miss all the fun?" She pffts out. "Not a chance." The minute she was nine months pregnant, she stepped away from her job even though she didn't know if being a stay-at-home mom was for her. But the minute she had Easton, it's like she was born to be a mom. She's up most of the nights with them, and not once has she complained and meant it. She has them in every single activity kids can be in. Gym, soccer, swimming, skating lessons, piano, art—you name it, my kids have been to at least one class.

"So how was everyone's day?" I walk over and pull Easton's plate away. "No cake pop, and you have two pieces left." I look at the plate. "I guess I'll eat it."

"Fine." He huffs in concession. "I'll eat it." He glares at me before glaring at his mother.

"I done," Evander declares, and I look at his demolished plate.

"You had less than me," Easton whines, and I have to laugh because I know for a fact that Evander eats the same, if not more, than Easton.

"Okay, here you go," Zoey says, handing them both a cake pop. "Then we can go to the park.

"Why don't you go change?" she urges me, and I run up the steps to our bedroom. The bed is made, and the pictures of us are also scattered around the room. I quickly get out of my suit, slipping on a pair of shorts and a T-shirt before going back down and finding her cleaning the kitchen. The two boys sit on the steps, waiting for me to put on my shoes.

It takes ten minutes for her to finish cleaning the kitchen before grabbing her little to-go bag she carries everywhere. It has everything you need when you have two boys who are not afraid to fall and get hurt. "I want to ride my bike," Easton says as soon as we step outside, walking over and grabbing his helmet and his bike.

"Me too," Evander mimics, grabbing his tricycle.

The four of us make our way to the park with the kids riding their bikes in front of us while Zoey and I walk behind them hand in hand. We spend two hours at the park, and I have to carry Evander back home in my arms while Zoey carries his tricycle.

"I'll take care of baths," I tell her, and she doesn't fight with me as she walks upstairs and heads for our bathroom. The boys drag their asses through the shower, and when they slide into bed, there isn't even a bedtime story. I kiss their heads before closing their doors a bit on the way out.

Walking into our bedroom in search of my wife, I find her sitting in the middle of the bed in one of my T-shirts. Her wet hair is combed through, and she's holding a piece of paper. "What's that?" I ask.

"It's what I wanted to talk to you about," she replies, and I suddenly get worried.

I sit beside her, seeing her name written in the middle of the white envelope. "The last time you gave me a white envelope, I got coupons that changed my world," I tease her, and she laughs. "I still have the pick which hole," I remind her.

"You used that one when we were on our anniversary trip the year after we got married," she retorts. "I just didn't collect the paper."

"Well, I still have it, so it never happened," I say, turning it over.

"Before you open that," she says, putting her hand in mine, "I want to say something."

"You're making me nervous," I tell her, leaning over to kiss her lips.

"I love you," she declares, blinking tears away. "Like when I sat down with you and told you what I wanted my life to be, it was a dream. But now." She smiles. "I live in a house with a white picket fence. I'm a stay-at-home mom and president of the parent committee at the preschool, and now the last thing on this list has been checked off."

"What?" I ask, thinking about her list when she told me what she wanted her life to be. A life I vowed to make come true and what I've busted my ass to do for the last six years. Making her never regret saying yes to me at a bar in Vegas.

"Open the envelope," she urges, and when I do, I pull out the black-and-white picture. I look back at her. "I now have two point five children." She brushes a tear away.

"You're pregnant?" I ask her, looking down at the little blob in the picture.

"Apparently, when you tell your husband you think now is a good time to have a baby, he pulls out all the stops to make sure you get your wish." She puts her hand on her stomach. "Thank you, Nash, for giving me the life I always dreamed of having."

"Thank you," I say, leaning over to kiss her, "for saying yes and giving me a chance to make all your dreams come true. I love you." I look into her eyes before I kiss her lips. The woman who owns my heart. The woman who I met on a beach and then got to marry me. The woman who my life would be empty without. The woman who I was meant to love.

www.ingramcontent.com/pod-product-compliance
Lightning Source LLC
Chambersburg PA
CBHW070315310726
48976CB00005B/1727